BRIAR

Midnight's Crown: Book 1

RIPLEY PROSERPINA

BRIAR
MIDNIGHT'S CROWN: BOOK 1

Copyright© 2017 by Ripley Proserpina

Copyright © 2017, Ripley Proserpina
First electronic publication: November 2017

Ripley Proserpina
www.ripleyproserpina.com

All Rights Are Reserved. No part of this book may be used or reproduced in any manner whatsoever without written permission, except in the case of brief quotations embodied in critical articles and reviews. The unauthorized reproduction or distribution of this copyrighted work is illegal. No part of this book may be scanned, uploaded or distributed via the Internet or any other means, electronic or print, without the author's permission.

NOTE FROM THE AUTHOR:
This book is a work of fiction. The names, characters, places, and incidents are products of the writer's imagination or have

been used fictitiously and are not to be construed as real. Any resemblance to persons, living or dead, actual events, locale or organizations is entirely coincidental. The author does not have any control over and does not assume any responsibility for third-party websites or their content.

Published in the United States of America

PROLOGUE

Briar knew what it was like to burn alive. She'd watched her skin blister and pop the moment a beam of sunlight touched her.

Long ago, on a beautiful summer day, with the smell of mown grass in her nose and the buzz of cicadas in her ears, she bounced with all the restrained excitement a five-year-old was capable of having. She stood on her toes, fingers pressed against the sliding glass door as her parents rolled back the cover on their brand new pool.

Sticky with zinc oxide to protect her fair skin from the rays of an early June sun, she waited. Her elbows stuck out like chicken wings, held away from her body by stiff plastic floaties bought especially for this first swim of the year.

She stood next to her brother, who huffed impatiently. "I'm going off the diving board first. You have to wait. I call dibs."

Her parents waved at them, and Briar and her brother launched themselves from the house, feet flying.

The wood was hot against the soles of her feet, and she jumped, the cool water taking her breath away. Liquid covered her head for just a second before she popped to the surface, and flames seared her from the top of her head to her tiny collarbones and shoulders.

A scream ripped from her throat, and in the days that followed, she was hoarse, her small baby voice only above a whisper. Hands plucked her from the pool, but still she screamed and thrashed, seeking to escape the pain from which there was no relief.

Soon, unfamiliar adults held a mask over her mouth and nose, tangy air blowing over her, and later, when the swelling in her lips and face receded, she could still taste it on her tongue.

Not much was as clear in those first few moments when Briar's life changed forever and the sun became her enemy.

There was a name for what she was, and while the kids at her school called her a vampire, she wasn't that. She was photosensitive, with, as the doctors would quote to her as she grew older, *an extreme sensitivity to ultraviolet light.*

A moment of sun, and her skin swelled and reddened, cracked and bled. There were no lazy days at the pool, no beach vacations.

For Briar, there would never be any track and field events, never a wedding in the backyard on a sunny day. Her life happened inside, curtains drawn.

And if she did venture out, she covered herself, head to toe, in special clothes that only made her stand out more.

She was part of the darkness now; her days in the sun were over.

CHAPTER 1
BRIAR

Briar Hale had waited four years for this day.

Four years of online classes, taking every prerequisite Boston College required and getting the best possible grades.

The leading researcher of the genetic syndrome, erythropoietic protoporphyria, or EPP, Professor Nors knew more than anyone else in the world about Briar's condition.

But the man was notoriously reclusive and never returned any of the emails Briar had sent him. Nor had he answered her questions about bone marrow and ferrochelatase catalyzing. A girl like her had a lot of time on her hands, and she'd spent that time searching for answers about why her body worked so differently than everyone else's.

A garbage truck went by, distracting her, and she waved her hand in front of her face to dissipate the sickeningly-sweet smell. Then, she let it drop to her side as she took in the scenery.

"Move."

Briar had been staring up at the gothic revival architecture, working up the courage to go inside for her first college class with other students.

Now, however, she narrowed her eyes at the man who spoke. Pointedly, she stared at the available sidewalk around her. In response, he merely raised a dark eyebrow bisected with a scar.

"Don't be a dick, Sylvain. Sorry, miss." A behemoth of a man with blond hair elbowed his friend and tipped his chin in an old world way that made her smile.

The dark man snorted, and her good feelings melted away. "Walk around me. I'm not taking up the entire sidewalk."

At five and a half feet, Briar was solidly average.

The dark man seemed to bulk up at her challenge, and for the first time, she really studied him. A foot taller than she was, he had tan skin, and shoulder-length, wavy brown hair. Broad shoulders and thick arms clad in a long-sleeve tee completed the lumberjack look he had going.

Sylvain.

She amended the occupation she'd mentally assigned him. Instead of a lumberjack, he looked like a man who lived alone in the Appalachian Mountains near her parents' home in Beckley, West Virginia. With the manners he displayed, it seemed a fitting characterization.

"What?" he asked, and she realized she'd been staring.

"I'm just wondering how long it's been since you've spoken to other humans," she mused, not trying to hide her sarcasm. "You seem out of practice."

His dark eyes widened for a second, but when his friend burst out laughing, they narrowed again. Mumbling something under his breath, he dipped his head and strode toward the building.

"Hope I don't have class with that guy," she muttered, and the light-haired man laughed again.

"Don't worry, you won't. Sylvain's too dumb for college.

Have a good day, miss. It's been a pleasure." Like he had earlier, the man addressed her formally. When he bowed, hand over his heart, Briar took a step back, surprised.

"Goodbye," she replied and watched as he followed Sylvain inside.

It took her a moment to gather herself and remember what her purpose was. She was used to deflecting snarky comments, so Sylvain hadn't bothered her as much as his friend's actions had. Those had left her off balance and confused. A part of her wondered if the man had been making fun of her *and* his friend.

Annoyed at herself for being distracted by a single unexpected blip, she straightened her shoulders and went inside. It was late afternoon, but sunlight still poured in from the windows. The outside of the building belied the bright, open interior. Light floors and stainless steel fixtures made the room seem full of light, and instinctively, Briar searched for the shadows.

Her skin was covered, white-buttoned gloves on her hands and long sleeves right over her wrists, but she knew what would happen if an inch of her skin came into contact with the sun. This room seemed to be designed to be in the light, no matter where she stood.

She'd been less nervous outside, which didn't make any sense.

But pain changed a person's brain, she reminded herself, and her reactions to things weren't always rational. There was no reason to hide at the edge of rooms. She was covered, and if she hadn't burned outside, she wouldn't burn inside.

Taking a deep breath to shore up her nerves, she searched for a map of the building, identified the auditorium where Professor Nors was lecturing, and made her way there.

As she suspected, all she needed to do was follow the hordes of people to find the hall. Professor Nors's mysteriousness made him that much more popular. If his communication with her was any indication, he would have a ton of other scientists and students dying to ask him questions or hear of his latest discoveries.

Briar caught her breath when she entered. Built like an amphitheater, the room was teeming with people, and the seats were quickly filling. Some had already given up and staked out a piece of the wall. Energy hummed through the room, as if they were fans waiting for a rock star to appear.

Briar moved as close to the front as possible, grateful, in this room at least, there were no windows. She was able to slide her hat off her head and remove her gloves and immediately felt more at ease. Those pieces of clothing were the things that made her stand out the most, identified her as different. Without them, she was another student. Pale, yes, but not glaringly obvious as *other*.

A hush descended, and from a side door came the man who must be Professor Nors. Whispers died away, the hall so quiet Briar wondered if anyone was breathing.

No doubt about it. He was a handsome man. He had pale skin, a shock of dark hair, square jaw, and full lips. His cheekbones looked carved from ice. But his entire countenance screamed, *stay back*.

"My name is Dr. Hudson Nors. I will be presenting my research on EPP and genetic screening. I will not be taking questions."

At those words, a wave of voices rose in denial, but Professor Nors lifted an eyebrow, and the room descended back into silence.

It was strange; she could be both amused and annoyed by this man. She had a million questions she wanted to ask, and would, if she had to chase him down to do so. She appreciated his damn-the-torpedoes attitude, but it wouldn't frighten her away. He could snarl as much as he wanted. She hadn't braved fire to run away scared now.

Briar studied the man standing twenty feet in front of her. He was the one person in the world who gave her any hope of living a normal life. A wave of gratitude swept over her, because no matter how unfriendly or weird he was, he was doing something for people like her.

Almost as if he felt her, he lifted his gaze and met Briar's curious stare. She didn't have a lot of experience with other people besides her immediate family, but he seemed confused. His dark eyebrows—two straight lines that slashed above his eyes—drew together, and he frowned.

"This lecture is a one-shot, please do not approach me. I have no desire to read your research or be part of your study."

Mister, we get it. Briar wrinkled her nose. He was laying it on a little heavy, but maybe he had no choice. There must be a reason for his actions. Perhaps other scientists had burned him in the past.

"Chromosome 18 is where our problem begins," the professor began, and the room plunged into darkness. A screen illuminated behind him. With a laser pointer, he indicated a section of a chromosome.

Science! Briar edged closer, perched on the end of her chair. Soon, she had no other thoughts except recessive and dominance patterns. His presentation, while not offering information Briar didn't already know, was different, coming from the horse's mouth, so to speak.

"As many of you know, there has been some success in Europe and Australia with use of the drug afamelanotide, but it hasn't been approved by the FDA for use here in the United States. Now, I received an interesting email weeks ago from a young college student that would put the rest of you Ph.D.'s to shame. This girl, who just graduated from college, suggested bone marrow transplants as a way to treat EPP."

Briar's head popped up. This was her! Her idea!

"Now, I haven't heard this idea from any other researcher, and while I, too, considered, and later rejected, this hypothesis, it was telling that the idea came outside of the scientific community. There are too few of us researching EPP. You'd do well to use this young lady as an example."

At his dismissal of her theory, she pulled her shoulders to her ears. Part of her was embarrassed her hypothesis was wrong, while the other was grateful he'd read her email. Thank goodness no one here knew who she was. She could just imagine the pointed looks.

And why was he calling her *young lady*? The professor looked only to be five or six years older than her!

The lecture went on. Her mind spun with the ideas and suppositions he posited, though most of them she'd heard before.

"Thank you for your interest. That is all." Professor Nors gathered his notes, and Briar sat up, clapping politely along with everyone else. Most of the audience was already standing, gathering their belongings or shuffling to the exit, but Briar stayed in her seat.

After preparing so long for this day, it was a supreme letdown. Oh, Professor Nors was brilliant. He had a commanding presence, but much of his lecture had touched on topics she'd already studied. With a flash, she realized she'd been hoping for a cure. That was something she hadn't allowed herself to want since grade school, a time when she still believed in Santa and the Easter Bunny. In those days, a miracle was as likely as finding a dollar bill from the Tooth Fairy beneath her pillow. Which was to say—totally possible.

Annoyed, she reached for her bag and pulled out her hat and gloves to hold tightly in her fists. She'd wallowed in self-pity enough. It was time for action, and the first thing she was going to do was find Professor Nors and ask her questions.

No—she would *demand* answers to her questions. She slapped the gloves into the palm of one hand, but as she did, one slipped from her grasp. It flew into the seats below hers, smacking in the face a young man waiting to exit the row.

He touched his cheek with a long-fingered hand before he bent at the waist to pick up her glove. "The last person who slapped me with a glove was challenging me to a duel." Bright, sea-green eyes met hers. "Is this yours?" he asked, flashing an even, white smile his dark face seemed to make even brighter.

"Um. Yes," Briar answered, mortified. "I apologize."

He reached forward. Did he want to hold her hand? No, he was merely waiting to drop the glove into her palm.

"No problem." He stared at her a moment longer, studying her face, gaze lingering on the place below her right eye, and Briar quickly dipped her head. He was staring at one of her multiple scars. The second burn she'd suffered, though not the worst, had been on her lips and face. A skin graft was required after the burn ruined the muscles in her cheek. Her smile was lopsided because of it.

"Bye," Briar whispered, facing away from him.

Hurry, hurry.

The line to leave the row was crawling along, and she could feel the young man's continued stare. Ignoring the impulse to cover herself, she instead stood straighter, and then with a deep breath, faced him. He smiled apologetically when she did. He knew he'd been caught, and he opened his mouth to speak, but someone tapped him on the shoulder and pointed to the now-quickly moving line. With a rueful grin, he walked away, down the stairs and out of the auditorium.

Briar followed suit, trailing along behind the line of

people while tugging on one glove. A dim hallway led back toward the atrium, and she went slowly in that direction while checking her watch.

When she left, she'd need to call her parents. They'd been anxious about her since she'd made the decision to live on her own. They wanted her in cloudy Beckley, where they could watch her and protect her. But she couldn't stay there a moment more.

She had things she wanted to do, and the place to do them was Boston, Massachusetts. All she needed to do was convince the anti-social Professor Nors to allow her to work with him, and her plan would be in motion.

Barking a laugh, she shook her head. After finally seeing the man, it seemed highly unlikely this part of her plan would work. Still, she was determined to try.

Light from the atrium spilled through the door. She placed her hat back on her head, and glanced up as she entered the open area. In front of her, a crowd had gathered, and Professor Nors's dark head towered above the group.

Apparently, she wasn't the only one who planned on ignoring his directive. Four or five rows of people encircled him. He shook his head and glanced around, searching for an escape.

It made Briar stop short. The man's face morphed from irritated to panicked, and his shoulders heaved like he was out of breath. Sympathy welled inside her. What could be causing him to look that way and how dense were the people around him for ignoring his very clear body language?

You were prepared to dismiss his wishes and corner him.

Canting her head, she regarded him and the people surrounding him closely. Most of the crowd was women, her age. She snapped her mouth shut. Were they groupies? Squinting and edging closer, Briar studied them. Eye-makeup, check. Rapid-blinking, check. All signs pointed to flirting.

From the corner of her eye, something white fluttered to the ground. Without thinking, she bent and reached for her glove.

Stupid.

In her excitement, she'd only put on one glove and her hat. Without thinking, she extended her hand into the beam of sunlight where the glove had fallen.

The pain was instantaneous and all-consuming. Her cry was louder than the din of voices, echoing and reverberating through the hall.

"Are you okay?" Someone took her shoulders, and though well intentioned, they dragged her further into the sunlight, holding her when she would have jerked away. "I think she's having a seizure."

"Let me go!" The skin on her hand swelled, and a searing sensation traveled from her wrist to her elbow. *No!* This wasn't part of the plan. She couldn't be injured, she was here to be normal—to study. Not to catch fire and smolder in front of the people she wanted to be her colleagues.

"Let her go." The voice was like a bucket of ice water. Barking directions, Professor Nors shrugged out of his suit coat. He draped the clothing over her arm and tugged her out of the sunlight.

Her arm felt like an exposed nerve, and her teeth chattered. A piece of her brain recognized the shock response that inevitably followed an injury.

"Marcus!" the professor called. "You'll be fine. I'm taking you to my lab. I can help you there. Marcus, hurry!"

"Got her."

Briar's knees buckled, but someone caught her. It was the man from earlier; the one with sea-green eyes and dark skin.

The one with the beautiful smile.

"Thank you," he answered.

Aw, shoot. *Said that out loud.*

"You did." He cradled her in his arms while she protected her injury.

"Call the hospital," she stuttered, forcing her lips to form the word. "It's a burn. Not a seizure."

"I'm aware of the nature of your injury." The walls blurred, but Professor Nors's face was perfectly clear. "What were you thinking? You can't be exposed to the sunlight."

Her stomach roiled, and she squeezed her eyes shut. *Please don't let me yak on these guys, please.* "I'm not hiding anymore," she said.

Paper crinkled as Marcus placed her carefully on a table.

"Let me see it."

But she couldn't move her arm. It would hurt too much. She knew what had to happen, but everything inside her rebelled. No more wrapping and unwrapping, no more wound care, or sloughing the skin if it was dead. She kept her eyes closed, not wanting to see how bad it was.

"Second degree," Professor Nors said. "Open your eyes."

Something in his voice demanded she listen, and she did. "Oh no." Her fingers were swollen, the ring she'd placed on her middle finger slowly turning her finger purple.

"We're going to cut it off. Marcus get me the—"

"Not my finger!" she cried.

Sighing, he rolled his eyes, and she relaxed. If he could roll his eyes at her, things weren't so bad. She annoyed him, and people about to lose limbs would be treated with more consideration than the way he treated her.

He snorted and shook his head. "Hydrogel, Marcus. And gauze."

"I don't work for you, Hud. Don't tell me what to do."

"Stop being an ass, and get me the goddamn metal cutters, Marcus!" A prick on her arm, and a warm hazy feeling filled her. "Morphine. You'll probably fall asleep."

"I always do." Her words were slurred. "I also barf when I wake up. So watch your shoes."

"Thanks for the warning, princess."

The morphine hit her hard and fast, and she closed her eyes. She wasn't sure who had spoken, because serious Professor Nors would never call her a nickname and smile at her—such a thing seemed unlikely.

"Knew you'd help me," she thought she said, right before the darkness swallowed her up.

CHAPTER 2
MARCUS

"What are you going to do with her?" Marcus asked Hudson as he placed hydrogel on the angry-looking burn on the girl's arm. The smell of her blood had dissipated, but only seconds ago, it filled his nose like a garden in full bloom.

It'd been a tiny prick, quickly wiped away with the alcohol pad Hudson had used to swab her skin, but it had been delicious. It threw him back in time, back to a garden that no longer existed and a flower that had been extinct for a thousand years.

The flower appeared in his mind. White with a dark purple center, nestled in thorny green leaves. He sucked in a breath, the scent of her blood coating his tongue like he'd sipped it.

A wildflower, it had grown at the base of the rocks that littered the barren hillside where he was born. He'd passed it a million times as he'd trekked up the hill, seen and dismissed it, and hadn't thought of it since he'd embraced this second life. But now he did, and he wondered how it was he could have forgotten it.

It took all his self-control to not bury his face in her neck and let his teeth slice her skin. He wanted more of the feeling her scent recalled—home, innocence, contentment. He had none of those things anymore, nor had he yearned for them. Yet he did now.

Snapping his mouth shut, he took in one breath and spun away, putting as much distance between him and the girl as possible. A roomful of people had seen him and Hudson with the girl. He couldn't afford a slip that would lead to his downfall and the girl's death.

"I'm going to wrap her arm and send her home. What did you think I was going to do with her?"

Marcus sighed, staring at the girl lying on the table in Hudson's lab. He'd come here for one reason only, to get the shot that allowed him to walk in daylight, and he didn't want to stay in his brother's lab longer than necessary. Every moment with Hudson was painful, dredging memories to the surface that he tried hard to keep buried.

But for some reason, he didn't want to leave until he was sure the girl was all right.

"How the hell should I know what you do?" Marcus snapped back.

The girl gave a small moan, and he eased forward. "Does she need more morphine, you think? A second longer in the sun..."

"I know. She's lucky not to have nerve damage."

"She's covered in scars." Marcus crept forward to point a finger at the one he'd seen earlier on her cheek, then another above her eyebrow. The hat she'd worn currently rested on a seat nearby, along with her white gloves and the sleeve of her shirt.

"Yes. I noticed." Hudson's voice was tight, and when Marcus glanced up at him, he caught him staring at Briar's lips before jumping to the pulse in her throat.

"When did you last eat?" he heard himself ask.

"None of your business, *brother.*" Hudson flung the words at him like a knife, and it found its mark. In time past, the word had meant they were family. Now it served to show how far apart they'd grown. "This is why I don't announce lectures. I have every pathetic human in the world turning up to beg me to heal them."

"They couldn't find someone further from being a saint," Marcus said.

Hudson spun, striding toward a small cooler and opening it to withdraw a syringe and scalpel. "Tilt your head," he directed, and Marcus did, exposing his jugular. He would heal quickly, so Hudson had to be fast. Cut and pump. His cold heart would pump the medicine through his veins, shooting him full of a drug that would allow him to walk in the light for six months or so before it wore off and he had to return to Hudson for another dose.

After a hundred years or more of not seeing his brothers, this new six month regime was hard to stomach. Often, Marcus left Hudson determined never to come to him again. He'd let the medicine wear off and go back to living at night. But then he'd watch a sunrise, and all his good intentions went out the window.

The cold steel sliced his skin before the burn of the medicine seared his veins, almost as if Hudson had filled the syringe with liquid sunlight and not hormones and peptides. He hissed; his fangs descending. The desire to snap, rip, and tear at the being hurting him was hard to quell, but he did it. His skin knit back together, and he pushed away from his brother, edging closer to the still unconscious form on the table.

"You should leave before Sylvain and Valen arrive." Hudson turned his back, and Marcus was again tempted to attack. He was an apex predator, and such a position left Hudson vulnerable.

But he needed Hudson's brain to keep perfecting the medicine that let them have a normal life. Marcus's own research into cloned human blood which would allow them to survive without killing, was progressing well. Between the four of them, they'd never been closer to defeating the curse they'd suffered from for centuries.

Perhaps it would be possible for them to live as men, and not vampires. Marcus sighed. A breakthrough seemed within his grasp and yet so far away.

"I know what you want to do, and I can assure you, despite my age, I can still best you," Hudson muttered.

"You have no idea what I want," Marcus retorted and slapped his palm against his neck, rubbing at the blood he scented there and then licked it from his palm. "And I'm not leaving here to let our brothers attack this girl. A crowd of people saw us leave with her Hudson. The last thing we need is for her body to roll into shore with the tide."

"Whose body?" Sylvain burst through the door like a cowboy into a saloon. Marcus narrowed his eyes. Their youngest brother was all bluster and brashness, walking like his cock dragged on the ground. *Neanderthal.*

Sylvain inhaled deeply and smiled, fangs descending. "Thanks, Hud. I haven't eaten since crossing the border."

Without thinking, Marcus leapt across the room, pushing Sylvain hard enough to shove him back into the door which groaned against the hinges. "Leave."

"What the—" Sylvain shook his head then growled. "Get your hands off me."

"Hey," Valen interrupted, "it's the girl."

Confused, Marcus let up on Sylvain, who swept his arms out and knocked him away. "Don't touch me. And what girl?"

"The one from outside." Valen had somehow managed to

get closer without Marcus tracking him, though Hudson stood close, watching him warily.

Interesting.

Valen hissed. "What happened? Who hurt her? Why does it smell like blood?" Valen's eyes darkened, the blue draining away to leave only the blown-out black pupil. The air crackled with electricity.

"How do you know her?" Hudson asked, diffusing the tension.

"She was in the way." Sylvain crossed his massive arms and cracked his neck. "I told her to move."

"You were rude," Valen added.

"I'm always rude," Sylvain countered.

Sylvain and Valen were night and day. Valen was light skinned, with long golden hair and bright blue eyes—every inch the Viking warrior. He towered over most humans. Ancient tribal tattoos ran down his neck and shoulders. Decades ago, he'd covered them up, but now he liked the looks he got. Of all of them, Valen was the most easy-going, but not now. He was eyeing Sylvain like he was ready to rip his head from his shoulders.

All over one unconscious girl.

"Whatever." Sylvain faced Hudson. "Can we do this thing so I can leave?"

Hudson nodded, and reached into the cooler for a vial of medicine. Like he had for Marcus, Hudson made a shallow cut and pumped the medicine directly into his vein. One heartbeat was enough to spray blood across the room before Sylvain's lightning fast healing began. He wiped his neck against his sleeve and, glaring at the rest of them, slammed out of the room.

"Hurry up." Valen's voice spurred Hudson on. "I need to catch him before he snacks on one of your colleagues." A second later, the medicine was administered, but Valen lingered by the door. "She smells like snow and ice," he mused, shaking his head as if to clear it of memories. "Like the sea. Who is she?"

The words stuck in Marcus's throat, but Hudson answered for him.

"No one." Hudson's voice was hard. Emotionless. "She's no one."

CHAPTER 3
HUDSON

She was no one, so why did saying so feel like a lie?

Marcus watched him, and Hudson had to pretend to be busy with test tubes and syringes. He pulled on a pair of rubber gloves and examined the girl's arm again. The hydrogel was taking down the swelling, but she'd still be dealing with pain for the next week.

"Who is she, really?" Marcus asked when the door closed behind Valen.

"How the hell should I know?" Hudson answered. "Clearly she has EPP, but that's all I've got."

There was a shuffling sound behind him, and then a zip. When he turned, Marcus had taken out the girl's wallet and was rifling through the pockets. "Briar Hale." Green eyes met his. "Know her?"

He did. She was the girl who'd sent him the question about bone marrow transplants. Her messages were smart, and he found the way her brain worked to be fascinating. The hypotheses she'd proposed were unique, and she was the first person in a long time he'd been tempted to write back.

But he shook his head. "No." It was a lie, and from the noise Marcus made, it was obvious he'd been caught.

"Semantics, Hudson."

"She's sent me emails. I've never met her."

"Asking for help?" Marcus asked.

Surprisingly, no. Briar had never asked for help. She'd asked *to* help. She'd asked about his research, his theories and techniques, but she'd never told him she had EPP or asked to participate in any of his studies. He should have known, though, from the depth of her knowledge that she had a personal stake in the research.

"No," he answered.

"How does she smell to you?" Marcus asked him suddenly.

"I wouldn't know." Hudson gestured to his nose, tilting his head back to reveal the nose plugs he'd inserted earlier. If he was going to be surrounded by humans, he couldn't smell them. He may have control over his instincts, but it was better not to tempt his determination. "Why?"

"Valen."

Hudson rolled his eyes. Valen had always been the most poetic. "Ice and snow, and the sea. Pathetic."

"She scents familiar to me as well, Hudson," Marcus whispered.

He whipped around. "No," he ground out. "There will never be anyone for all of us again. We are not a family anymore. This?" He held up an empty vial. "This is the only thing I will share with any of you. Once your research, and mine, is complete, we can go our separate ways and never see each other again."

"Is that what you truly want?" Marcus asked, eyes boring into Hudson's.

A groan sounded from the human before he could answer. "Briar?" Marcus said her name low, and Hudson swallowed the urge to growl. What did he care if Marcus said her name? It was nothing to him. "Briar, you're safe."

Hardly. She was in a basement lab with two cold-blooded killers who were as likely to drain her dry as hand her a glass of water.

"Watch out," she said before she retched. He heard the splatter of vomit on tiles.

"You did warn me." Marcus chuckled.

Which unsettled him. Marcus didn't laugh.

"I'll get the mop," he heard himself say.

"No. Wait," Briar called out to him. "I'll do it." The paper on the table crinkled as if she was trying to sit up. Forcing himself not to glance back, he found a mop and bucket in a supply closet and wheeled it to the mess. "I can do it," she repeated.

"With one hand?" Hudson asked, making sure his voice stayed cold and remote.

"Yes," she answered. She slid from the table, and her feet slapped against the floor. "Here." Hand outstretched, she waited, but he didn't give it to her. Finally, she wrestled the mop from him with one hand. Shock was the only excuse he had for how she was able to get it away from him.

"You don't have to do that," he said and reached for towels to scoop up the puke. Her pale skin was flushed, and she held her wounded arm tucked tight into her side. But as he watched, he had to admit she was able to work just fine with one hand. "Not the first time you've done this, is it?" He realized.

"No," she answered, and the flush deepened. Like earlier, his gaze was drawn to her neck and the skipping pulse point.

Marcus reached for the handle. "Let me."

She shook her head, impressing Hudson with her stubbornness. "I can do it. It's gross."

Swiftly, she mopped the spot and pushed the bucket back

to the closet. Resting the handle on her shoulder, she struggled to open the door, but wrestled it open before either he or Marcus could help her. "Again. I'm really sorry," she said. "I just need a plastic bag or something to put around my arm, and then I'll be out of your hair."

"I'll take you home," he offered. What was wrong with him?

"I was just leaving," Marcus interrupted. "I know how busy you are with your research, Hudson. I can see her home. Safely."

Ah. Marcus wanted time with her. Why was that? "I'm finished here." He wasn't, but he would come back.

"It's okay," Briar replied, glancing between the two of them, confused. "I got it."

Marcus moved fast, picking up her bag and then hoisting it over his shoulder, but Hudson snagged her wallet from the counter. "I'd like to hear more about your hypotheses, Briar. I read your emails, and your ideas were interesting."

Marcus's mouth dropped open, but Briar smiled.

"You read them?" Her eyes opened wide, and he could see flecks of gray in them. Briar looked like a strong breeze could blow her away. Slight, she was half a foot smaller than him, with tiny bird-like bones, narrow shoulders, small wrists. Not classically pretty, but wholesome, with freckles across her pale skin, and blue veins visible beneath her eyes and at her temples. Even her hair was wispy. Long, golden-brown strands curled at the ends and grazed her shoulders.

"Yes," Hudson answered, tearing his eyes from hers and focusing on the wallet he still held in his hands. "Here."

Instinctively, she reached for it with her burned hand and sucked in a breath.

"Give it here, Hudson." Marcus pulled it out of his hands and stuffed it into the bag. "I can drive you home if you're intent on leaving."

"I am." She smiled, a small gap between her front teeth. "But I'm good." Holding out a hand, the uninjured one this time, she meaningfully eyed the bag in Marcus's hands.

"She wants her bag," Hudson told him helpfully, earning a glare.

"I'll drive you home," Marcus told her, still staring at him.

"I took the T. I don't need a ride."

"The T is full of germs, and is busy. You could get bumped."

Marcus made a good point. So—"Let me drive you home, Briar. I can tell you all about the research I've started." Hudson smiled blandly at Marcus, and tilted his head—daring Marcus to challenge him.

"Are you sure?" Briar's voice was nervous and tired. "I'll take it if you're offering. But I need a bag. In case I get carsick."

Hudson grabbed a bag and his coat, opened the lab door, and gestured for her to lead. "My pleasure."

"You're an ass," Marcus whispered tonelessly, and Hudson smiled, this time for real. "Why do you even care? Is it just to show me up?"

Hudson refused to answer. Not only because he had no answer, but because it was none of Marcus's business what his motivation was. Swiftly, he led the way through the building.

"My hat and gloves." Briar panted, and he slowed, waiting for her to catch up with him.

"I put them in your bag," Marcus told her. "But you shouldn't need them. The sun has set."

Hudson matched his stride to hers. Outside, the air had cooled dramatically, and Briar sighed, as if it soothed her. As for him, the night allowed his other senses a chance to expand. His hearing sharpened, and his night vision focused. He could hear the heartbeat, not only of Briar, but of the individual students walking in a group across campus. A couple walked by, and he could feel the heat coming off the woman when the man took her hand.

Briar shivered in her one-sleeved shirt, and he refocused. "Come on. I'm parked right over there." He pointed to his black sedan with the heavily tinted windows and unlocked the doors with the key fob. As they approached, he threw out, "See you in six months, Marcus."

Marcus ground to a halt, and Hudson was grateful for the darkness. The anger Marcus broadcasted was loud and clear, but it left him off balance. What did he care if this girl, who he'd never see again, knew his brother hated him?

"Right," Marcus ground out through clenched teeth. "It was a pleasure meeting you, Briar."

"Thank you for your help." It sounded as if every word took an enormous amount of effort, and he felt a stab of unease. He'd let this girl leave his lab without taking her vitals or stats. He'd covered her arm, wrapped it, and that was it.

Without stopping to second-guess himself, he eased Briar into the seat, and reached over her head to flip on the dome light. "Look at me," he directed. Her pupils constricted, the blue so light it was nearly the same color as the rest of her iris, an unnerving shade that made him feel as if she was staring through him. "Hand." Holding out his palm, he waited for her to put her hand in his and then grasped her wrist to take her pulse. It was even, and her pupils responded to light as she followed his gaze. Not shock then. "When you get home, eat something sugary, and lie down. Do you have a primary care doctor? Can you see them tomorrow?"

Marcus knelt on the pavement next to him, observing Briar as closely as he did, and Hudson fought not to body check him. "Why are you still here?"

Huffing a sigh, Briar stood and edged past them. "I should go."

This time, he didn't stop himself from ramming into

Marcus, who fell sideways into the car. From the thud, there would probably be a Marcus-size dent on his fender. *Worth it.*

Briar waved, but there was Sylvain, lingering in the shadows, watching Briar like a wolf watched sheep. His brother should be long gone by now. "Briar. I apologize. Marcus and I are—we—" How to explain what he and Marcus were to each other? Best friends? Brothers? Family? They were all of those things and none of them.

"We are constantly ribbing each other. We forget what that can look like to h—people." Marcus, silver-tongued bastard, perfectly encapsulated what he struggled to convey.

"Um..." She scooted toward the open door and stood up. The girl was ready to flee.

She can't. Not with Sylvain out there.

She tiptoed away. The distance between them increased, but Hudson didn't want her to leave. He didn't know what it was about her, but if she disappeared and he never saw her again, he'd lose something.

Something he wasn't ready to lose.

Marcus side-eyed Sylvain and held out a hand to Briar. "We'll behave. Promise."

She tucked her injured arm against her chest with her good arm, and stepped closer. "No more fighting?"

"Not tonight," Marcus smiled, and she smiled in return. *Damn him.*

Lifting one light brown brow, she stared at Hudson, waiting. "I'm done," he promised and opened the passenger side door.

The side of her mouth lifted. She came closer then reached for the handle to the back seat and slid in.

He shut the door, and Marcus sighed before jogging around to the passenger side. He flashed Hudson a cocky grin, a dare to stop him from getting in the car.

Rather than answer, he got into the driver's seat. "What's your address?" he asked Briar, gruffer than he meant.

"I'm near Davis Square."

"Somerville?" Traffic put them forty-five minutes away.

"Sorry," she apologized. "I found a sublet there. I'm commuting until I can get closer to Chestnut Hill."

"You're a student?" Marcus asked.

"Yes. Graduate student."

"In?" Hudson asked, then winced at his tone. He wasn't used to talking to people these days.

"Biology."

"I'm not taking on graduate research assistants," he barked. Briar peaked his interest, and she shouldn't. This drive, the next forty-five minutes, would be the only time he would have with her. Better to let her know up front what to expect.

"I'm aware you haven't had assistants."

"You're the worst," Marcus whispered, lower than a human could hear.

"But you are lecturing this semester," Briar continued. "And perhaps you can recommend a professor who would be interested? Are any other professors helping with the study you mentioned earlier? I could help them—"

"Williams in genetics, perhaps. Or Lewis in chemistry. You're aware of the mutation—"

"Yes!" She cut him off excitedly. "I was hoping to examine my genes using the software available at a university. I have EPP and since the mutation is found on the X chromosome..."

Smiling, he met her eyes in the rearview mirror, but she trailed off, staring out the window. The grin fell from his lips. "Is that all?"

"You know all this. I don't need to regurgitate your research."

Next to him, Marcus inhaled and slowly hissed a breath out his teeth. A second later, he opened the window, clenching his jaw as the cold night air blew in. It reminded him that both Valen and Marcus had found her scent intoxicating, and he wondered if her scent had become too overpowering and tempting for him.

Older than Marcus, Hudson had more control over his instincts than any of his brothers. Relying on the darkness to hide what he did, he quickly exhaled, caught the nose plugs in his hand, and stuffed them in his pocket.

He immediately wished he hadn't.

Intoxicating wasn't the word for Briar's scent. More than a thousand years ago, Hudson had stood in a vineyard, and plucked a grape off the vine to toss in his mouth. It was right before he'd been turned into a vampire, but he'd forever associate that moment with the bright sun, cloudless sky, and sweetness coating his tongue.

Uncaring, he swerved to the side of the road. He threw the car into park and jumped out, ignoring the angry honks and yells of other drivers.

Where were his nose plugs? He sucked in mouthfuls of clean air, digging in his pocket for them and put them back in. Fisting his hands at his sides, he focused on calming the beast inside him intent on the girl in the back. This was more than a familiar scent—more than a temptation.

The scent triggered a response in him that left him shaken to his core.

Mine.

Hudson dug his fingers into the roof of the car as if it was clay, while the beast he'd always kept leashed gnashed and roared inside him, *Briar is mine!*

CHAPTER 4
BRIAR

"Drive her home," Professor Nors growled to Marcus, and ran away.

He darted through traffic so fast, Briar had trouble following him before he blended into the masses of people ambling between restaurants and shops.

"Is—" she began.

"He's fine. Agoraphobia," Marcus explained.

"But agoraphobia is—"

"I meant claustrophobia."

"Since we're stopped, I can get out here. We're only a few blocks from my apartment." Making a move to undo her seatbelt, she stopped when Marcus got in the front seat and slammed the door shut.

"I'll drive you to your door." Gone was the good-natured jokester. He seemed distant now, mind on something else. Probably Professor Nors, who'd done a great impression of a deer caught in headlights earlier.

Part of her wanted to argue, but another part was plain tired and would rather sit in the back of the car like it was a taxi than walk three blocks and risk jostling her injury. What a day. She chuckled.

"What?" Marcus asked.

Letting her head fall against the seat, she shook her head.

"Come on," he cajoled, some of his humor back.

"I was thinking—" Rubbing her forehead, she searched for the words. "I came to Boston College to meet Professor Nors and learn more about his research. And I did it. No one thought I could. My parents are so angry at me for doing this, and my brother is annoyed. He thinks I'm being dramatic. But I did it."

Marcus rolled to a stop and parked, shifting in the seat to see her better. "You did. Now what?"

"Class on Monday."

"Good luck."

Briar smiled. "You teach here as well?" She wondered if she'd be able to find a class with him.

He shook his head. "No." Silence descended. She waited for him to fill it, but he didn't. Awkwardly, she came to understand that he was waiting for her to leave.

Handle in hand, she pushed open the door then twisted her body to get the bag next to her. She almost expected him to offer to walk her to the door—both he and Professor Nors had been so concerned about her injury. It seemed strange he was suddenly letting her fumble with her bag and rifle for her keys in the cold.

"Thank you, Marcus," she said. "And, um, if you're ever in Boston again..." She gestured with her head to her house. "You know where to find me."

"Nice to meet you, Briar," he answered, and she heard what he didn't say. It was highly unlikely she'd see him again.

"Goodbye." Using her butt, she knocked the door shut and hurried to her door. She rested her bag on her feet and fumbled with the lock, holding the doorknob in place with her hip so she could jiggle it the way the landlord had showed her when she'd moved in. Once it was open, she glanced behind her, but the car was gone. Sighing, she shut the door and threw the deadbolt. One more flight of steps, and then she had three more locks to open before she was in her apartment. It was early yet, but the only thing she wanted to do was drop, face first, onto the mattress.

The locks took the last bit of energy she had, and she didn't even bother taking off her boots when she shut the door behind her. She dragged herself to her bed and sat heavily on the mattress before carefully lying back.

Her arm was starting to throb again, and she'd have to start a Tylenol and ibuprofen cocktail to keep the pain at bay. God, she'd really messed things up.

First, she'd made a fool of herself in front of Professor Nors, and potentially every other graduate student studying biology at BC. Then she'd puked on Hot Marcus. She snorted at the nickname, Hot Marcus.

Though if she planned to assign names based on hotness, then Professor Hudson would have to be Hot Professor Hudson Nors.

Or Professor Hotson. *No!* If she gave him that nickname, started thinking of him that way, she'd probably say, "Nice to see you again, Professor Hotson" or something equally embarrassing.

Not that he'd say anything to her, or that she'd even see him again. First off, people didn't say hello to her. She looked too weird when she was in her sun-defense get-up. No one wanted to be seen with the girl wearing an ugly hat and strange gloves.

It was still early fall. In New England, where Indian summer was possible, she'd be wearing long sleeves and pants when the sun was blazing and it was eighty degrees.

Briar took a deep breath. Her mind raced, something

which went hand-in-hand with her physical exhaustion and pain. Whenever she hurt, she became completely overwhelmed with her life, threw a pity party, cried, and then fell asleep.

Knowing it was her typical pattern didn't make the process any easier—it just made her feel crazy.

Briar stared at the ugly, water-stained ceiling and felt the first tears trickle down the side of her face. So here she was. The ugly, scarred freak, who'd made a fool of herself on her very first day at the college she'd dreamed of attending since she was sixteen years old.

She should really get up and fix her bandages. Call her mother the way she promised. But instead, Briar flipped onto her good side and shut her eyes.

Windows! Her eyes popped open. She had drawn the blackout curtains, thank goodness. Relieved she wouldn't burn like a vampire when the sun came up, she squeezed her eyes shut, made a mental list of all her deficiencies, and fell asleep.

BRIAR HAD DREAMS THAT PUT HORROR MOVIES TO SHAME.

Blood.

Everywhere in her dreams, there was blood.

She'd find herself in rooms where the blood dripped down the windows like rain. Sometimes, it fell on her face, streaking into her eyes, so when she wiped them clear, her palms were stained red.

She dreamed of stabbing, felt the steel against her bones as the knife slid between her ribs.

And she dreamed of burning—the sunlight burned her to ash. She watched her skin curl like a match held to paper, and felt the heat, first discomfort and then the raging sear of the light on her. There was nothing to protect her, to come between her and the sun.

The flames crept closer and closer to her face, and when she opened her mouth to scream, she sucked the fire right into her lungs and awoke with a gasp.

During the night, she'd twisted, pinning her injured arm under her body. Now it ached and throbbed, the inflamed nerve endings screaming at her. Carefully, she sat, and slid off the bed. The clock next to the bed showed it was still early morning, and her plan for the day had to include a call to her mother and then a trip in full body armor to campus tonight.

After popping a couple Tylenol, she carefully removed the wrappings Professor Nors had placed on her arm.

God, it was ugly, but not as bad as she'd thought. The professor had moved fast last night and probably saved her from a deeper tissue burn. It was red and swollen, but not blistered, and covered the top of her hand and part of her lower arm to her elbow. Her stupid move could have ended a lot worse, and it reminded her just how dangerous her plan was.

She'd been lucky, and it was never a good idea for her to rely on luck. Yesterday had served as a reminder of how careful she needed to be, of how many fail-safes would be necessary for her to live a relatively normal and independent life.

Okay. No more removing gloves.

Thinking back on her time in the lecture, she tried to pinpoint the decisions she'd made that led to her injuries— taking off her hat and gloves, for sure, rolling up her sleeves in the heat of the lecture hall.

Extra deodorant. The hat stays on. Reminder on my phone at the end of each class. She made notes of the changes she'd make in her routine. More than anything, she wanted this degree and to attend college here, a thousand miles away from her family. She'd do whatever she needed to make it work.

By the time she called her mother, the swelling had gone down further, aided by lying on the couch and keeping her arm propped above her head.

"You didn't call yesterday," Mom started right off.

"I got in late from the lecture. Next time, I'll text you."

"Briar..." There was the long-suffering sigh she expected, and for the next fifteen minutes, she listened to her mother enumerate everything that could possibly go wrong—the injuries she could suffer, the impact it would have not only on her life, but on her parents—which led to a succession of bullet-pointed sacrifices her parents had made because of her diagnosis, including but not limited to, buying a house in West Virginia and leaving their extended family in South Carolina. "And I never got to take pictures of you going to prom."

Mom's litany of disappointments generally ended with the prom, so this was the time where Briar was expected to step in. "You've been the best, Mom. And I wouldn't be here, in graduate school, without your support. I know you're proud of me." This was the track she took—deflect, deflect, deflect. "How's Jamie?"

Her brother was a great distraction, and like she hoped, Mom went off on the latest Jamie-drama. Finally, there was a pause in the one-sided conversation, a sign her mom was wrapping it up. "You're going to call me tonight, or text me, when you finish whatever you have happening. I need to know when you're in for the evening and safe."

It wasn't too much to ask, Briar decided, at least not now, at the very beginning of this separation. Soon enough, she'd let a day go by without messaging, and before they knew what had happened, she'd be contacting her parents like a normal twenty-something.

"I promise, Mom. I will."

"Goodbye, Briar. Be safe."

"Love you. Say hi to Dad for me?"

Her mother made a lip-smacking kissing noise. "Of course. Bye, sweets."

"Bye, Mom." She hung up the phone, feeling like she'd run a race. A slight throb in her arm reminded her it was time for her second dose of pain pills, the ibuprofen chaser to the earlier Tylenol.

Swallowing the pills, she stared at herself in the green-tinged bathroom mirror and studied her face intently. Lightly, she touched her fingers to her cheek and the slightly raised and puffy skin graft she'd had to have as a child. From there, she touched a small white scar in the center of her lower lip, then tugged her shirt to view her collarbones. Her first burn had been the worst— shoulders, the back of her neck, collarbones—they'd taken the direct hit of the sun. It'd only been luck that she'd emerged from the water with her face tilted toward the pool.

Cupping her cheeks in her hands, she examined her face. It could have been her face that melted, not her back. As it was, her scars horrified her. An ever-present reminder of the need to *be careful*. She couldn't forget again.

Mentally, she groaned. Would there ever be a time when she forgot the mess she'd made the night before? She'd thrown up in front Professor Nors and Marcus. Now, if she was ever to see them again, she'd picture the sight she must have made—screaming, sweating, and then, the *piece de resistance:* barfing.

In order to distract herself from reliving her embarrassment, Briar forced herself to turn her thoughts to her graduate program and opened her laptop. Just the idea of taking classes with some of the most acclaimed researchers in the world made her pulse race. On Monday, she would have a molecular biology class, and then a meeting with her graduate research advisor to take the first steps in defining what her thesis would be.

She'd been thinking about her research and thesis since she'd made the decision to study biology. What caused her genes to mutate?

Opening her old files, she scanned articles she'd already read a thousand times, but the answers weren't there. Why had this happened to her and how could she stop it from happening to anyone else?

The darkness was no place to live. Briar opened a new tab on her computer and searched for Professor Nors. She'd saved his articles to her computer, but it was his faculty profile page she wanted to read. Unlike the other professors, his didn't list office hours or class schedule. Somehow, he managed to lecture on a whim and focus primarily on his research.

What had made him run away last night?

His face, when people in the atrium at the lecture hall had surrounded him, had been panicked, eyes skittering as if to find the nearest exit and escape. The man had gone from caring, to distant, to considerate, to angry, and then back to distant—a series of emotions that were impossible for her to follow.

Her phone chimed, and she glanced down and then at the blackout curtains. It was dusk. Standing, gloves in place, she flicked the curtain to the side, allowing a small shaft of light through. Without checking the weather on her phone, she had no idea what sort of day it was. A warm Indian summer or a brisk New England autumn day—it didn't matter when she had to wait for the night.

No. Things were different now. She'd made the decision to rejoin the day and take whatever precautions she must in order to be part of the light.

Ironically, it was dark out. Heavy, gray clouds hung low in the sky, and the cars speeding by her apartment splashed water onto the sidewalk. The people on the street held umbrellas above their heads, hurrying to wherever they were going.

Clouds and rain. The best possible weather for a girl like her. Donning her hat, Briar slid her gloves onto her hands and her backpack on her back, fairly bouncing outside. The other wonderful thing about the rain was that she didn't standout in her hat and gloves. People assumed she was cold, not odd.

She locked the door to her apartment and faced the street. Her plan was to make it back to BC and explore the campus more. She wanted to see McMullen Museum, though it would probably be closed. Even in the dark and the rain, it'd be beautiful because it was *hers*. Her college. Her plan. Her future.

The T, Boston's subway system, wasn't hard to find. Soon, she was on her way to Brighton. Briar tried not to stare at the people coming and going, or rubberneck every time the train made a stop. West Virginia was a long way from Boston and couldn't be more different.

Beckley, her hometown, was nestled in the Appalachian Mountains, which made it feel closed in on all sides. Boston wasn't like that. Yes, there was a lot of leafy greenness, but everything was so stately. Houses were built side-by-side— stone, mortar, brick, leaded glass.

"Commonwealth Avenue. End of Green Line." A robotic voice announced as the train came to a jerking halt. She was one of only a few people left on the train, but she was nearly crushed at the influx of people trying to get on. Elbowed and shoved, Briar had to stand on the sidewalk to get her bearings. In the time she'd been traveling, the rain had stopped and the streetlights had come on. The darkness surrounded her like a blanket—*safety*.

A wide drive led to the McMullen Museum, but she could make out the building, windows still bright, from the sidewalk. The interior section of the building was illuminated and made of glass. While she wanted to appreciate the architecture, the survival part of her brain made a note of the glass-enclosed stairwell and how she'd have to avoid it if she was ever to get inside.

A wrought-iron gate stood open, and she started up the drive. Behind her, the sidewalk was crowded with people leaving BC and headed to the T she'd just left into the city. It was Saturday night, and even though she was trying to fit in, she managed to stand apart again. She wanted to explore the campus and get into the museum, while everyone else was looking for a bar or excitement.

The closer she got to the entrance, the more uncertain she grew. The last twenty-four hours made her wary, and with her luck, she'd end up tripping through the plate-glass window.

Forcing herself to step forward, she peered in through the door, trying to make out some of the exhibits. Supposedly, there were beautiful Renaissance tapestries inside.

"Museum reopens at ten tomorrow," a deep voice said, and Briar jumped, spinning and covering her heart with her hand.

"Yes. I know." She smiled nervously at the security guard, trying to convey how non-threatening she was. Imagine if it was daylight, and she was wearing her protective clothing. She'd look like a cat burglarizing gardener. "Sorry," she continued. "I was trying to peek."

"You a student here?" he asked.

Reaching into her purse, she took out her wallet and showed him her BC student ID. "Yes, sir."

"Came to a museum instead of finding a party?" He had a thick Boston accent, and the word "party" came out "pah-ty."

"Yes, sir." She wasn't going to explain her day-is-night, night-is-day schedule. Truth be told, she'd be a fantastic party animal. She'd been staying up all night for years. Now, slowly but surely, she was becoming diurnal again—active during daylight hours.

"The museums in the city stay open later." There it was again, *late-ah*. This might be her favorite part of being in Boston.

"I start school Monday. I'm a graduate student," she explained. "No parties for this girl, and I'm still exploring."

At that, he sighed and rubbed his hand down his face. "Uh. I probably shouldn't do this, but I'm locking up anyway. Come inside, and you can check out the tapestries on the lower level. You've got fifteen minutes."

"Thank you." She hadn't expected to get inside. A private tour—for fifteen minutes anyway.

Boots clicking against the stone steps, she followed the guard inside. A woman, hair gathered in a bun, glanced up when they came inside. "Hello." Her eyes flicked to the guard, and she raised her eyebrows in question.

"Student. I'm giving her a couple minutes as we shut down."

"Okay."

Briar had expected more sideways glances and suspicion, but both guards waved her on her way. "Thank you," she said as she walked by the desk, eyes already trained on the muted-red tapestry she saw hanging on a wall.

The closer she got, the clearer the image became. A man wearing a red cape knelt at another man's feet. She read the small plate. *Emperor Caesar Augustus Receiving the Spoils of War.* The cape held her attention because the rest of the tapestry was done in beautiful golds and blues. It swirled around the man's neck, spilling onto the ground. One step closer, and she stopped. Suddenly, the cape stopped being a cape, and instead became blood. Blood poured from the supplicant's neck, pooling at Caesar's feet.

Moving away quickly, she passed a series of tapestries about Venus and Adonis. What was the story with them? Venus was the goddess of love, and Adonis was handsome. She knew that much.

"Adonis's beauty attracts the goddess, but he is young and only interested in the hunt. Venus sees him and falls in love with him. She begs him for a kiss, and he refuses. He tries to get away, but she holds on to him and won't let him escape."

"Awful woman," Briar replied, shifting to see who spoke.

"Hello." It was the man from yesterday, the rude one.

"You?"

"Me." Bright, white teeth flashed in a bitter smile. His handsome face was serious as he fixed his attention on the tapestry again. "One of those women who wouldn't take no for an answer. Are you like that?" He faced her suddenly, and she stepped back at the hard, cold glare he gave her.

"I suppose with some things." The words felt as if they were pulled from her. She didn't want to answer him or confide in him when he looked at her that way.

"With men?"

Her face tingled where heat seeped into her cheeks, and she cursed her pale skin. She didn't have any experience with men, and she knew it had to be obvious. Therefore, he had to be making fun of her. Instead of answering, she stepped around him to stare at the next picture. More blood.

No.

Another red cape.

She read the title: *Desperata Venus Retia Comburit*. "What does that mean?" she whispered, forgetting about the angry man in the face of Venus's sadness and Adonis dying on the blood-red cape beneath him.

"Adonis died, gored to death by a wild boar."

"Was she the boar?" Briar asked, remembering other stories of gods and goddesses taking the form of animals in order to harm mortals.

"No, but some believe it was due to her interference that Adonis went hunting the next day and was killed," he answered.

"How?" Interest piqued, she forgot about his earlier rudeness and waited for him to answer.

"If she hadn't stopped him from hunting in order to beg a kiss, he'd not have gone out into the woods the second day," he said after a moment's pause. His dark eyes flicked toward her forehead, and then down to her cheek, and lower, to her neck. Self-consciously, she covered her throat with her hand, not wanting him to see the puckered, melted skin there.

"How'd you get inside here?" he asked.

"The guard let me in," she answered quietly.

"Miss?" a voice called, and she spun. The female guard strode toward her. "We need to close. I'll escort you out."

"All right. Are you—" The words stuck in her throat. The man was gone. Spinning, she examined every corner of the room, but there was only her and the guard. "Where..."

"Miss, please." The woman's voice held a hint of impatience, and Briar hurried to follow her directions. They'd been so nice to let her in. She didn't want to make a bigger nuisance of herself.

A moment later, she found herself on the stone steps again, completely confused. She stood, waiting to see if perhaps the man would be escorted out as well, but no one came and the lights in the entrance shut off, a clear dismissal. Whoever the man was, he was obviously not coming out. Taking her phone out of her pocket, Briar checked the time and sighed. A forty-five minute train ride, a fifteen-minute exploration of the museum, and now what?

Her injured arm ached, and she was tired. Excitement and stress and hurt all combined to do her in. Home it was.

Ambling down the driveway, she struggled against a sense of failure. She should be doing more, introducing herself to the people walking by, making friends.

This was the problem with her. She'd lived her life so closeted that now she was free to make her own decisions, she wanted to do everything, all at once.

Her mind went to the man at the museum. He was interesting, she decided. Yeah, he'd been grumpy, but maybe he'd had a bad day.

She thought about the way he'd behaved the day before, biting her head off for standing in his way—maybe he'd had a bad week, or maybe he wasn't good with people. He'd had a glimmer of niceness tonight.

Briar suddenly stopped in the center of the sidewalk, aware she'd been walking for a while and hadn't happened upon the T station. This wasn't Commonwealth Avenue.

She'd gone the wrong way when she'd left the museum. Pulling her phone from her pocket, she thumbed into the maps app, but it flashed a battery symbol at her and died.

Perfect.

Backtracking, she headed in the direction she thought the museum was. But the longer she walked, the more unsure she became. What had been a busy street was now a quiet neighborhood. On one side of her sat the houses, while on the other was a grassy incline and forest. If she'd done what she suspected, on the other side of that forest was Commonwealth Avenue.

After waiting for a car to pass, she crossed the road, climbed over a low stone wall, and walked into the woods. She could hear traffic, but otherwise it was quiet, her feet shuffling through the dead leaves on the forest floor the only sound.

Above her head, the clouds broke and the moon illuminated the woods. Two eyes, low to the ground, flashed. Briar gasped, and jumped back, but the clouds covered the moon, obscuring anything else she may have seen.

Her heart pounded in her chest, and the back of her neck itched, like someone was staring at her. It made her lift her shoulders to her ears and whirl around, squinting into the darkness. Okay. This was dumb. She admitted it. Rushing into the woods, hoping to make her way to the T station, instead of staying on a well-lit, residential street was a stupid move.

Lesson learned.

She whirled, took a step back toward the street and stopped. An arm, cold as ice, with fingers sharp, wrapped around her waist and pulled her back. A chill seeped into her skin from her back to her neck, and she froze.

"You smell... so good." A voice like a snake, sibilant, curling and hissing, wound its way into her ear. "And not altogether human. Do you smell her?"

From the corner of her eye, something glowed. Like her gaze had thrown a switch, two eyes lit up. She glanced down, then immediately wished she hadn't. Something crawled at her feet. White, vaguely human, with yellow eyes and long, distorted limbs, the being stared at her. Man or woman, she had no idea. The clouds parted, and she gasped. It wasn't animal, but its mouth was wide, reaching from one side of its face to the other, and its tongue was black, tasting the air.

"I smell her. Human, yes. But more." Long fingers reached for her body, and she jerked, but the person who held her only tightened his grip, fingers digging painfully into her side. Using her body as a prop, the thing at her feet dragged itself upright until it was eye-to-eye with her, its fetid breath washing over her face.

In that moment, something clicked into place for Briar.

Through her fear, she felt wonder. Of course something like this would exist. If she was possible, a person who would burn up when the sun touched her skin, the world could devise a creature as twisted as this one.

Like her brother had always teased, she was a mutant. But God help her if these were the other X-Men.

"One of us?" the person holding her asked.

"Perhaps. There's one way to know for sure." Briar twisted her head to see the person who held her, but they tsked, and the creature in front of her curled a moist hand around her chin. "No, love. Watch me. Watch me while I taste you."

Briar kicked, struggling, as the lips and black tongue came closer to her face. She cried out. When she did, her mouth was smothered by a hand, the cold searing her as surely as the sun did.

In all her preparations for the real world, never once had she considered having to fight another person for her life. Her mind blanked for a second before coming back online with a vengeance. Letting her weight fall, she threw the person holding her off-balance, and the creature holding her face, fell back. She landed on top of it, and it was just as disgusting as she suspected. Unlike the man who stopped her, this thing was soft. Her hands, when she threw them out to brace herself, sunk into its skin. It let out a cry of pain, and she rolled to the side.

Without glancing behind her, she pushed herself to her feet. Her arm folded from the weight, pain shooting through her as a reminder of the injury she'd suffered yesterday, but she muscled through it. Behind her, the thing was silent, but she knew it was after her. In her mind's eye, she saw them both, one slithering after her on its belly, arms and legs propelling it forward like a spider, while the other one chased after her on silent feet.

Her lungs burned, but it didn't matter. Safety was ahead.

The streetlights shone through the trees—fifty feet, forty, twenty, ten. Something caught on her ankle, and she went down. Before she could open her mouth to scream, the creature was on her, yawning maw open to display rows of blackened fangs.

It dove toward her, and instinctively she shut her eyes, but the pain she expected never came. The soft weight of the thing left her, and she heard a thud, as if it had been thrown onto the ground.

Twisting, she pushed herself up, hands up, ready to fight. But the woods were empty. There was no creature, and no evil buddy. The wind blew, rustling the leaves innocently, while behind her, headlights of a passing car illuminated the neighborhood for a second.

Lifting a shaking hand to her face, she touched her skin. Maybe it was all in her head, but she imagined the creature had left a film of filth on her. Her hand, when she studied it, was clean.

Briar took a wobbling step toward the light, and then another, and another, until she was scurrying and sliding down the hill and back onto the sidewalk. Not caring which way she was going, she ran. She ran until the road met up with another, and she suddenly and inexplicably found herself back in front of the museum, panting and sweating.

Students walked by her, totally unconcerned there was a man-beast in the woods with a mutant sidekick. They were dressed up, boots and short dresses, high-heels and scarves. Headed downtown.

Briar followed them, staying in their shadows. Trailing them the way she imagined the creature had trailed her, stupid and oblivious, through the woods.

CHAPTER 5
SYLVAIN

Sylvain lifted the tree branch to impale the crawler. His hands shook, and he saw Briar's face, freckles stark against her white skin, as the crawler leaned in to bite her. Driving the sharp end of the branch into its soft, rotting skin, he felt only satisfaction. Pinned to the ground now, Sylvain reached down, and tugged its head from its body.

For a second, the head gave a cry and hiss, but disintegrated into dust. He whirled, ready to race into the forest to chase the soldier who'd dared to put its cold hands on the girl, but it was gone, much like he expected. Soldiers were vampires, but not like him. They were cold, and their minds were not their own. More sentient beings could use the soldiers to carry out the tasks they didn't want to do.

Soldiers were excellent, expendable assassins.

But in all of Sylvain's long life, he'd never seen a crawler and a soldier work in tandem. Nor had he seen one crawler so close to a residential area like this one. This was a wealthy neighborhood, well lit. It was the sort of neighborhood where, if someone went missing, they would be noticed.

And what the hell was Briar doing, walking through the woods at night?

Angrily, he marched through the woods toward the street, not caring if he was quiet, or hidden. He heard Briar's voice in his head, her soft, slightly southern-accented drawl as she answered his questions.

Stupid girl. This wasn't fucking Arkansas, or wherever the hell she was from. She needed to be more careful. Smarter.

When he found her, he'd—

Sylvain stopped.

He'd do what, exactly? He couldn't even answer what it was that had led him to her tonight. Why he'd continued to think about her and the way she smelled, like apple blossoms in the old orchards around his family's farmhouse.

His heart beat, a heavy thump in his chest. *No.* He didn't think of the before time, the farmhouse, or his family. A scream cut through the night, and he threw his hands over his ears.

No.

"Sylvain."

He heard the scream again. His wife. He knew what came next, but was helpless to stop it. Through the night, his son's voice echoed through his brain as his small boy cried out in fear. The woods disappeared, becoming older woods, darker woods. A forest so thick the light couldn't penetrate the overlapping branches, leaving the forest floor spongy and mossy.

Ahead of him, his cabin—the one he'd spent months building, chopping down trees, splitting the logs, hauling them with his horse over to the site he'd cleared with Juliette. But now it was burning, flames reaching so high, they scorched the trees.

Sylvain ran for the cabin, eyes on the flames spilling from the window. He knew Juliette and Jacques were inside, dying.

But before he could get to them, something slammed into him, pinning him to the ground.

"Sylvain!" Valen was merely a shadow against the flames. Pain exploded along the side of his face, and suddenly the flames were gone. "Sylvain!"

He twisted, dislodging his oldest friend. "Get off me, Valen."

Despite not having eaten for four-hundred years, his stomach rebelled as if he had. The image of the cabin, seeing and hearing his family burn to death—it felt as real as it had when it first happened.

"Why are you here?" he spat, guilt assaulting him momentarily when his friend's face pinched.

"I followed you."

"Don't need you to babysit me." He huffed, standing and brushing the leaves off his jacket. "You can go."

"I know that." Valen's sad voice made Sylvain only angrier, and he lashed out.

"There's no reason for us to be together once Hudson has dosed us. It'd be better for all of us if we went our separate ways."

The clouds broke, turning Valen's blond hair silvery white in the moonlight. Facing Sylvain, Valen chuckled. "You're such an asshole. But you're my brother, and I won't leave you."

Sylvain stared at him, taking in the stubborn set of his jaw and shoulders. The man would follow him to the ends of the earth, when all Sylvain wanted to do was walk off it and fall into nothingness. "We're not a family anymore, Valen. I'm done pretending. You're a stranger as far as I'm concerned."

"Damn you." The hurt in Valen's voice nearly undid him, but Sylvain didn't let himself look away.

"I'm already damned," he answered, and before Valen

could respond, he ran. Like the coward he was, and the coward he'd always be.

❦

Sylvain tracked the girl the rest of the night, aware of every hour that passed and every minute that brought him closer to sunrise.

In the old days, he'd have memorized her scent and followed it. Discounting the scent of horses or other humans, he'd have found her trail like it was a golden thread, and all he had to do was wind it in his hand.

The modern world made that impossible. He could wait for a train, but it may not be the same train, the same car. Ironic, when this era was all about things happening at the speed of light, and designing things to deliver whatever humans wanted as soon as the thought occurred to them.

For him, though, a creature who relied on his senses, this world only confounded him and made things more difficult.

Why did he even need to find her? It wasn't to make sure she was okay. He didn't care. Didn't care if the crawler ripped her to pieces or the soldier fed off her until she fell, pale and lifeless, to the ground.

In a flash, he saw just that. Briar's scars, whiter than white against a bloodless face. Fear, like he hadn't felt in a lifetime, stabbed him in the belly.

What the fuck was that?

Halting where he was, he very nearly turned around and ran in the opposite direction. Away from whatever it was the girl brought out in him.

But there it was again. He'd gone a good distance, from Brighton to Davis Square, when he found her. Apple blossoms and something else.

He tracked it to some coffee shop across the street from yet another coffee shop.

There she was—as if a spotlight had illuminated her just for him. Through the window, he watched her sip her coffee, the cup shaking and spilling liquid onto the table. If he'd been close, he knew he would have smelled her fear, and he hated that—hated she'd been afraid and he'd been too late to keep her safe.

"What are you doing here?"

Years of practice kept him from showing his surprise. He answered Marcus as sarcastically as he could. "Do you suddenly own the city? Am I not allowed to stay here?"

"Jesus, Sylvain. Are you ever able to answer a simple question?" Marcus stared at the small figure in the window.

"What are you doing here?" he asked, watching a fascinating range of emotions play across Marcus's face.

"I work here."

"Do you?" Sylvain crossed his arms and raised an eyebrow. "Making coffee?"

"Shut up," Marcus ground out. "Forget it."

The door to the shop opened, and a wave of apple blossom-tinted air struck Sylvain in the face. It was so strong, he closed his eyes, breathing deeply.

"You feel it, too," Marcus whispered.

"No, I don't," he answered immediately and opened his eyes to see Marcus staring at him in wonder and bemusement.

"You do. I feel it. Hudson feels it. Valen felt it."

"No." His voice choked. "I don't feel anything." He wouldn't let himself feel anything again. He refused. The last time he had, the last time any of them had, it had torn them apart, left them the shells they now were.

It could never happen again.

CHAPTER 6
MARCUS

Sylvain could deny it all he wanted, but this was the most emotion he'd shown in two hundred years, and the only thing that had changed was the presence of this girl.

"She's like us, in a way," Marcus said, causing Sylvain to snort derisively.

"Oh, is she?"

"The sun burns her like it would us. She's part of the darkness."

"There's nothing dark about her," Sylvain retorted before pressing his lips together, but Marcus smiled. His friend had admitted more about his feelings than he'd meant to. "Why doesn't Hudson give her the same medicine he gives us?"

Marcus shook his head. "I'm sure he would, but it doesn't work on humans. He's tried in the past. No effect."

"And your research?"

"I concern myself with blood, Sylvain. I don't save people." No. His research was purely selfish. Blood was his focus—creating a never-ending food source for them. Hudson was the one who cared about more than himself, even if he pretended otherwise.

"Why are you here, Sylvain? Really?" he tried again. "I saw you last night. So did Hudson. Watching her."

"You're watching her, too."

"I am."

"Why?" Sylvain faced him, chin tilted down, eyes flicking over his shoulder and at the sidewalk before finally settling on his.

"She smells like home," he said.

Eyes wide, Sylvain shook his head. "No, she doesn't."

"Yes," Marcus answered. "Wildflowers. Ice and the sea to Valen. And she's important to Hudson. You didn't see him last night. He ran away. Scented her and jumped out of the car."

"No." Sylvain raked his fingers through his long hair. "Valen doesn't care about her. If he did, he would have helped her tonight."

Anger flared inside Marcus. "Why would he need to help her? What happened? What did you do?" He moved closer to the window and narrowed his eyes. Briar continued to shake. Alternately sipping her coffee and rubbing her eyes, she appeared deep in thought. He peered closer. Caught in her hair was a leaf, and the elbow of her jacket was dark, wet. His eyes flashed to her neck, checking for wounds, but he saw nothing. "What did you do, Sylvain?"

"Nothing." Sylvain stepped back, holding out his hands. "Calm the fuck down, Marcus. You're flashing fang."

One deep breath followed another, and another, until he could be sure he wouldn't rip Sylvain's head off.

"Tell me what happened."

"I followed her." He swallowed hard, turning to stare at Briar, and his voice softened. "I don't know why. Since last night. Couldn't think of anything except her. Shit!" He spun away, walking a few steps down the street only to return. "You're right. You're fucking right. She smells like home, and it's all I can think about."

Marcus knew what he meant. Since last night, when he'd dropped her off at home with no intention of ever seeing her again, he hadn't been able to stop thinking about her. As he'd driven back to BC, his chest had tightened exponentially. He'd parked Hudson's car, stuck the keys under the seat, and run all the way back to Davis Square, only to stand outside her building. He left when the clouds gathered and it began to rain, forcing himself to go to his lab. There, he'd gorged on blood, thinking maybe it would satisfy him.

But it wasn't blood he wanted. He was a goddamned vampire, and he didn't want blood.

He wanted Briar.

The rest of the day, he'd fought himself. Each time he'd wanted to step outside the lab, he'd forced himself back inside.

"I'm going in," he muttered.

"What?" Sylvain slapped his hand against his shoulder. "No. You can't."

"Why the hell not? Maybe I'm going crazy. I'm going in there, and I'm going to see what it is between us. Maybe it's something, or maybe I'm just hungry."

A growl rumbled from Sylvain's throat, and Marcus smirked. "You're welcome to join me."

"Fuck you, Marcus." Without a backwards glance, Sylvain marched down the street then disappeared around a corner.

Now that his brother was gone, so was his bravado. As a scientist, though, Marcus was curious. What was it about Briar, besides her tantalizing smell, that drew them to her? There was only one way to find out.

He strode through the doors and directly to the spot

where she was mopping up another coffee spill. A pile of stained, wet napkins showed it wasn't the first one she'd had.

"Did any of the coffee make it into your mouth?" he joked. Briar's frightened stare met his. All laughter left him, and he had to smother the snarl threatening to escape. "What happened?" he asked, mentally planning on seeking out Sylvain and killing him. He could scent a faint trace of his brother lingering on her.

She remained silent, gaze flickering from him to the door and around the shop. Trembling, she crushed the napkin in her fist and lowered it to her lap. The injury suffered earlier must have been paining her because she cradled it close to her chest. Her hand, wrapped in bandages, was gray with dirt and speckled with pieces of grass and leaves.

Grabbing a chair, he sat it next to hers and cupped her face in his hand. Immediately, her eyes shut and she let out a breath. "Briar," he whispered. "Are you all right?"

A small frown appeared between her eyebrows, drawing them low, but she nodded and opened her eyes. "Marcus." His name was a sigh, and though he couldn't remember telling her his name, he liked the shape of her mouth as she formed it. "I think so."

Carefully, he let his hand slip from her face, trailing down her neck to sneakily check for puncture wounds. Sniffing, he found no trace of blood, but what the coffee and baked goods masked earlier, became more pronounced.

Rot.

Rot, and filth, and decay.

"What did you see? Briar." He kicked the chair away, knelt next to her, and wrapped her good hand in his. "What happened?"

"You won't believe me." Her voice shook, and he cursed. Sylvain was somehow involved in this, though he didn't know how. Whatever it was she'd seen had shaken her to her core and left her here, stinking of the worst of his kind.

"I believe you," he whispered. "Whatever it is. I will believe you."

"You're a scientist, like Professor Nors. What I saw shouldn't exist."

"Because I'm a scientist, I'll believe you. But more than that, Briar, I'll believe you because it will be your eyes that saw it." He leapt without thinking, and free falling, waited for her to catch him.

Clearing her throat, Briar's eyes darted around the shop before she began. "It crawled, and spoke. It had fangs. And it wanted to taste me."

Marcus shut his eyes so she wouldn't see his rage. Holding his breath, he forced it down.

Down.

Down, into a box and then shut the box and stuffed it into a closet.

A crawler. That was the stench. The rot. Crawlers were vampires, but not like him. They were what happened when a turning went wrong, and without conscience, its creator let it live. All of them had the potential to be crawlers, and it was only luck that left him humanesque.

"I believe you." He opened his eyes, squeezing her hand tightly. "I believe you."

"You do?"

"Yes. Are you all right? Did it bite you?"

Slowly, Briar shook her head. "No. But..." Disentangling her fingers from his, she touched her side. "There was another one. It scratched me."

Jacket buttoned, he didn't see what she meant, but when she pulled the two sides apart, he saw rends in the fabric of her shirt. "Show me." His voice was deep, angry. She paled.

Trembling, she lifted the edge, exposing white skin.

Across her side were four deep-purple bruises and then scratches, not deep enough to draw blood, but red. "The crawler did this?"

"No," she answered and had to clear her throat again. "The other one. He didn't crawl, but I never saw him."

Did Sylvain do this?

"Him?" If Sylvain had hurt her, if he'd been the one to bruise her soft skin, Marcus would tear him to shreds. "Did you recognize his voice? Was there anything familiar about him?"

"No. But he was cold. Like ice. He held me still while the thing pulled itself up my body, and his skin was so cold—it was like it burned me."

His shoulders slumped in relief. *Thank God.* The cold. It was a giveaway. A soldier then. Mindless, it took orders and followed them. It was like a robot—give them a task, press enter, and it went to work. Why in the world would it have bothered Briar? To that end, why the hell was there a crawler and a soldier together, in Boston?

Marcus's skin itched, and he shivered. "Where, Briar?"

She shook her head from side to side. "I don't even know. I went to McMullen." A far-off smile appeared on her face. "They let me in. Even though it was closed, and I got to see the tapestries. Venus and Adonis." There was that tiny pucker between her brows again. "I talked to the man from yesterday, and then I got lost."

"In the museum? And what man from yesterday?"

He took her hand in his again, and her face heated, blood rushing from her neck to her face. The scar below her eye turned splotchy, and one small red shape, like a crescent appeared. *Fascinating.* He reached for it without thinking, touching the pad of his thumb to the tiny outline. She shifted uncomfortably beneath his examination, eyes downcast, and he knew it was because of what he'd done yesterday, staring at her scar.

But it didn't bother him.

His eyesight was good, better than a human's. He could make out every flaw, if it could be called that, marring her skin. Letting his gaze drift from her face, he paused on her neck. It hurt him, for some reason, to see the results of the pain she suffered.

"Don't look," she whispered, and his eyes shot to hers. "Please? It's ugly."

Shaking his head, he lifted both hands to her neck before wrapping his fingers around her small throat and skimmed them along the puckered skin. "It's not. Not at all."

The scent of fear and hurt disappeared, replaced with the hypnotizing one from yesterday—wildflowers and heat.

"I didn't think I'd see you again," she said. "After last night. I thought you were leaving."

"I meant to," he replied honestly. "Had every intention of going to work and not returning."

"Then it's luck to see you here?" She canted her head to the side, and he realized she was issuing a challenge. Would he answer honestly?

Challenge accepted. "In a way. I knew you lived here and came hoping to see you," he replied.

"Oh," she whispered, a smile curling the ends of her lips.

"You never answered my question." He needed to pull her back on track.

"Which one?"

"Which man did you see again?" The words were difficult to push out. Was there already some human who found her as interesting as he, and his brothers, did? An ache formed in his chest. What would he do?

Dammit! This was a mistake. He'd come in here to see if

there was a connection with Briar that went beyond scent, and the answer to his question was indisputably, yes. Her blushes and smiles captivated him, but her honesty knocked him off his feet. She didn't know him, but he'd told her to trust him, and she had.

He'd leapt, and she'd caught him.

"I met a man on my way to Professor Nors lecture." She laughed. "Actually, I was in the way of a man while on my way to the lecture. He grumped at me, but his friend apologized for him, and I don't think he's actually as grumpy as he seems. Just out of practice talking to people."

"Ah." The ache turned into something good. Something hopeful. A grumpy man with a friend in tow who apologized for his grumpiness? "Sylvain and Valen."

"Tall?" She held her hand above her head. "Dark hair?" Finally, she brushed her fingers through her eyebrow. "A scar?"

Definitely Sylvain.

"Yes." *Son of a bitch*. If he didn't know better, he'd say fate had thrown this girl in their path. "That's Sylvain. He's a—" *He's a what? A friend? My brother?* "He's family."

Tilting her head to the side, she considered him. "You don't look alike."

Marcus barked a laugh. "We wouldn't. Adopted."

"And Valen? He's the blond man? The one who looks like a Viking?"

Now Marcus couldn't stop laughing. She'd come closer than she realized. Valen *was* a Viking.

"How strange," she mused. "I can't believe I met your family on my very first day of school."

"I don't know," Marcus replied. "Maybe it was meant to be."

Briar's gaze went over his shoulder, and she shuddered. "You really believe me?"

She was thinking about what she'd seen tonight. "I really

do," he answered. But he couldn't tell her it was real, he couldn't tell her what he knew. Not yet. Not until he'd spoken to his brothers.

When had he begun to think of them as brothers again? Two hundred years had passed since they'd gone their separate ways. In that time, he'd forced himself to think of them by name, if he let himself think of them at all. Now he declared them family and talked about them to a girl.

Not just any girl. A voice in his mind whispered. *Yours.*

Marcus inhaled again. Wildflowers and heat. Yes. She was his.

CHAPTER 7
BRIAR

Something strange was happening, and it wasn't the horror movie extras who'd accosted her in the woods outside of BC. It was this feeling inside her—the one of calm and contentment. She'd been sitting, sipping and spilling her coffee, afraid with every gust of wind that the creatures from earlier would slide through the door, when she looked up into the concerned face of Marcus.

For a second, she didn't know what to think. It was like a dream coming to life, and she was afraid if she blinked, he'd disappear.

He'd asked her what was wrong, and for once, she hadn't put on a brave face and stated, *nothing*. She'd told him the truth—the unbelievable truth—and he'd accepted it.

What was more? He wasn't lying. His gaze held hers, and when he'd said, "I believe you," she knew, whole-heartedly, he did.

The more they talked, the straighter she sat. Her hands steadied, but her blush intensified. She could feel the heat on her neck, under her cheeks, and she was starting to sweat.

"Do you need to leave?" she asked suddenly, interrupting him when he asked if she wanted another coffee.

His green eyes narrowed. "No. Why? Do you want me to leave?" He watched her closely.

"No!" she replied quickly. "But it's getting late and I don't know if you have to work. I'm kind of a night owl." That was putting it lightly. "My days and nights have been all switched around."

"Because you have EPP?"

He knew. Of course he knew; he was a scientist, and he was friends, or colleagues, whatever, with Professor Nors, who would have recognized her symptoms immediately.

"Yes," she answered, and then, because she couldn't *not* ask, "Does it freak you out?"

Her words had him sitting back in his chair. "What?"

"My—" What should she call it? Illness? Syndrome? "EPP. Does it freak you out? I understand if it does. It's one thing to know about it, it's another to know someone who stays up all night and burns up in the sun like a vampire."

"It doesn't freak me out," he answered.

"I lost friends, or never made them." *Shut up!* Why was she spilling her guts to him? Warning him off of being her friend?

"It doesn't freak me out," he repeated, and pinned her with a stare.

"We're closing in ten minutes," the barista called over the counter to them.

Briar stood. "I'll be right back." Carefully, she picked up her cup to return to the counter, but Marcus swept it away from her.

"I've got it."

She couldn't help but follow him with her gaze. His figure commanded attention. Straight-backed, broad-shouldered, he walked with purpose. Briar caught the barista watching him, and she shrugged, like, *can't help it,* and Briar agreed. Her gaze was glued to him, but when he dropped the cup into the dirty dish bin, she quickly stared at the table, not wanting to be caught ogling her new friend.

"Can I walk you home?" he asked.

Focusing on the table, she nodded, and when she had hidden her thoughts, she met his stare. "Yes, please."

He waited for her to stand and push in her chair before he placed a hand on the small of her back to lead her out of the shop. No one had ever done that before, and it was all she could think about as they left the bright interior of the coffee shop and went out into the chilly night.

When he dropped his hand, she sighed. It had been nice, like he was staking his claim.

They walked in silence through the busy streets. Even though it was late, bars were still open and groups of people were leaving one to enter another. As they passed, the door opened, music blaring, and then faded when it closed.

"Wow," she said. "Great soundproofing."

Marcus side-eyed her, and smiled. "Are you moving closer to Chestnut Hill?"

"I'm still looking, but it's only an hour way."

"Only in Boston can seven miles equate to an hour of travel."

"I'm learning. I rented the apartment while I was still home, so it didn't look bad. Seven miles was ten minutes where I grew up," she answered.

"Where are you from? I can hear an accent."

Briar laughed. "I have an accent? Funny."

The side of his mouth lifted. "I don't have an accent."

"Fine. You're the only one without one. But I actually love it. It's exactly like I thought it would sound." She thought of the guard from earlier. "I'm from West Virginia. Though not originally. I was born in South Carolina. It's where my grandparents are. We moved to Beckley because it's one of the cloudiest cities in America. Are you from Boston?" she asked, but he wasn't paying attention.

"Here you go." They'd arrived at her house, and except for the one bar, she couldn't remember the walk.

"Oh." She stared at the apartment house. "So. Thanks." Should she invite him in? Give him her number? Their conversation felt like the first steps to friendship, but what if he was just being nice? The last time she'd suggested seeing him again, he'd shut her down.

"Can I call you?"

"Yeah," she answered. The words tripped over her tongue. "I don't know anyone. It'd be nice to have a friend." She took the phone he held out to her, and entered her number before handing it back.

His eyebrows drew together, but then his face cleared. "Okay. I'm going to go. Wave to me from the window?"

"My apartment is in the back." She pointed. "But the stairs are there. I'll wave to you from the top. Okay?"

He nodded, walking with her up the steps and waiting until she'd unlocked the door. He stood so close, when she glanced up, she could see the dark scruff of beard along his jaw. Curling her fingers so not to graze his face with her hand, she cleared her throat. "Night, Marcus."

"Goodnight, Briar."

She closed the door behind her, turning the locks before hurrying up the wooden steps. Two apartments made up the second floor, but there was a narrow hallway with a window at one end. It took her a moment to locate him, his dark hair and clothes made him blend into the night.

"Goodnight," she whispered, waving.

He lifted one hand in reply before he turned his back and dashed down the street.

Two nights in a row, Briar had been offered a challenge,

and on both, she liked to think she met it. Once inside her apartment, though, her momentary pride bled away. Drawing the curtains, anxiety began to curl in her stomach.

A challenge. She rolled her eyes at herself. Something was out in the woods—a monster. She had seen, and survived, a monster.

What was she supposed to do now?

The thing, with its pale skin and black mouth, burned the back of her eyelids. What was it Marcus had called it? A crawler.

She shuddered. It was the perfect name for the creature. Suddenly, she pictured it, scaling the side of her house, its weird, disjointed body contorting itself around corners and through her window.

Shaking her head to force the image out of her mind, she went into the bathroom and twisted the shower knob toward "hot" as far as it would go. She stood there, waiting for the steam to fill the room, and then turned down the temperature. Any warmer and the heat would make her burn feel worse.

Without Marcus to distract her, her mind kept replaying the voice of the man who held her and the way the creature had felt, grasping her clothing to hoist itself face-to-face.

What genetic mutation had caused that thing?

Grabbing the soap, she scrubbed her skin, lingering on those places where the creature and man had touched her. The ghost of their bodies stayed on hers. Using a facecloth, and one hand, she scoured her skin until it reddened.

Hair dripping, she tugged a t-shirt over her head and sleep shorts and went to find her computer. There had to be an explanation for the thing she saw because she came back to the same idea, over and over. If someone like her could exist, anything was possible.

First, she searched the traits she'd seen—*pale skin, black mouth, hairless, hyper-mobility.* Sure enough, the constellation of symptoms came up with a syndrome.

Reading the description, she shook her head. Nope. Not the right one, but her anxiety was alleviated. There was a logical explanation for what she saw, and not only that, it'd only taken one cursory internet search.

Briar closed the laptop, yawning. Carefully, she stretched her arms over her head. First one, then the injured arm. It felt better, even with the jarring she'd given it in the woods earlier. She could extend it and flex her fingers, all without suffering debilitating pain.

Her phone was still in her jacket. She grabbed it and plugged it in. So much for her resolutions to use her phone for reminders and smart planning. She hadn't even charged it sufficiently. Not only hadn't she reminded herself to wear her protective gear, she couldn't even access it for a simple map to lead her back to the T station. Her independence and decision-making needed some more work.

But not right now. Right now, she was done. Crawling into her bed, she pulled the covers over her head and snuggled into the sheets. She could put weight on her arm, and turned on her side, tucking her legs up to her chest.

Each mistake she made was a lesson learned. Hopefully, her quota of lessons learned through stupidity was met and she could finally focus on what she came to Boston to do—go to school.

CHAPTER 8
VALEN

Valen Larsson didn't give up. He couldn't. No matter how many times his brothers—because that's what they were, his brothers—dismissed him, insulted him, or pushed him away, he came back. It's what family did. They stuck together through war, and peace, and famine, and blight.

He knew what it was like to lose the family of his birth and all of his tribe. So when he'd finally found another one, he'd committed to them.

Sylvain could run away as often as he liked, but Valen would be there. His brother stood in the darkness, growling under his breath at him and at Marcus, who'd walked the girl from yesterday to her house.

"Why are we here?" Valen asked, though he knew. He wouldn't give it away, not yet. His brothers were still struggling to understand what was happening, but as soon as he'd smelled the girl, *Briar Hale,* he'd known she was the one for them. A seer, it was Valen's gift, and curse, to recognize the signs the universe sent them. In this case, the giant arrow pointing to the girl who had his brother, Sylvain, tied up in knots.

And apparently, Marcus, as well.

It made him infinitely curious.

Sylvain had sought her out.

Sylvain—who refused to admit to any reason for standing outside Briar's window, except hunger. But Valen had seen Sylvain like this before, and he knew what it meant, even if his brother didn't.

A vision hit Valen, harder than he'd ever been hit before, and the busy city neighborhood disappeared. Sylvain held Briar in his arms, blocking out the sun with his body, curled over her form as if to protect her.

And then he was back, standing next to Sylvain, who filled the night with a constant growl.

Valen fisted his hands and crossed his arms. They ached with the remembered weight of her, slight though it'd been, as if he'd been inhabiting his brother's body.

He closed his eyes, revisiting every detail he could remember. Her pale eyelids, crossed with thin veins, golden freckles across her nose, and a scar below her eye.

"Why are you still growling?" he asked Sylvain. It was getting annoying.

Facing Valen, Sylvain raised his scarred eyebrow. "Not me."

Oh.

"Are we standing here all night?"

Sylvain continued to watch him, shuttering his confusion quickly. He flashed a glance toward the house, so fast Valen nearly missed it, and shook his head. "No. No reason to stay."

If Valen left with him, Sylvain would only return. He knew his brother like he knew himself, and though he'd fight the urge, he'd give in eventually.

Valen needed time. He needed to consider what he'd seen

and how it made him feel. Then he had to think about Briar. This girl was different. Four hundred years ago, something unheard of happened. Four vampires left their master to form their own family. They'd lived together, hunted together, existed through centuries.

Then one day, they met a human. A woman—Annie.

In this new world, in a country where the humans burned witches, revolted against kings, and made slaves, they fell in love. And Annie fell in love with them.

He and his brothers took her, like they had every right to her, and made her one of them. They made her one of them, and they hadn't even asked permission.

Annie wasn't made for the night. She wasn't built for hunting, and persevering, and *surviving*. Valen and his brothers, they weren't enough to hold her, and one day, when the sun rose, she walked into a field and let the flames consume her.

Two hundred years ago, he was too proud, and too late.

Too proud to admit they'd done something they shouldn't, and too late to save the woman they thought would complete their family.

It had broken them.

Sylvain. Valen had restrained him to keep him from going mad.

Hudson. The distant scientist, a man who'd lived eons, almost as long as Valen, only got colder and more distant.

Marcus. He'd hidden his pain behind parties and humor.

And him. What had he done? He'd survived to keep his brothers alive, focusing on their pain and not his own. If he did, if he let himself think too long, he'd remember how this all was his fault. How the moment he met Annie, he'd had a vision of flames, and a vision of his brothers running, scattering to all ends of the earth. He'd remember how he ignored all the warnings the universe gave him about Annie and did what he wanted because it *felt* right.

Valen shifted, retreating into the shadows to leap the chain-link fence and sneak into the backyard. He'd overheard Marcus talking to her and knew he wouldn't be able to see a thing at the front of the house. There was one tree, half dead, in the yard along with a molded patio set. Everything about the place spoke of neglect. No one took pride in their homes anymore.

He wasn't ready to leave. Not yet. Let Sylvain sulk around Boston, kicking curbs and cars.

All night he stood there, staring up at the apartment until the sun rose and the sky turned bright blue. It'd be a hard day for her if she chose to come outside. A rusty hinge swung, and next door, someone let out a small dog. It sensed him, and rushed to the fence, barking frantically.

"Tyson!" the person called. "Get back here!"

Cigarette smoke wafted toward him, and he hid himself around a corner until the smell dissipated and the yappy dog had done his business and gone inside.

The street got busier, people heading to work, or school—or hell, what day was it?——Sunday? Church, maybe. He wouldn't be able to stay here much longer without someone spotting him. He was great at blending, but at six feet, three inches, leaning against a house for hours on end was going to get him noticed.

The curtains in the window didn't so much as twitch, and after a while, he straightened and headed into the street. As he turned the corner, the front door opened, and a figure emerged, bright blue shirt meeting white gloves with a floppy brimmed hat.

Briar.

Whirling around, she startled and jumped back. "Holy cow, you scared me!" Dark sunglasses hid most of her face, but the hat shadowed what wasn't covered. "I don't expect anyone to know me! You're Sylvain's buddy."

He chuckled. *Buddy.* It sounded as if he and Sylvain were youths who had, what did humans call them nowadays? Playdates.

"...And Marcus's brother."

Her words had him choking. He'd been so distracted by the vision of a playdate with Sylvain, he'd missed that she was still talking. "Marcus told you?"

"Sylvain is his brother, yes. He told me."

Ah. Even so. Marcus was confiding in her. Interesting.

"I'm Valen Larrsen," He resisted his old habit of bowing slightly at the waist. "Where are you off to?" he asked when she shifted from side to side.

"School," she answered. "I'm going to the bookstore."

He nodded, then scraped his hands through his hair. This was harder than he expected. "You eat?"

"I do," she answered slowly. "Do you?"

No. But he could fake it for her. "I can."

She lifted one brow, reminding him of Sylvain. Her lips curled as he remained silent, waiting.

Finally, he understood she waited for him to ask. "Do you want to have breakfast with me?"

The smile disappeared, and he winced. He'd moved too fast, come on too strong. He should have known.

"Why?" Briar lifted a gloved finger to the glasses, scooting them down her nose a tiny bit to peer at him from beneath them.

Shit. Why? Weren't girls supposed to blush and bite their lip and nod coyly? Instead she was looking at him confused. She really wanted to know.

"You seem nice."

"I seem..." She paused, pushing her glasses in place. "Nice?"

"Yes." If he spent time with her, he could answer her question even more honestly. Something about her drew all of them to her, but he was determined not to do what he'd done with Annie. They'd never gotten to know her, and maybe that had been the time. Then, people married after weeks, not years. Lifelong commitments were made without any second-guessing, but it was probably due to the short life expectancies.

White teeth dug into her lower lip, gnawing nervously. She was waiting for him to speak. "What's wrong with nice? Kindness is an under-appreciated quality."

Now, she smiled, and there was the blush he'd been expecting "I'd like to have breakfast with you."

"Thank you," he replied. Contentment and anticipation filled him. He'd done it. He'd gone out on a limb, and she'd said yes.

"Do you know Boston well?" she asked, as they began to walk.

"Yes," he answered. He couldn't tell her about arriving before the Pilgrims, albeit, further north and in a longship. "I know it quite well."

The hat she wore grazed his arm, the wide brim tickling his elbow. "Why do you wear the hat?" He scanned her, taking in her clothes. It was a warm day, not uncommon for September in New England. By midmorning, it would be what the Bostonians called *a scorch-ah*. "And gloves?"

If he hadn't been watching her so closely, he'd have missed the way her shoulders squared before she spoke. "I have a condition called EPP. I'm sensitive to ultraviolet light."

This sounded like something Hudson would understand. "You mean the sun?"

"Yes," she answered.

"Allergic?"

"In a sense." She shrugged and stopped, facing him. "I

have extreme reactions to the sunlight. If my skin is exposed, I'll burn."

Burn. The word echoed in his brain, and he saw Annie, the fire whipping her hair into red flames.

"Want to skip breakfast?"

Shaking his head, he came back to the present and found her staring at the ground, scuffing the toe of her shoe on the sidewalk. "No," he answered. "I want to get there faster. What are you doing outside if you can burn up?" He touched her back to guide her, hurrying toward the first place that looked like it had food. "A place in back, please," he told the hostess, while positioning Briar directly in front of him so his body blocked the sun coming through the plate-glass window. He angled her seat against a back wall, and made sure his shadow would provide the cover she needed before seating himself.

She followed him with her gaze, her lips turned up. "I'm not going to catch fire," she joked.

"I don't know what could happen. Now, please. If you don't mind, explain."

Her smile only grew wider. "I like you, Valen." *Honest.* He liked her, as well.

"When I say burn, I mean my skin burns, like the worst sunburn you could ever have. And if I stay too long, I won't catch fire, but my skin will..." She pulled off her glasses and placed them on the table, glancing up at him while touching a scar on her cheek. "It isn't pretty."

The length and width of his thumb, the scar was white, old. "The sun did that?"

"Yes," she answered. "If I'm not careful."

"You were burned at Hud's lecture."

A flush stained her cheeks, pink on one side, splotchy on the other. "Yeah. I was dumb. Dropped my glove and reached for it with bare skin."

An alarm went off on her phone, and she peered down at it. Valen read it from his seat across from her. *Wear your gloves! Put your hat on!*

"Not dumb," he argued, gesturing with his chin to the phone.

"I'm not used to the daylight," she admitted, fiddling with the buttons at her wrist.

Valen sat back, taking in her outfit. Now that he knew what it was meant to do, it looked different. What he thought was merely a long-sleeve shirt, had to be more. "What's it made of? Your suit of armor?" He smiled, hoping to lighten her mood, and it did the trick.

"This old thing?" She plucked at the fabric. "Polyester and titanium dioxide."

"Titanium dioxide?" He had no idea what she was talking about.

"It's a chemical that refracts light. So I won't get burned."

A waitress appeared by the table, pad in hand. "What can I get you two?"

Briar grimaced and grabbed the menu. "Sorry. Um. Yogurt and granola please."

"And you?" the woman asked, while writing down Briar's order.

"Toast, please."

"White, wheat or rye?"

Didn't matter. He wouldn't taste it anyway. "White, please."

"Anything else? Coffee?"

"Yes, coffee, please," Briar replied.

"No, thank you, ma'am," he answered.

"Toast and water?" The waitress's brows went to her hairline.

"Yes, ma'am."

She walked away, shaking her head.

"You have nice manners," Briar observed. "I like the way you talk to people."

It didn't come easy to him. Actions were how he communicated. Staying near Sylvain was how he showed his brother he cared. He didn't know how to respond to Briar, and so he stayed quiet, tapping his fingers on the counter and studying the restaurant.

"Do you think I can take my hat off?"

"Why?" He studied her. If it kept her safe, there was no reason to remove it.

"It's pretty dark back here, the light's not touching me. I think I can do it."

"Why would you take it off? I don't understand."

Studying the walls and the window, she didn't seem to hear him. She stuck a gloved hand into the space between their table and the one next to them. "Hmm."

He snagged her hand as she brought it back and folded it onto the table, snug between both of his. His giant paws dwarfed hers, made him feel freakish, and he drew them back, sticking them in his lap. "Don't risk it, please, Briar."

She made a moue, and waved her hand. "Look around, Valen."

Twisting, he did. The chair creaked beneath his weight, reminding him of how huge he was compared to most humans. He half-expected all eyes to be on him, but they weren't. No one was watching them.

"I'm getting the side-eye. It's weird for someone to wear a hat in a restaurant."

The side-eye?

He studied the humans closer, and didn't see any eyes staring at them. As for hats, there were at least two different male humans wearing backwards baseball hats, and one female wearing a flat-brimmed cap. Understanding coursed through him. "Briar," he said carefully, "so what if they look at you? I see three more people wearing hats."

She scanned the room, face flushed, but her smile grew and her shoulders relaxed. He'd done that. "You're right." Adjusting, she sat up straighter and folded her hands on the table. "How long have you been friends with Sylvain?" she asked as if dismissing the topic from her mind.

"A long time, little one." The name slipped his lips without any thought, but it fit. Compared to his massive size, she was tiny, and while his voice boomed, and he had to make a concerted effort to keep it from carrying across the restaurant, hers was quiet and smooth. The consonants rolled together in an unfamiliar, at least in New England, way. "Sylvain was an explorer. Liked to work on his own. I met him in the Bay of Fundy."

"I don't know where that is," she replied, leaning forward in her seat and smiling self-deprecatingly.

"In the Gulf of Maine, between New Brunswick and Nova Scotia."

"I didn't know there was such a thing as the Gulf of Maine. Is it far from here?" she asked.

"Very far," he replied, thinking of the hours it took now, and the weeks, or months it could take when the only means of transportation was horse. Or their feet.

"Is it near Prince Edward Island?" she asked. "I love Anne of Green Gables."

"South of PEI, and a bit east."

"Is that where you're from?" Her head tilted to the side as she studied him. "You have a bit of an accent."

Did he? Usually he was much more careful with his speech, making sure no one could identify his origins. How had he let it slip?

"In a roundabout way," he began when the waitress returned with their meals.

"Here you go." She placed the toast in front of him and Briar's yogurt next to it. He slid the bowl across to her.

"You need silverware?" he asked, glancing down at the table.

"Yes. And my coffee," she observed, glancing toward the waitress. "Excuse me ma'am."

The waitress, who'd been bussing the table next to them, spun. Half a steak and a sharp knife flew away from her. The steak hit the floor with a slap, but the knife nicked the back of Briar's hand, filling the air with the scent of her blood. *Ice and snow, the sea.* The most delicious scent he'd ever encountered.

"Ouch!"

"Oh my God, I'm so sorry!" the woman apologized, slapping a napkin over the shallow cut.

Valen's fangs descended immediately, and he clapped his hand over his mouth. He couldn't breathe, and for a second, couldn't move. The monster inside him woke up and roared, ravenous.

"It's okay," Briar assured her, glancing up when Valen pushed his chair back and stumbled away from the table.

Keeping his head angled away from her, he apologized. *No!* The monster clawed at him through his skin. It wanted nothing more than a taste of her blood. "I have to go. Now. I'm sorry."

He didn't wait to hear what she said or care if anyone stared at him as he shouldered past the smaller, weaker humans who suddenly became more than roadblocks. With his monster awake, they were prey, and he wanted to hunt.

CHAPTER 9
BRIAR

Valen shot out of his seat and elbowed his way through the crowd toward the exit. Not once did he glance back at her in his hurry outside.

"Probably the blood," the waitress said, and Briar nodded. That had to be it. Poor Valen. On the sidewalk, his blond head dashed by the window and out of sight.

"Yes," she murmured, feeling guilty. "Can I get the check?"

"Of course, sweetheart. I am sorry."

"It was an accident. It's fine," she assured the woman.

Briar had made sure her hat was secure and her gloves in place by the time the waitress returned. As she counted out the cash and tip, she wondered how she could get ahold of Valen to apologize. Marcus would be the answer, most likely. As a friend of a friend, he could at least pass the message onto Sylvain.

Eyes on the ground, Briar picked her way out of the restaurant, covering her face with the oversized glasses before she exited. No matter what Valen said, she knew she stood out, and the last thing she needed to cement her belief was to catch the sideways glances or confused, but loaded, stare between friends.

Glasses in place, Briar scanned the street for any sign Valen had stayed nearby. But even on her tiptoes, there was no blond head towering over people, or sunny smiling face.

Her plan had been a little hijacked, but it was possible to get back on track. She let herself revel in her freedom a second, proud of herself for being out in the daylight and taking risks. In two days, she'd made two friends. Not bad for this West Virginian freak.

The T wasn't far, and in a matter of moments, she'd swiped her pass, and stood waiting with a crowd of people for the Red Line. She tucked her sunglasses in her bag but left her hat on. There were times when the train went above ground, and she couldn't be sure she wouldn't need her protective gear, as much as she wanted to strip off the hat and gloves and shove them next to her sunglasses.

Allowing herself to stare, she noted all the ways people were dressed. One man was in a three-piece suit, shoes shined to perfection. A couple of girls wore crop tops and short shorts with sneakers, while another girl, probably the same age or younger, wore a long dress. Boys wore baseball caps, and one woman had on a straw fedora.

Valen was right. She could blend. It was up to her to wear her clothes with confidence. This shirt? Boring though it may be, kept her from roasting, and as ugly as her hat was, she didn't have third degree burns or melted skin on her face.

Mostly. A voice inside her reminded her, and she touched a gloved finger to her cheek. It didn't feel like anything there. Most of the nerves were dead, and while she could feel hard pressure, anything lighter was dulled.

Would she feel a kiss? She ghosted a finger across the skin. Nothing.

"Attention passengers. The next Red Line train to Porter Square Station is approaching."

Briar edged closer to the platform along with the rest of the crowd. The train blew into the station, a gust of wind tossing her hair back. Quickly, she touched her hat, holding it in place. As the train came to a stop, the wind settled and she could let go. Someone nudged her from behind, and she lost her balance, tripping a little.

The wind blew again, as the doors to the train opened, and the passengers flooded out, tossing her hair around her face and over her shoulders. Something wet and slimy touched her neck and she slapped her hand there, glancing toward the ceiling to see what had leaked on her.

A voice spoke right in her ear. "I knew you'd taste delicious." A chill drifted over her neck, and she jerked away, whirling toward the voice. But no one was there. The other passengers were entering the train, and she was at the edge of the crowd, with nothing behind her except the tiled wall.

Freaked out, she shoved her way on the train, ignoring the angry glowers sent her way. As the doors closed, she let out a breath and squeezed her shoulder to her ear, trying to dislodge the slick feeling on her skin.

It was in her head. It had to be.

"Next stop, Porter Square Station," a mechanical voice announced.

All in my head.

She needed to relax. She was fine. Everything was fine.

The train jolted, then moved forward. She grasped the bar next to her, glancing up as she did so, into the icy white eyes of a man who stood outside, on the platform. He stared back, smiling. Unable to look away, all she could do was gasp when he lifted a white hand, fingers curling in a mocking wave, and then he was gone. There was a blur of white and black, and then nothing.

The lights came up in the train as it entered a tunnel, and Briar was left staring at her wide-eyed reflection.

She touched her neck, skimming the glove along her skin and then staring at it. Nothing. Gripping the pole with both hands, she leaned her head against it, sighing. This was altogether too much action for a Sunday morning.

❧

AN HOUR LATER, BRIAR ARRIVED AT THE CAMPUS BOOKSTORE off of Commonwealth Avenue and was surprised to find she was more comfortable. The city was starting to feel like home. When she'd arrived a week ago, Boston had been overwhelming. A week in, she was discovering Boston had nooks and hamlets.

BC was its own community, and if she lived on campus, she'd probably not need to leave for anything. All of her needs would be met. She'd live in a dorm and eat at a dining hall.

There had been graduate housing available, and she'd considered it. But she wanted to be independent, and though she never had a true college experience, she decided to skip it.

She was twenty-two, and if most twenty-two-year-olds lived in their own apartments, so would she.

Briar had forgone calling the bookstore ahead to arrange to buy all of her books. Most of the books she'd been able to find online, but there were some, specific journal articles compiled by her teachers and then bound by the college's printers, only available at BC.

The bookstore was packed, and Briar had to elbow her way past students milling around, staring at their phones in the middle of aisles to get to the Biology section.

"Holy cow."

Online bookstores, with their price matching, hadn't prepared her to come face-to-face with the required-reading, full-price, textbook.

"You can rent them." A young man reached a hand past her, picking up one of the books she'd been staring at in disbelief.

"Rent them?"

"Yes. Did you read online? Some of these books, like the one you're eyeballing there for one-hundred and six dollars, can be rented and returned after finals." The man stepped away, picking up another book and folding his arms around them. "It's a good idea. Things get expensive."

"They do." No more twenty dollar yogurt breakfasts for her. "Thanks."

"No problem. Look for the sticker, it'll tell you whether or not you can rent. It saves time to do it online."

It would. She knew when deciding to come to the bookstore that all of it could have been accomplished online, but she was picky when it came to books. It wasn't until she saw the book, held it and skimmed through the pages that she could decide if it was the book for her. She cracked the spine of one in her hands. It was a used version, highlighted everywhere. *No, thank you.* Placing it carefully on the ground, she chose another book. This one had no highlighting, but underlined paragraphs in ink, along with notes.

I'll make my own notes, thank you very much.

This book joined the first at her feet. Each subsequent book went into the discard pile, and she shook her head. This was going to take a while.

Eventually, she became aware of someone watching her and glanced up. The young man was gone, and in his place was Professor Nors.

"Oh!" She dropped the book, but he was faster, catching it

before it could drop and topple the tower of textbooks she'd made.

"None of them make the grade?" he asked, kneeling and arranging the books back in place. She didn't say anything, even though she wasn't finished looking. There was a pile of books behind the pile she'd just made, and another one behind that. Somewhere in there was the perfect book, no highlighting, no notes, maybe the spine hadn't even been cracked.

"I have this book." He made a face at the title. "You can borrow it."

"Thank you," she replied, "but I need my own. I want to write in it."

"Then you can have it," he countered.

A strange anxiety twisted her stomach. He'd be saving her a lot of money, but the idea of taking something else from him after what happened the other day, didn't seem right. "I can't."

"Why not?" His blue eyes narrowed. "I have it. I'm never going to read it. I know everything in it. In fact, I believe I edited..." his voice trailed off as he opened the cover. "Yes. I did. I edited it."

"Are you sure?" she asked, and he sighed.

"I wouldn't offer if I wasn't sure."

He was as snippy as Sylvain! What was in the water in Boston?

"All right then," she said, meeting his glare. "Thank you very much. I accept."

"Good," he answered gruffly and rubbed the back of his hand against his jaw. "What other books do you need?"

Briar knelt, transferring her pile back beneath the shelf. "I need to find the selected journal articles for my *Recombinant DNA Technology* class and the books for my *DNA Viruses and Cancer* class."

"Searching for a cure?" he asked, and she ground her teeth together. Maybe he didn't mean to be, but he was condescending. Everything about him, from his crossed arms and glare, to his tone, was belittling.

"What's wrong with that?" she countered, mirroring his body language. "You said yourself I had good ideas. But I don't know enough yet. Who's to say if I discover why my genes mutated, it wouldn't lead to other discoveries for things like cancer or—"

"You're going to discover the cure for cancer."

"Maybe," she replied. "I don't know." Spinning, she grabbed the book off the top of the pile. "Forget it. I don't want your book. Thanks anyway." Southern manners dictated she say thank you and, "It was nice to see you again. Have a good day."

"What are you doing?" he asked when she ignored him, striding purposefully to another aisle. "I asked you a question."

Crossing her arms, she turned. She bit on the inside of her lip and looked anywhere but at him. "I'm finding my books."

"I'm trying to help you."

"No, you're not," she replied. She never thought she'd be disappointed after meeting her hero. "You're making fun of me and making me feel stupid and small."

His eyes widened, and he took a step back, as if she'd dealt him a blow. "I—" He stuffed his hands into his pockets, and then removed them before stuffing them back again. Pacing, he scuffed the back of his hand against his face. "I'm sorry. I don't know why I said that. You're right. I was very rude."

He did look sorry, and a little bit sick. Briar mashed her lips together, biting the side of her lip with her teeth and dropped her arms before sticking out her hand. It was a little awkward because she'd burned her right hand, and had to shake with her left. "Apology accepted, Professor Nors."

He stared at her hand for so long Briar wondered if he wouldn't take it, but as she was about to draw it back, his hand shot out and gripped hers. His hand was cool and gentle as he squeezed once and released her. "Thank you, Briar."

"You're welcome."

His gaze dropped to the book in her hands, and he reached for it, glancing back up at her before taking it. "Will you accept my book instead of buying this one?"

Briar was going to cut her lip with the way she was gnawing on it. Professor Nors made her head spin, but like with Sylvain, it seemed more to do with his own discomfort than how he really felt about her.

"Do you think I'm stupid?" she asked.

"No," he answered. "I read your admission application for graduate school. You're anything but stupid. Naive, not stupid."

"Why naive?"

He reached for a paper-bound book and held it up. At the bottom it read, *Section One, Recombinant DNA Technology,* and she nodded. He opened it, skimming the pages and snorted before he continued to walk.

"You're very hopeful, perhaps that's a better word to describe my impression than naive. I've been working at this a long time—"

"And you haven't given up," she interrupted.

"No," he allowed. "I haven't, but I recognize discoveries are made gradually, over decades or even centuries."

"You think I expect too much of myself." She understood now. Her mother and father had said something similar to her when she informed them of her major and her plans for graduate school. They wanted to know what she possibly thought she could accomplish, a girl who had to stay inside all the time.

Well. Look at her now. Not only was she out, in the daytime, but she was buying books with Professor Hudson Nors.

"Yes," he agreed. "Partially. I think you expect too much of science. There are some things even science can't explain, at least not yet."

She nodded, facing him. "That's the thing, though," she began. "So what if it doesn't happen in my lifetime. I could make a discovery some other scientist uses to solve the mystery of my condition. Maybe, one day, when I'm old, I'll be walking in this bookstore with one of my students, and she'll be the one to discover how to cure EPP. You never know." Tapping him on the arm, she then pointed to a book on the top shelf. "Can you get me a used copy, please?"

He stared at her, shaking his head. Dismissing her for the moment, he twisted, snagging the book. "How old do you think I am?" he asked, handing it to her.

Opening it, she fanned the pages, and found it was full of highlighted sections, and even worse, doodles. "Try the next one, please," she directed.

He got it and gave it to her, waiting.

"I don't know, not much older than me. Your articles go back about ten years, so I assume you're in your thirties."

"Something like that," he muttered. This book wasn't much better than the first, and without her asking, he grabbed another one, opening it for her and thumbing through the pages. "This one looks good."

"Thank you." She added it to the pile of books she already had and gestured with her head to another aisle. They walked silently until she found the department she needed.

"Art history?" he asked. "Do you really think you'll have time for an elective?"

"Sure," she replied. "It's what I'm here to do. What am I supposed to do with my time?"

"Don't you want to go out and do college kid stuff?" He stared at her so intently, she broke away and chose the glossiest, newest book in the pile she could find. She choked a little at the price, but ignored it.

"For this you'll pay full price?"

Sighing, she set the pile on the floor and reached for a used copy. "Look." Sitting cross-legged, she opened one book and then the used copy. "Are you going to sit?"

Professor Nors glanced around before hiking his pants to sit. She smiled at him. Wearing a tailored suit, he made quite a sight, criss-cross applesauce, next to her.

"Now, look." Placing the new book on his lap, she arranged the used book above it. "This book has been bought and resold so many times the pages are folded and the pictures are faded. Art doesn't change, though our interpretations might. The Mona Lisa is always the Mona Lisa, so these books exchange hands a lot. I want a brand new copy to keep so I can see everything. Every detail."

Adjusting her position, she knelt and bent over the page, staring. Professor Nors cleared his throat, and she glanced up. She hadn't meant to get so close to him, but they were a breath away. His eyes, she thought they were blue, but she could see now they were blue around the outside, with a ring of gold around the pupil. His skin was so pale, it looked like porcelain. His lips were blood red, and she smiled. He was the male version of Snow White.

"What?" Those red lips spoke.

"Nothing." She tore her eyes from his lips and sat back, laughing a little.

"Tell me."

She gathered her books, standing on tiptoes to place the used copy back on the pile.

"Briar." His tone held a warning. He wasn't going to give up.

"You remind me of Snow White," she said, walking away toward the register.

"Excuse me," she heard him say to someone, and then he called after her. "Wait."

The line to the register was long, and she stood in place, arms wrapped around her books, perusing the pens and shot glasses nearby.

"I said, wait." Brushing his hands down his suit, he sighed. "Why am I like Snow White?"

"Hair as black as night, skin as white as snow, lips as red as blood," she repeated the line she'd heard a million times during her childhood.

As soon as she'd said the word *blood*, his eyes went hard and cold. He didn't like that.

"Stop by my office when you're done here," he said. "I'll get you the book."

Guilt swamped her. She hadn't meant to hurt his feelings. "I'm sorry. I wasn't making fun of you."

"I have things to do, Briar. It was nice to see you again." Now he was doing what she had earlier, dismissing her with distant politeness.

"All right," she whispered. "It was nice to see you, too."

Shoulders straight and back stiff, he left her. Mentally, she kicked herself. What had she been thinking? She really needed to learn how to talk to people.

CHAPTER 10
HUDSON

It wasn't Briar's fault. Hudson knew, when he left her so abruptly, she thought she'd offended him. She thought she'd sent him beelining for the door, but that wasn't it.

She did, however, get him thinking about blood, and he didn't trust himself around her.

He'd sought her out. Knowing she ventured to campus and hoping to run into her, he'd spent the last two days fairly haunting the bookstore, library, and biology department. This morning had been dumb luck. He'd stopped by the bookstore on his way to his lab, not really expecting to see her there. But there she was.

Blood. Blood. Blood. Lips as red as blood.

Hudson had taken a risk today. He didn't wear his nose plugs, trusting the sheer number of humans would help him control his beast. It had helped, but what helped more was Briar.

She was a fascinating combination of sweetness and fire.

Sweet poison.

That was what Marcus called it in the old days when they'd spent a decade or so in Savannah, Georgia. The ladies were able to whip them with their tongues all while smiling genteelly.

But there was nothing wily about Briar. Rather than verbally lash him, she fell back on manners, choosing to retreat and not attack.

Do you think I'm stupid?

The question came from her heart, and he could tear out his own throat for insinuating as much.

Her scent had called to him. He wanted the flash of memory again, but there was more to her than an intriguing scent. It may have been what lured him to her, but it was her mind that kept him by her side.

Hudson took his ID out of his pocket, swiping it on the keypad to unlock his lab. His white lab coat hung by the door, and he shrugged into it as he walked to his computer.

The lab was quiet, empty, the way he liked it. Usually.

Today, however, the quiet pressed in on him. The hum of the processors, irritating.

After opening his email, he scanned his inbox, part of him hoping for an email from Briar with more ideas. There was nothing.

An award he had to travel to Europe to accept, an offer to lecture at Harvard, another offer, this time of tenure at Oxford. He forwarded them to his personal assistant, a human he'd never met, but with whom he corresponded solely electronically. All events and awards were managed by his PA, he just needed to wait for the itinerary.

Hudson closed the email, calling up a model of a double helix, and drumming his fingers as he stared at it. With a click, he zoomed in on one section, again, and then again, finding the chromosome pair and then the section he wanted.

Chromosome 18. All it took was a slight mutation, a gene unable to encode and suddenly, a baby was born who couldn't walk in the sun.

But why? What was it about this little thing, right there, that made the difference between walking in sunlight or hiding in the shadows? And why couldn't he make a medicine for him and his brothers that would translate to humans?

He studied the model in front of him, considering the enzyme at the heart of the mutation, FECH, or ferrochelatase. This enzyme was important for a lot of reasons, not the least of which was its role in converting organic compounds into heme B, an oxygen carrier in blood.

It all comes back to blood.

Could blood be the answer? Did it start or end with blood?

Hudson tapped his fingers on the table before spinning away from his computer. Working quickly, not allowing his mind to ponder Briar, he instead considered blood.

He found his samples from people with EPP and placed them under the microscope. Adding a compound, he watched, waiting to see if it converted.

The day flew by. Hudson didn't think about anything except blood and sunlight. He worked like a fiend, like a *beast*. A beast like him didn't need breaks, or to use the bathroom. He didn't need sleep.

Even though the sun no longer controlled his body, he still felt the tug, deep inside him, to obey. His kind, like the myths of old stated, did sleep during the day. The discovery he'd made, and the one which brought his brothers back to him twice a year, not only allowed them to walk in the sun, but made resting unnecessary.

At times, he would crash. Awake for days and nights on end, the sun would rise one morning, and he'd collapse. Hours later, as the sun went down, he'd awaken, lying wherever he'd fallen. No one had the code to his lab besides his brothers, and no one checked on him.

Like the emptiness earlier, something about the idea of

lying, unmoving, no one knowing or caring he'd collapsed, bothered him. There were no windows in the lab, no possibility of him sleeping all night only to be burned to ash when the sun rose, so it wasn't that.

It was the loneliness. It was no one caring.

Hudson pushed the microscope away, pressed the heels of his hands into his eyes, and stretched his neck from side to side.

For the first time, he allowed himself to think about his brothers living similar lives. Marcus lived ten miles away, and the only time he saw him was when he dosed him with medicine. What did Marcus do all day? What if something happened to him? What if he died and Hudson never knew?

He'd know, wouldn't he?

His brother's laughing face filled his mind, and Hudson gasped at the pain the thought of a world without Marcus gave him.

If there was anyone he should worry about, however, it was Sylvain. Sylvain'd been harboring a death wish since Annie, even if he'd never admit it.

Annie.

Remember her?

Over time, her face had grown hazy, but the pain he associated with her hadn't. It was as sharp as it had been the day Marcus arrived to tell him of her fate. He hadn't believed it.

They'd told her they loved her and given her eternal life. Who threw that away?

Hudson knew their kind was immortal, but he didn't know they could live without their souls. In the instant Marcus informed him of her death, he'd gone cold inside. The warmth he'd felt for Annie and his brothers retreated and hardened. It crystallized and froze.

"Thank you for telling me," he'd said. "You can go now."

Valen'd come next. Sylvain had disappeared, and Valen wanted Hudson's help to find him. "This is our family!"

If Valen thought his pleas would move Hudson, he was wrong. Nothing would move Hudson to act. He couldn't bring himself to dig up emotion when everything he thought he'd cared about was gone.

Time had passed, and Hudson stayed the same. He recognized it now. All vampires had the potential of freezing. Why interact with the world when it would only change? Humans died, even the gods disappeared. What could Hudson do to change that?

A spark grew inside him now, melting the ice around his heart, but it had all started with Briar.

If he could go back in time, he wouldn't have let this happen. His brothers had needed him, and he'd brushed them aside, too mired in his own guilt and hurt to care about theirs.

Valen had sensed it, and Marcus, too. There was something about the girl that called to them and woke them up.

Hudson thought of Annie, and then Briar, wondering if it was the same pull all of them had felt.

It had to be different. Annie had never challenged him, never asked him questions that made him angry and threw him off-balance.

Annie had been easy to love. Her sweetness appealed to all of them, and it had seemed the most natural thing in the world for him and his brothers to agree to share her, and then, when faced with her mortality, turn her into one of them.

Briar was a product of the modern age. That had to be what he found so fascinating about her.

Do you think I'm stupid?

No. He most definitely did not. Hudson's thoughts

swirled. He needed to make some changes and see about coming back to life.

※

Harvard had changed in the hundred years since Hudson had taught there. Divinity Avenue's landmarks were the same, but the departments were very different. Marcus's department was Regenerative Biology, a perfect fit for a vampire. Years ago, they'd worked as a team, making breakthroughs in things like blood transfusions. Like many scientists, their interests and specialties started with a personal investment, but unlike other vampires, their work hadn't been an excuse to insinuate themselves into human society.

Blood was always the focus, but as a means to take humans out of the equation, not to have easy access to them as a food source.

After Annie's death, Marcus continued studying blood diseases, and in the nineteen sixties, Hudson had seen a name, *Mark Filipelli,* obviously a play on his brother's name, *Marcus Phoneician,* as co-author of research related to hemophilia and sickle cell anemia.

Stem cell research was his brother's area of expertise now. Hudson, despite his best intentions, followed Marcus's research with interest. If Marcus could clone blood, using his research with stem cells, vampires would no longer need humans; those vampires who refused to use animals to slack their thirst could stop murdering people.

Hudson walked inside, studying the map of labs and offices to find Marcus.

He was in the basement, of course. Allowing himself a smile, Hudson wound his way there, studying with interest the various labeled research teams and their area of study.

At least, that's what he told himself. He was taking his

time because he was interested in other's research, but the truth of the matter was, he was nervous.

For the first time, Hudson sought out Marcus, not the other way around, and he wasn't sure of his reception. In less than seventy-two hours, Hudson had done an about-face. No longer wanting to keep his brothers at arm's length, he recognized the stupidity of rejecting the only family he had.

And he and Marcus had been the original brothers, finding each other when mysticism and mythology ruled, and creatures like him were named gods, or worse, demons.

"Hudson?" Marcus's voice echoed down the tiled corridor.

Bracing himself, Hudson faced him.

"What are you doing here?" Head tilted in confusion, Marcus approached him. "I'll find you later," he told the two young men who kept pace next to him.

"Students?" he asked.

"Doctoral candidates and lab assistants," Marcus confirmed. "What are you doing here?"

"Do you have an office?" They were too exposed, and Hudson couldn't lower his voice enough for the sound not to travel. Not only that, he needed some privacy for what he needed to say. Or what he thought he needed to say. He hadn't really allowed himself to think too much about what to say to Marcus. He'd had an epiphany and come straight here.

Now, however, his mind was racing, struggling to find the words to explain.

"This way." Marcus gestured down the hall. Hudson trailed behind him, following as he unlocked the door. "Sit."

An ache grew in Hudson's chest as he studied the walls. Unlike Hudson, who'd taken every item reminding him of his brothers and Annie, and threw it away, Marcus's office was a shrine to their family. A palm-sized oil painting of Annie hung behind him, while on his bookshelves were leather bound books he and Hudson had written together. A model replica of a Viking longship sat on his desk, and a buffalo skin rug, probably one of Sylvain's trophies, lay in front of his chair.

"Not very politically correct," Hudson observed as he sat. "What do the students think of it?"

"I tell them it's a reminder of human excess and the danger we face when we believe we should conquer nature," he replied. "But most of them think it's from Crate & Barrel, so the conversation doesn't happen often."

Hudson chuckled, leaning his elbow on the padded leather arm of the chair.

"Why are you here, Hudson?" Marcus asked, all joking absent from his voice.

"How can you stand to look at her?" Hudson ignored his question for a third time. His gaze glued to Annie. The miniature was a perfect rendering of their wife. Long dark tresses swept away from the golden skin and rosy cheeks. Somehow, the painter had even managed to get the twinkle of her brown eyes. "Doesn't it rip out your heart?" His voice was choked, and he cleared his throat. Everywhere he looked was a reminder of what he'd lost. The room was a tomb.

"Those were the happiest times of my life, Hudson," Marcus replied. "My brothers by my side, work I loved, a woman who loved us all, however briefly. Why wouldn't I want to be surrounded by it all?"

"I never understood you," Hudson whispered.

"I've always said there's no one like me," Marcus teased.

"You're perfect for this era," Hudson said. "Believing you're unique and special."

Marcus leaned back in the chair, smiling widely. "I really am."

"I miss our family," Hudson said abruptly. "I miss my brothers. This life is too long to live alone with no purpose."

"You have your work," Marcus cut in.

"My work." Hudson scoffed. "It's a distraction from my feelings. From facing what I lost—from what I did."

"You didn't do anything we didn't all agree on."

Hudson shook his head. It had been his idea to turn Annie, and his arguments had convinced his brothers. His fangs descended at the memory of sinking them through her soft skin, and the way her blood had flowed over his tongue and down his throat. Her death, and the disintegration of their family, rested squarely on his shoulders.

"Hudson." Marcus's sharp tone yanked him from his memories. "Why now?"

"You'll laugh."

"I always laugh, and I'll probably tease you mercilessly as well, but I need to know. The years are endless for our kind. I want to know if I do this and rebuild our family, it won't be torn away from me again." Peering up at his oldest friend and brother, he found Marcus's gaze on Annie's portrait. He continued to stare before he sucked in a deep breath and faced Hudson. "Well?"

"Briar. The girl."

Marcus shot out of his chair. It slammed into the wall behind him, and in a move no human's eyes could track, he'd wrapped his fingers around Hudson's throat. Lip curling, Marcus hissed at him. "Not for a woman."

"Not for a woman," Hudson choked out. "Because of a woman. The time I've spent with her—"

"You've been spending time with her? When?"

"I left her not long ago. I'm not asking because I want to turn her, or to share her." Or was he? The draw he had to her was undeniable, and her scent called to all of them. He dismissed the thought. This was about his family. He had to keep his focus on them. "She reminds me of home, which reminds me of my brothers. The last time I was happy."

Slowly, Marcus uncurled his fingers, releasing him. "She

reminds me of home as well. When I'm with her, I think of places I thought I'd forgotten."

"But she's young," Hudson replied, before shaking his head. "I can't think about her now. I want to fix what I broke, Marcus. Will you forgive me?"

Turning away, Marcus laced his hands behind his dark head, staring silently at his bookshelf. The clock ticked away the seconds, and still Marcus didn't speak. The steady, slow thump of his heart began to override the clock, and Hudson closed his eyes, letting his senses expand. A heartbeat. A breath. The slow whoosh of blood in his veins, like wind blowing through the long grasses of a field. It was hypnotizing.

"I forgave you for Annie long ago." Marcus spoke deliberately, each word heavy. "I don't know if I can forget these years and how you've pushed us all away, but I forgive you. I want to be a family again, too." Eyes shining, Marcus met his gaze. "You fucking suck, Hud, and I'm going to enjoy watching Sylvain kick your ass."

Hudson barked a laugh, relief making him slump. "I'm sure you will."

CHAPTER 11

MARCUS

Reuniting with his brothers was the last thing Marcus expected when he'd arrived at work, but it made perfect sense. Ever since meeting Briar, he'd sensed things were changing.

"What does this mean?" he asked Hudson.

He shook his head and shrugged. "I don't know. Going back to the way it was seems unlikely, but being friends again is possible."

"Valen will be relieved. Sylvain, though."

"Sylvain." It wasn't the first time the two of them had considered their youngest brother and shaken their heads.

Marcus barked out a laugh. "Look at us. Same old shit with Sylvain, different day."

"True. So, uh." Hudson paused. "Can I see your lab?"

"Yeah," he answered, rubbing his hand over his short, coarse hair. "Of course."

And just like that, he had a brother again.

While Marcus explained his research, Hudson listened, asked questions, and pointed out flaws in reasoning. The hours ticked by, and he didn't even notice. For a vampire, time didn't have much meaning. Since losing Annie, and then his brothers, it'd felt endless. Marcus had had to force himself to pay attention. He may have seemed lighthearted, but it was an act. The truth was, some days he couldn't remember the names of his students or distinguish one from the other.

Evening had fallen when he walked Hudson to the doors leading to Divinity Avenue. "What happens now?" Marcus asked. The day had cooled significantly, and he could smell autumn on the wind blowing off the Charles River.

"See you tomorrow? My lab? Maybe we can work through some of the issues I'm having with heme B."

"I was always smarter than you," he replied. "Hasn't changed in two hundred years." He slapped Hudson on the back, hard enough to push him forward. "I'll see if I can get you on the right track."

"You're still an ass." But Hudson smiled, holding out his hand.

"Brothers don't shake hands," Marcus quoted, and Hudson hurried down the steps.

"Forget it."

"See you tomorrow, brother!"

"Yeah, yeah," Hudson answered, but even without seeing his face, Marcus could hear the smile in his voice.

Marcus kicked his heel against a step before heading back into his office. The first thing he saw when he opened the door was Annie's miniature. He'd rescued it from the destruction Sylvain wrought in the aftermath of her death. Hudson had stared at his office like he was face to face with a ghost, whereas Marcus had become inoculated against the pain these items used to cause.

Lifting the portrait from the wall, he brought it closer to his face. Each individual brush stroke, minute and precise, was still visible. The office was windowless, and he didn't have to worry about the portrait fading.

His memory sparked, and he closed his eyes, trying to recall her skin and the way it felt beneath his hands. He waited for the pain her memory would bring, but it didn't come. Instead, another set of eyes, these palest blue, appeared.

The change had begun with Briar, and he had to see her. After placing the portrait on the wall, he left. With her face in the forefront of her mind, he dashed through the city. Humans would sense a strong wind, maybe one that pushed them back or whipped their hair around their head, but they wouldn't see him.

Strange, once he thought of Briar, anxiety rose inside him. He tried to reason with himself. She wasn't in danger. He barely knew her. But reason was lost on him, and for the first time in a long time, he struggled with his vampiric side. The vampire wanted to stake claim, and possess her. Had he been any younger, any less practiced, he may have done it.

Scents assailed him, and he jerked to a halt. Sylvain, Valen, Hudson. All of them had been here, but there was something else. Another creature reeking of rot and garbage. Scanning the road, he searched for the source of the scent.

It was too bright.

Leaping up, he smashed one streetlight. It helped a little, but not enough. Faster than any eye could see, he leapt from one light to the next, smashing them until the street was dark and the only light came from illuminated apartments. *Better.* Now there were shadows in which to hide.

Marcus sucked in a lungful of air. While crawlers all smelled of rot, there was still a uniqueness that set apart one creature from another. He'd smelled it on Briar last night, and the one he smelled now was the same.

Fangs erupted from his gums, anger tingeing his vision red. He would kill this thing. It was sniffing around Briar, and Briar was *his*.

Shit. His? *Mine.* The vampire was in complete agreement with the thought. The wind blew, rustling the leaves about his head and slapping him in the face with another scent.

Soldier. No. What he took to be one soldier was wrong, there were many soldiers. Each of their scents overlapping one another. He growled. This many soldiers meant one thing, someone was leading them here.

Did another vampire have his eye on Briar?

Over my dead body.

Without giving it another thought, Marcus rushed up the steps then leaned on the buzzer to her apartment.

"Hello?" He hadn't realized until the moment he heard her voice how afraid he'd been.

"It's Marcus. Can I come up?" His voice shook, and he fisted his hands, digging deep for a measure of control.

"Marcus? Sure. Of course. Hold on." Above him a door slammed, and feet pounded down the steps. He counted each lock as it was thrown until the door opened, and Briar stood there, breathless, wearing what were clearly pajamas.

"What time is it?" When had Hudson left? Had he gotten her out of bed?

Her cheeks reddened, the tiny crescent appearing on her cheek. "About seven."

"Were you asleep?"

Biting her lip, she lifted a hand to smooth her hair. "No. Um. You want to come up?"

"Yes." He passed her as she held the door open for him. He watched as she threw the locks. There were three of them, but they wouldn't be enough to keep out a vampire intent on entry.

"Are you hungry?" she asked, leading the way upstairs.

He breathed in, her wildflower scent stronger in the narrow stairwell. *Famished.* "I ate."

"Okay." Her door remained opened. She must have

hurried out to let him in. He smiled, pleased with the picture of her rushing to meet him, but as he stepped inside, the smile was wiped from his face.

"This is where you live?" he asked horrified, studying the apartment. It was a hovel. The small oven dinged, so old it didn't have a digital timer. "Is that safe to use?"

"Wipe that look from your face," she answered, opening the oven door to remove a pizza. She flipped the dial and shrugged off the oven mitt. "Boston is expensive."

"How much is a place like this?"

Her face grew redder, and she bit her lip, whirling toward a drawer to remove a pizza cutter. Each movement was jerky. He'd hurt her feelings.

"I'm sorry," he apologized. "It's been a long time since I've seen student housing."

"There's no excuse for bad manners," she muttered. "Can I get you something to drink? Are you sure you aren't hungry?"

Quickly hiding the smile threatening, he shook his head. "No, thank you." She'd chastised him with one breath and tried to feed him with the next.

There was no table. In fact, there was no living room. Her bed was in the center of the room, the kitchen to one side and what he thought must be a bathroom through a door.

"Where do you sit?" he asked without thinking. "I'm sorry. Ignore me."

"You can sit on the…" Her eyes landed on the bed, and she straightened her shoulders. "The bed. It's clean."

Perching on the end, he waited for her to join him. She placed a cup of water on the bedside table before sliding on and settling herself cross-legged. "I feel weird eating in front of you."

"I'm not hungry, promise." But with each passing moment, the urge to bite was growing.

Balancing the pizza on her lap, Briar gathered her hair and secured it into a ponytail at the base of her neck, exposing the long white column of her throat. Her pulse thumped gently. *Bite.*

"It's nice to see you."

He startled, meeting her eyes. "Yes. I was in the neighborhood. And I wanted to see you."

"I'm glad," she answered. "Even though you've insulted my apartment."

"Have you seen anything strange?" He took her by surprise, and she dropped the pizza onto the plate.

"Anything?"

"Like you saw last night. The crawlers."

She shook her head, but her pulse leapt. Beneath the wildflower scent came a slow bloom of fear, and the combination was mouthwatering. What it would she taste like? Eyes glued to her throat, he edged forward.

"I've been thinking about it. Perhaps it was a prank. Like a frat hazing, you know? Someone pledging?"

He couldn't process what she was saying through the fog of hunger. His entire being was centered on her throat. Her skin.

"Marcus?" Her pink lips formed his name, and he blinked.

Somehow he'd crept across the bed until he was inches from her mouth. Closing his eyes, he let her breath caress his face. Her skin was warm, pulse thudding beneath his fingers. When had he gripped her throat?

With a jerk, he threw himself backward, knocking into the wall so hard the picture frames on her bureau fell over.

"Are you okay, Marcus?" Briar shoved the plate onto the bed and stood.

"No," he croaked. He covered his mouth, hiding his fangs. He had to taste her. There would be nothing as delicious as her blood, and he was so hungry.

The vampire hissed. *Famished.*

No. He was stronger than the vampire. Worry had brought him to her home, and the last thing he intended was to hurt her. But now, faced with her and the bouquet of her scent, all he could think about was blood.

His teeth would slice into her skin, and her blood would drip down her throat, staining the t-shirt she wore. She'd sink back into the bed as he hovered over her, tongue licking the droplets from her shoulder to the puncture wounds he'd make. In his mind, he could see himself, and his dick jumped.

Pushing past her, he threw open her door.

"Marcus!" she called, but he ignored her.

Never had he come so close to feeding.

Blood.

The vampire clawed inside him, wanting out, but he shoved him back down. "No."

Emerging onto the dark street, Marcus sucked in a breath and tasted rot. In a split second, he'd changed from rational man to a creature ruled by his desires. He *desired* blood, and if he couldn't have Briar's, he would hunt.

Marcus let the vampire have his skin: He'd let the only thing that mattered sate his hunger.

CHAPTER 12
BRIAR

Briar's heart thudded against her chest. Marcus had frightened and confused her. The way he stared at her, watching her speak, eyes dropping to her throat, she couldn't tell if he wanted to murder her or kiss her.

He'd left as if something was chasing him, and she couldn't help feeling as if he'd done it for her. But that was crazy.

Appetite gone, Briar picked up her plate, wrapped her pizza and shoved it in the small refrigerator that stood waist high. She dismissed the idea that Marcus wanted to kiss her, but she couldn't deny there was something... hungry about the way he'd watched her. She'd had his complete focus, and it had made her heart pound.

She wasn't sure if that was a good thing.

Needing a distraction, she grabbed the bag of books she'd bought at the bookstore and flopped on her bed. She pulled out the art history book and began to flip through the glossy pages. Tomorrow was her first day of classes, and she would be stopping by Professor Nors's office to pick up the book he'd promised her.

Her stomach fluttered thinking about him. What was wrong with her? She wanted Marcus to kiss her, thought Professor Nors was handsome—*Hotson* Nors—and had breakfast with Valen this morning.

Shaking her head, she instead focused on the page in front of her. *A Portrait of Miss Elizabeth Linley.* Briar propped her chin in her hand, staring at the beautiful woman. Dark eyes in a pale white face, stared away from the artist, exposing her white throat.

For the rest of the evening, Briar looked through her book, examining each picture, pausing on those that she found especially interesting. The last thing she remembered was staring at *View of the Landscape near the Catskills* and reading a short passage about the Hudson River painters when her eyes shot open.

Pain radiated along her hand, and she blinked rapidly, trying to make sense of what she saw. Blue sky and sunshine poured through her windows.

Acting instinctively, she rolled, hitting the floor with a teeth-rattling thump and crawled beneath her bed. Had she forgotten to draw the curtains?

No. The curtains always stayed drawn, and while she might pull them to the side to see the weather, they remained shut, protecting her from the sun. Edging toward the bedskirt, she examined the floor and gasped. The blackout curtains had been torn from the rods, piled into a messy heap.

Her heart pounded, and she crawled toward the other side of the bed, peeking beneath the bedskirt and avoiding the sunlight hitting the end of the bed. Her door was wide open.

Bile burned her throat. Who would have broken into her house and torn her curtains off? For that matter, who knew she had EPP? Any longer in the sun and she would have burned.

Drawing her arm toward her face, she examined the skin.

It was a little red, but it was nowhere near as bad as it could have been.

Her entire apartment was flooded with light, and while she could avoid the sun here for a little while, eventually there would be nowhere to hide.

She was going to have to crawl from under the bed, wrap herself in a blanket, and escape into the bathroom. Her clothes were in there, all laid out for her first day of school.

Eyes filling with tears, Briar pressed her face against the cool wood floor.

This was going to hurt.

Blasting from beneath the bed, she grabbed the first thing she saw, the curtain, and wrapped it over her head. It covered her, but not fast enough. It was like being blasted by a water cannon. The pain was instantaneous. All she could do was muscle through and dive into the bathroom, slamming the door shut.

Sobbing now, she turned on the shower, stripped, and got inside. The cool water dissipated the heat, but beneath the surface, her nerve endings flared.

It happened sometimes. Her body responded to exposure as if the burn was much worse than it was. The doctor told her it was her body's way of surviving. By lying to her, making her believe the burn was worse, it could guarantee that next time she'd remember and not burn herself again.

As if she needed a reminder. Briar huddled beneath the stream, shoulders shaking as she tried to calm her breathing. "I'm okay." Her voice bounced off the tiles. "I'm okay."

Someone tried to kill me.

"I'm okay." Her voice broke, and she let the tears overwhelm her. Who would do this? Who had she made so angry they'd break into her apartment to hurt her?

Inexplicably, her thoughts went to Sylvain and the way he looked at her with distaste one moment and amusement the next. But no. Sylvain knew nothing about her, except she snuck around museums after hours.

Once she let the tears flow, she couldn't stop them. All of her dreams seemed to crash around her. What had she been thinking, wanting a normal life?

There would be no school for her, no books and research. No time with Marcus or breakfast with random friends of friends like Valen. Those things weren't for people like her.

With an immense effort, Briar shut the water off. The towel she patted her skin with may have well been sandpaper. It grated against her skin, and she sobbed harder. Dressed now, she covered herself with the curtain. Her hand shook as she grasped the knob, but she yanked it open anyway.

She rushed to the bed, grabbed her cell phone and ran back into the bathroom, slamming the door. Dialing 911 was like the death knell to her hopes. Her parents would hear about this, and they'd be on the next plane to Boston. Or worse, they'd send her brother, Jamie, after her.

Jamie would have a field day with the "I told you so's."

"911, what is your emergency?"

Briar explained what happened as calmly as she could, but soon she was crying again, hiccuping and choking.

"Ma'am, calm down. I have first responders on their way to you. Can you let them into your apartment?"

"The building door is locked," she explained. "But I can do it."

It would mean another foray into the daylight, which, unlike yesterday when she was full of excitement, was her enemy today. Nearby, sirens blared, prompting her to move. The curtain went around her head again, and she hurried downstairs, throwing the locks on the door in time to see the first fire engines and ambulances pull to a stop.

"Come with us, miss," the paramedic directed, and she shook her head.

"I can't. I'll burn."

The man exchanged a glance with the other paramedic. "Miss. You won't burn. You're covered. We're going to take you to the hospital and the police will make sure your apartment is safe."

"You don't understand." Had she not explained this to the dispatcher? "If I go into the sun, I'll burn."

With her words, something in their demeanor changed. "We understand." His tone was polite, but the way they walked toward her, hands out, put her on guard, and she stepped back, onto the stairs. "Are you burning now?"

"I'm all right as long as I stay out of the sun," she replied, and there was the look again.

In a split second, she understood what happened. She *had* explained her situation to the dispatcher, and they thought she was crazy. "You don't understand," she tried again. "I have a condition. Erythropoietic protoporphyria. It means I burn when I come into contact with UV light. I'm not crazy."

Her last words were her undoing. Someone grabbed her from behind, and the curtain fell off her, leaving her face and head fully exposed. Screaming, she kicked and jerked. She turned her head as far from the sunlight as she could, but it caught her, burning her ear. "Let me go!" she screamed, her voice breaking. "Please!"

"Hey!" a deep voice yelled, and then. "Hey!"

Something was thrown over her head, and then, just as she collapsed, two strong arms wrapped around her.

"Sir, back up."

"Don't touch her, you fucking idiot. She's allergic to sunlight. You could have killed her." *Sylvain.*

"Sylvain," she choked from beneath whatever covered her. She gripped him, digging her fingers into his arm. "Please don't let me go."

"Sir, she's—"

She spun, and the covering was gently removed from her head. "Look, fucker."

He'd led them into a dark corner of the stairwell, away from the light. Sylvain stood at her back, holding her up while a police officer, Taser drawn, and the two paramedics stared at her in horror.

"Shiiiiit," the paramedic said. "Sir, you have to let us help her."

"I'm not crazy," she stuttered over the words, holding even tighter to Sylvain. "I don't want to burn, Sylvain. Please."

"You won't burn, Briar. I've got you."

Her ear throbbed in time with her heartbeat. Oh God, how bad was it?

"Miss," the first paramedic said. "You have a pretty bad burn, and we need to treat you. Please. We'll do whatever you need to get you from here to the bus and to the hospital. What was that thing called?" His eyes flickered to Sylvain.

"Erythropoietic protoporphyria." He didn't even trip over the word.

"EPP," Briar whispered.

The throbbing was overwhelming her, and her body was starting to shut down. She could feel it, a bone-deep fatigue that had her vision tunneling and darkness hovering around the edges.

"Stay with me," Sylvain whispered. "Talk to me. What are you doing today?"

Her eyes fluttered closed, and she let herself lean against him. "I was supposed to have class. It's my first day of school."

"What class?" he asked. His voice was soothing when he wasn't barking at her.

"Regenerative DNA Technology and Molecular Biology. And Professor Nors has a book for me. But it doesn't matter anymore."

"Why doesn't it matter?" He shook her, and she opened her eyes. "Briar, stay with me. Why doesn't it matter?"

"I'm not normal. Why'd I think I could do this? I don't belong here."

"You're giving up?" His chest rumbled as if he was growling. "Didn't think you were a quitter."

"Someone ripped the blackout curtains from my windows, Sylvain." Why was he being so mean? "Some jerk must have thought it was funny to mess with the freak."

"So you're going to have a pity party? Get new curtains."

"Sir, we're ready."

"No!" Her eyes had closed again, but now she forced them open and spun, gripping Sylvain's shirt in both her hands. "No. Sylvain. They think I'm crazy. Please don't let them take me." Even as the words left her lips, she knew she was being illogical and paranoid.

"I'll go with you," he replied and dropped a kiss on her forehead. His lips were cool, and she allowed herself to rest there, pressing herself a little harder against him.

"You won't leave me alone?"

"No." It was a promise.

"Okay."

"Miss. Briar. We're going to put these blankets over your head. Can you get on the gurney?"

The paramedics had wheeled the gurney to the door, but it still sat in the sunlight. "I can't."

"Here." Sylvain held out a hand for the blankets and the paramedic tossed them to him. "I'm going to put them around you and lift you, okay?"

She nodded and sucked in a breath. Sylvain shook out the blankets, dark eyes following his movements as he settled it over her head. He held out another hand and caught the next. "Ready?"

"Yes."

He gave her a small smile, just a tilt of his lips, and covered her face and head. The next thing she knew, he'd scooped her beneath her knees, settling her against his chest and lifted her. "I have her," he said.

Around her, the paramedics directed him to the ambulance, where he placed her carefully on a gurney already inside. They strapped her in place, but Sylvain took her hand, lacing his fingers with hers as the paramedics shut the doors.

"Four minutes," someone said. "How you doing, Briar?"

Sylvain squeezed her hand, and she squeezed back. "Okay," she answered. She hadn't passed out, and Sylvain hadn't left. She could do this.

"You with me?" Sylvain asked.

"I'm with you," she answered.

CHAPTER 13
SYLVAIN

S ylvain thanked whatever instinct it was that brought him to Briar's door. Long ago, he'd given up ignoring his urges. When he was hungry, he ate. When he was angry, he fought.

And when he wanted to lay eyes on the girl who'd filled his thoughts, he found her.

Her covered form shivered beneath the blankets on the gurney. Her hand, small, warm, held his with a grip tight enough to bruise had he been human.

"Sylvain?"

"I'm here, blossom. Holding your hand."

He shook his head. No endearments. She was a distraction, a novelty, nothing more. But even as he had the thought, he knew he was lying to himself.

Every so often, her body would jerk, and he imagined her eyes closing, her body trying to force her to sleep. He'd asked her to stay with him, and she had, fighting her exhaustion.

"We have a bay ready, and our doctors are prepared," the paramedic informed them.

Growling, Sylvain stared daggers at the man. It was their

fault she was injured at all. He'd seen the moments before they dragged her into the sunlight. Her skin was flushed, but not burned, but the instant the sun had touched her skin, it swelled and blistered.

He would never forget it. Flames flashed in front of his eyes, and he shut them tight. No. This wasn't like Annie. Briar was human, and she would heal.

"Did you see it, Sylvain?" she asked. "How bad is it?"

It had been bad, but for some reason, his bluntness left him, and though he tried, he couldn't find the right words.

She sighed. "Must be pretty bad if you have nothing sarcastic to say."

"There are good doctors here, Briar. They'll help you." It fell flat even to his ears.

The doors opened with a crash, and Briar jerked. "You'll stay?"

Would he? Sylvain hadn't been inside a human hospital in years, hadn't allowed himself the temptation. A place full of weakened prey was too alluring.

"Please?"

Could he do this? *Worst thing that happens is you murder everyone.*

"Yes. I will." He'd tamp down the desire to feed, and focus on the girl holding onto his hand like a lifeline.

The gurney was lifted, but still he held on, contorting his massive form to fit through the door. Beneath the blanket, Briar shook. The humans pushing the bed rushed her into the hospital, through the emergency room to a bay with no windows.

"Sir, we need you to wait outside." At six and a half feet, Sylvain took up a lot of space, but Briar held onto him.

"I want him to stay," she replied as the blankets were removed.

Oh, Briar. Sylvain clenched the fist of his free hand, struggling not to murder the paramedics. He couldn't take his eyes off the damage done to her body. When dragged into the daylight, she'd twisted away from the sun. From her earlobe down to the middle of her neck had been struck by the brunt of the rays.

One patch of skin, the length of his finger, was melted, exposing, in one spot, muscle. He stared at the damage, hissing through his teeth. *Later.* He would find out where these men lived, and he'd devour them. He'd rip their heads from their body. No. He'd build a fire and hold them over it and *then* rip their heads from their body.

Sylvain shut his eyes, trying to get ahold of himself, and when he opened them, he met Briar's sad gaze. The doctors bent over her, lights shining on the wound while the nurses prepared something in the corner. A tear streaked down her face, catching on her lips before rolling over her chin. "Almost made it."

"I don't understand," he rasped, bending at the waist.

"I thought I'd gotten the worst of the burns behind me, and I hadn't melted off my face. Should have knocked on wood or something."

He stroked her head without thinking. "It's on your neck." His gaze flicked to the doctors as they inserted a needle near the wound, numbing it he guessed. "It's far back, near your ear. Your hair will cover it."

"I still have my ear?"

God. Humans were too fragile. He had burned before, melted the skin to the bone. Within hours it had regrown, not a scar remained from any damage done to his body since being turned.

"You do," he answered. "The lobe is red. The worse burn is on your neck."

"We have a plastic surgeon on call, Miss Hale. We're going to transfer you to the burn unit, and he'll meet us there."

"How did you get your scar?" she asked, not appearing to have heard the doctors.

He chuckled. Received well before he was turned, he'd carry it for eternity. It had been a long time since he'd thought about it, but now he raised his finger to his eyebrow, tracing its length. "A brother."

"Marcus?" she asked, and he froze.

"Marcus?"

"He said you were family, brothers. Did he do that to you?"

It took him a moment to find his voice. "No. Marcus—no. I was a boy. Made my younger brother so angry he threw a hatchet at me. Took us both by surprise."

"A hatchet?" she asked, eyebrows lifting. "Like an ax?"

He nodded. "Yes."

"Briar, we're going to give you some medicine to relax you. It may make you sleepy."

"Okay," she answered, eyes still on his scar. "You're lucky you didn't lose your eye."

Her scent changed, becoming more metallic and hiding the familiar smell of apple blossoms. It filled the room, and as her eyes closed, the other scents suddenly slapped him in the face. As her fingers loosened and her hand fell away, Sylvain's predator came alive. Five heartbeats, pumping blood, thudded in his ears. The smell of their blood called to him.

The paramedics would be first. One by one, the predator chose his victims. He'd drain them for hurting Briar. After, he'd take care of the nurses and doctor. He wouldn't kill them, but he'd weaken them so when they awoke, they'd have no idea what had happened.

A low rumble left his chest, jerking him to a halt. He couldn't murder a room full of medical personnel. "I'm stepping out," he told a nurse, his voice rough.

Without waiting to hear her answer, he burst out of the

room, and was hit in the face with the overwhelming smell of blood. The chaos of the emergency department assailed him.

Prey was everywhere.

Holding his breath, he stared at the floor and rushed through the ward before he burst outside. He sucked in air, but it was tinged with too much humanity.

There was no choice but to run. If he didn't want to become a mass murderer, he had to put distance between himself and the hospital. Taking off, the world became a blur. His senses wanted to expand outward, taste the air, zero in on the sounds of the city, but he blocked the impulse, running as fast and as far as he could. He didn't stop until he reached the ocean.

He leapt, diving into the water, kicking his feet to propel him deeper and deeper beneath the waves. There, in the murky depths, with no air, the blackness so complete it could be space, his predator finally settled.

Slowly, he got control of himself. He would not murder the stupid humans, he would not hold their flailing limbs over fire to teach them a lesson.

Expelling the air from his lungs, he floated to the surface, blasting out a mouthful of water and shaking his hair out of his face.

"Nice day for a swim." On the shore, Valen watched him with narrowed eyes, his tattooed arms folded over his chest. "Care to explain?"

Sylvain flipped onto his back, staring up at the sky. He kicked, diving beneath the water and swam smoothly toward Valen until his feet touched the sandy bottom.

Drenched, he slogged to the shore, making sure to shake his hair and soak his friend. "Dammit, Sylvain!"

Sylvain ran his hands through his hair, pulling it to one side and squeezed the ends. "I needed a break."

"From what, old friend?"

"Humans. I didn't murder any. You're welcome."

Valen chuckled. "Well done, then."

"But I need your clothes now. I have to go back to the hospital."

"No way!" Valen burst out, and Sylvain smiled at the modern phrase.

"I can't go back in wet clothes, I'll make a scene." He enjoyed the look of shock on Valen's face.

"You can come to my house. I have clothes there." Marcus stepped across the sand, and Sylvain growled.

"What are you doing here?" he asked.

"I was tracking something, but I lost the trail. Strange coincidence finding you both here," Marcus began. "But I'm glad."

Valen glanced over at him, and Sylvain shrugged. Damned if he knew what Marcus meant. "Let's go." Sylvain didn't have time to decipher Marcus's bullshit. Briar could awaken any minute, and he needed to get back there.

"Why do you need to go to the hospital?" Marcus asked as he led the way to a row of brownstones. Glancing around him, Sylvain realized he'd run to Back Bay. Marcus would have to live in the ritziest part of town.

"I just do." No reason to share his secrets.

He followed Marcus up the steps, waiting for him to unlock the heavy wooden door and lead them into a gleaming entryway. He stood for a moment, dripping on the floor, filled with a sick satisfaction about dirtying the pristine interior.

"This way," Marcus said, without mention of the dripping or the fact that Sylvain and Valen still wore their boots. Inordinately disappointed, Sylvain followed him.

"Hey."

"Fuck." Sylvain didn't need to turn around to know Hudson was behind him. How had he not scented their oldest brother when he'd entered the house? "Are you fucking kidding me?" He spun to face Marcus. "I need a shirt, not a god damned family reunion. Forget it. I'll just rob someone."

Spinning on his heel, he strode to the door, but Hudson stepped in front of him.

"Out of my way," he said through gritted teeth. Already he was making plans. He could grab a human, steal his clothes and toss him in an alley. If this asshole got out of his way, he could make it back to the hospital in a matter of minutes.

"Sylvain. Wait. I want to talk to you." Holding out his hands, Hudson's eyes entreated him to listen. For a second, he was tempted. And curious. As if Hudson could see his indecision, he attacked. "I want to talk to you both." Hudson's gaze flicked to Valen. "To ask your forgiveness."

Sylvain didn't know how to respond. Never had he expected to hear those words leave Hudson's mouth. His brother stared at him, eyes wide with honesty. What the hell was happening? Where was his cold, distant brother?

This was not the Hudson of the past two hundred years.

This is your brother. A memory assaulted him of Hudson seated across a candlelit table, laughing at some story Valen told while Marcus cracked jokes from the other end.

Shaking his head, Sylvain dislodged the vision. "Why?" It wasn't the question he meant to ask, or even what he meant to say. *Fuck off,* or *get out of my way,* had been on the tip of his tongue.

"I owe you an apology," Hudson replied. He glanced at Marcus. "For Annie, for abandoning our family, for throwing it away."

For Annie. Sylvain shook his head. "Don't talk about her." He couldn't bear it. None of them knew the amount of courage it had taken him to fall in love with Annie. After everything he'd lost in his human life, Annie was supposed to be his redemption. Instead, she was the one who hammered the nail into his heart, making sure it stayed dead.

"Sylvain. I know—we all know—what you lost as a man. I never meant for it to happen again."

Deep inside him, his dead heart thumped. Placing a hand over it, he dug his fingers into his chest. "Please stop." He couldn't take it. The only way to endure this life was not to care.

But you already care.

These thoughts were tearing him apart. First Briar, now his brothers. It was too much. "I can't."

"I accept your apology," Valen said to Hudson.

"Of course you do, you've never lost anything," Sylvain snapped.

"Never—" Wide-eyed, Valen dropped his crossed arms and pushed Sylvain against the wall. "You think I've lost nothing?" He shoved him again, tossing him through the sheetrock into the bricks behind them. "You selfish bastard."

"Selfish?" Sylvain shook the dust from his hair and launched himself at Valen. Together, they fell onto the stairs, breaking the railing. Sylvain caught a fist across his face, and he tasted blood. It awoke the predator, who'd been watching the fight with interest. With a roar, he leapt to his feet, releasing the berserker who was always ready to throw down.

Valen answered his roar with one of his own, and they attacked one another with renewed vigor. And glee.

Sylvain couldn't remember feeling so good. Each hit he took sent stars exploding through his brain. Eventually, though, Marcus and Hudson waded into the melee and dragged them apart.

"Just like the old days," Marcus joked, winking at Hudson who shrugged.

"Are you ready to listen?" Valen asked, wiping the back of his mouth with his hand. Before his eyes, the gash on Valen's forehead knitted, and his nose, which was mashed in the center, reshaped itself.

He was, but no way would Sylvain say it. Instead he stood, arms crossed, glaring at the floor. With not a small amount of pride, he noticed long, fresh gashes in the mahogany floor.

"Can we be a family again?" Hudson approached him, but Sylvain merely glared at the floor. "Will you forgive me and be my brother?"

Forgive him.

The truth was, the blame didn't rest on Hudson's shoulders more than the rest of them. He'd let Hudson believe it, because it was easier that way. Hudson's guilt kept him far away from Sylvain, and nothing punished him more than the absence of his brothers.

Rubbing his neck, he winced when he dragged his hand across puncture marks. "You son of a bitch, Valen." He met his brother's smug face. "You bit me."

"I was trying to make you throw a punch. Each blow you landed felt like a kiss." Valen puckered his lips, and Sylvain jerked toward him, but Hudson slapped a hand on his chest.

"Even now, you need your brother to keep you safe," Valen goaded. "I won't hurt him too badly, Hudson. You can let our baby brother go."

"Baby brother..." Sylvain swiped Hudson's hand off his chest. "You—"

Valen stepped forward, and smacked Sylvain's shoulder, cupping his arm and dragging him forward into a bone-crushing hug. "I missed you, brother."

"You've been dogging me for two hundred years. What the hell are you talking about?"

The behemoth rustled his hair and shoved him away. "Tell Hudson you forgive him."

Throwing his gaze to the ceiling, Sylvain sighed. "I fucking forgive you. Now I need to go. Get me the fancy fucking clothes you promised me, Marcus, and get out of my way."

"What's at the hospital?" Marcus asked, opening a closet and throwing him a pair of jeans and t-shirt.

Shrugging out of his clothes, he threw his wet shirt at Valen's face, where it landed with a slap.

"Briar?" Valen dragged the shirt to his nose, breathing in deeply. "Hurt." Valen strode toward him, menace in every step. "Why is she hurt?"

"Burned."

His words threw his brothers into a tailspin; they shouted questions at him, except for Marcus, who bolted through the door.

"I forgot," Hudson spoke through clenched teeth. "She was supposed to come to my office today for a book. I didn't even remember."

"She wouldn't have made it." Sylvain remembered the girl's voice when she told him what someone had done to her. "She was injured this morning." He buttoned the jeans and shoved his feet back into the wet boots.

"I want to see her," Valen stated.

"Fine," Sylvain answered. "Let's go."

"Are we running or driving?" Hudson grabbed a set of keys from the side table.

"Running," he and Valen answered at the same time, and he smiled. *Brothers.*

CHAPTER 14
MARCUS

One thought repeated over and over in Marcus's brain as he blurred through the city streets. He'd left her. He'd left her.

First, he'd nearly fed on her, and then he'd left Briar, unprotected. Not knowing how she'd been injured didn't stop him from heaping the blame on himself. Somehow, he was responsible. He knew it.

The hospital was busy, humans streaming in and out of the doors, their scent teasing his senses. Last night, after leaving Briar, he'd hunted, gorging himself on the animals he found in the forests of western Massachusetts. A trip that would have taken humans hours in a car, with his speed and stamina, took only minutes. Animal blood could fill him, provide him with the necessary requirements for survival, but it didn't slake his thirst.

There was only one thing that would, he suspected, but he could never let it happen. He'd never let himself feed from Briar. No matter what.

"Briar Hale," he replied to the nurse sitting at the desk in the emergency department.

"Are you family?" she asked.

"Yes," he answered. He was a doctor well versed with the rules and regulations of hospitals, and not above lying to find the answers he needed.

"She's been transferred to the burn ward," the nurse replied, and pulled out a map and highlighter to show him where it was.

"Thanks," he answered, forcing himself to slow. The hospital was full of cameras, and unlike the ancient belief that vampires couldn't appear on film, or in mirrors, the opposite was true. The last thing he and his brothers needed was to be recorded flashing from one room to another. He jogged through the hospital, cursing the need to go human speed. Then, after he pushed the button for the elevator, cursed human technology, which was still slower than he could move as a vampire.

"Briar Hale?" he asked, as soon as he exited the elevator. He had no compunction about ignoring the humans waiting patiently for the nurse's attention. If they chose to follow the rules, that was on them.

"Room two—"

The elevator doors dinged behind him, and he smelled them, metallic and stale: soldiers.

Whirling to face them, he froze when he saw their faces, and who they protected. It couldn't be.

"Asher." His maker. How was he able to walk around during daylight? With soldiers, no less, who should be sleeping?

"Marcus." No one who saw Asher Olympus would know they stared at a being as old as recorded time. "Hello."

The humans, the sights and sounds of the hospital, all of it blended into the background. It was noise and haze.

"What are you doing here?" *What are you doing alive?*

Asher cocked his head, gesturing to a window. It was

useless to deny his request. Nothing would stop the ancient vampire if he decided to kill Marcus and murder the entire wing of the hospital. He was powerful enough to wipe it all out before the humans realized what was happening and were able to grab their cell phones.

"There's been a disturbance in the force," Asher began, and catching Marcus's open-mouthed shock, laughed. It would fool anyone who listened. They'd think him witty, good-natured, but they'd be wrong. The vampire camouflaged himself like the deadliest of animals. He wrapped sophistication and culture around his shoulders, but it was all an act.

At his heart, Asher was the purest form of evil Marcus had ever encountered.

"Did you do this?" Marcus asked.

"Did I do what? Give you eternal life, and receive nothing from my sons but hatred and disgust?" The smile left his face. Asher would never be anything but youthful. His appearance —broad shoulders, long, dark hair, and golden, gleaming skin —would never change. It was only when Marcus met his eyes that he saw the true age of the vampire. In their black depths was nothing but ice. "Do you mean, have I watched and waited for four hundred years for my opportunity? Yes. I *did* do that."

Marcus swallowed. There was nothing in this universe he feared like he did Asher. No matter how many centuries passed, the vampire still had the ability to make him feel weak and useless.

"But what are you doing here, son?" Was it possible Asher hadn't hurt Briar? Were the crawlers and soldiers he smelled around her apartments due to coincidence? "Shouldn't you be with your newly reunited family, and not here, distracted by *dinner?*"

Question answered. "You did this."

"Of course I did, you stupid fool." Waving a hand, the

vampire brushed off his question with an annoyed flutter. "Consider it a warning."

"A warning?"

"Yes, a warning. Return to me, or I'll destroy everything you care about."

"I just met her." Marcus was grasping at straws, but even if Briar had been someone to whom he'd lent fare for the bus, Asher would kill her without hesitation. All he had to do was show kindness, and his maker, his *father*, smote that thing, or person.

"Tell your brothers." Without a backward glance, they disappeared. Technology would prove to be no hurdle for him. Asher was powerful enough to appear merely a blip on camera.

The elevator dinged, and the doors opened, revealing his brothers. Hudson's nostrils flared, and his pupils expanded, turning the blue to black. "Asher."

"Impossible." Valen choked.

Sylvain didn't answer. He dashed past them, elbowing Marcus in his haste. Striding after him, Marcus realized how often he hid his vampiric side. His first instinct had been to ask the nurse for the number of Briar's room, rather than follow her scent, like Sylvain did now.

The wildflower aroma was faint, overlaid with pain and medicine. Sylvain opened a door, pausing briefly to glance back at them before walking inside. Valen closed in on him, but he and Hudson were last, and he had to elbow his way forward. The room was small, and Marcus suddenly felt like a giant. Shoulder to shoulder, he and his brothers took up most of the space that wasn't taken up by the hospital bed in which Briar lay.

Sylvain went right to her side, taking her hand in his and covering it.

Marcus stared at her small form and cursed his cowardice. He should have murdered Asher long ago.

Head wrapped in a bandage, Briar's face had the flushed rosy hue of someone who'd fallen asleep on the beach.

"She woke up this morning and someone had torn down her blackout curtains," Sylvain said to no one in particular. "I found myself there. Again." He breathed out a laugh, shaking his head. "Got there when the cops did."

"How bad is it?" Hudson asked, moving to the other side of the bed. His gaze lingered on the bandage, and he inhaled. "She's in a lot of pain, and they've given her a big dose of morphine."

"Bad."

"Who did it?" Valen asked. The Viking was ready for battle.

"This—" Sylvain pointed to the bandage on her neck and her ear. "This is from the cops and paramedics who dragged her into the sunlight."

"Show them to me," Valen ground out.

Marcus didn't make a sound, but Valen had his complete support. Except—"The cops didn't take down the curtains."

Hudson reached for Briar's face, turning her head to the side. "That's the worst of the burns. The rest must have happened from brief exposure."

Knowing his next words would throw their lives into more chaos, Marcus hesitated. He'd just gotten his brothers back. The most he could hope for was they would stand and fight together. He opened his mouth to speak, but Hudson beat him to it. "Asher did this."

"*I recognized his foul stench when I was brought on board,*" Marcus quoted.

"Enough with the jokes!" Valen spat. "This is serious."

"I know," Marcus replied. Hudson's focus remained on Briar. Marcus waited for his brother to back him up, but he didn't say a word. "The only one who stayed longer than me with the sick fuck was Hudson. Didn't call them the Dark Ages for nothing, right Hud?"

"Shut up, Marcus. Christ." Hudson sighed and stepped away from the bed.

"Back off," Sylvain called over his shoulder to Valen. "You're being paranoid. Asher doesn't give two shits about us anymore."

"Of course he does," Hudson replied, dryly. "We left him. Betrayed him. All he had to do was wait."

"For what?" Sylvain asked.

Briar groaned, thrashing on the bed before the morphine pushed her back to sleep.

"For us to care," Marcus answered for Hudson. "We've spent two hundred years miserable and alone. Do you think it's a coincidence he finds us when we come together again?"

"Or show interest in a human," Valen added.

"Exactly," Hudson agreed. "He's been waiting for the opportunity to punish us, and now it's here."

"I never understood the fucker," Sylvain mused. "Lives, what, four thousand years? You think he'd learn to let shit go."

"He thinks he's a god, Sylvain." Hudson clasped his hands behind his back, strode to the door, and leaned against the wall. "He walks in daylight, commands armies of soldiers, and bestows eternal life." His head dropped and he shook it. "We have to destroy him."

Sylvain and Valen nodded.

"Are you crazy?" Marcus asked. Surely Hudson couldn't be serious. Asher was the strongest vampire in existence, and who were they? Two doctors, a Viking, and a moody bastard.

And now they had an even bigger weakness.

"He got the name *Asher* for a reason Hudson. He's obliterated as many vampires as he's created." Marcus approached

Hudson angrily, grabbing his shoulder. "We don't stand a chance."

"Speak for yourself," Valen huffed. "I haven't fought a battle in a long time, but I remember how to fight."

"Marcus." Hudson grasped his hand where Marcus held his shoulder and squeezed once before releasing him. "We don't have a choice."

"I'm not leaving," Sylvain retorted. "I'm not running. He wants a fight? Bring it."

"Insane," Marcus threw out. Sylvain flipped him off.

"He's powerful," Hudson said, "but he's always underestimated us. And now we have something he doesn't."

"What?" Marcus couldn't believe his brothers. They were talking about suicide. And murder. Because their maker was going to kill them, and then he'd kill Briar, and maybe the Back Bay of Boston while he was at it, just for shits and giggles.

Hudson glanced toward the still form in the bed, and then gazed at his brothers. "Something to fight for."

CHAPTER 15
BRIAR

Angry voices pulled Briar from her happy, floaty place. She'd been drifting in and out of awareness, heard Sylvain, and went back to sleep. He'd kept his promise not to leave her, and if he was here, then she was safe.

The second time she came around, however, it was to a roomful of arguing. She blinked her eyes against the darkness, squinting to focus on the shadowy forms gathered around her bed.

"Sylvain?" she called, trying to distinguish one giant man from another, but the person who turned was Professor Nors, not Sylvain.

Suddenly, each person crowded closer. Sylvain was there, yes, but also Professor Nors, Marcus, and Valen.

"Professor Nors? Why are you here?"

"Hudson," he replied, his voice low. When he met her eyes it turned anxious. "Please call me Hudson."

"We were worried." *And Valen?*

"How are you all here?" she asked, and wondered for a second if her injury had resulted in some kind of waking fantasy. Of course, she was more than happy to keep this one going. A room full of beautiful men, concerned about her? Yes, please.

"Sylvain told us," Professor Nors—*no*—*Hudson*—answered.

"And so you all came?"

"Yes," Valen replied, like it was the most obvious thing in the world. But it wasn't to her.

"Why?" she asked again. She was no one to them. A friend, maybe. Nothing more.

Valen glanced at Hudson, and she wondered if they'd actually tell her. That they knew each other was clear. Sylvain was related to Marcus, but besides being colleagues, how were Marcus and Hudson connected? And what about Valen? He was a friend of Sylvain's, but one breakfast didn't mean he cared about her.

"Valen, Marcus, and Hudson are my brothers," Sylvain answered.

"You don't look anything alike," she observed and winced. "Sorry. Blame the morphine barely masking the throbbing pain."

Valen laughed, and Marcus chuckled, shaking his head. "No. We don't."

"They were concerned about you." Sylvain and Hudson stared at each other. "We want to be your friends."

Friends. Why did the word sound hollow to her? She wanted friends. She *needed* friends, but it didn't quite sum up the spark of interest she had in each of them.

So it's better if we're friends. I can't very well date them all. Not that they'd want to date me. I mean—look at me.

Which reminded her..."How bad is it?" She lifted her hand to her face, seeking out the bandages. Her entire head was wrapped, but the gauze bulked near her ear and down her neck. "Third degree?"

Hudson's face was sad, and he nodded. "Third degree on

your neck, second on your earlobe, the rest of your face is not even a first degree burn."

She barked a laugh and lowered her eyes to the blanket, trying to hide the tears prickling. "At least it'll match the rest of me." She grazed her collarbones and shoulders. "Not my face. Bright side? Right?" But her tears spilled over, dropping onto the back of her hands when she clasped them on her lap. "Shoot. I have to call my parents. They'll want me to come home." *Forget being friends.* She couldn't be their friend from West Virginia. "You guys probably have things to do. Don't feel like you have to stick around."

"I want to," Sylvain replied.

"We can wait," Marcus agreed. "There's nothing pressing." With that, each of them found a place closer to her. Sylvain dragged a chair to the bed, making it even with her head, and propped his feet on the bottom near hers while Marcus and Valen took up spots on either side of her.

"I'm sorry you missed the first day of classes," Hudson began, kindly. "I'll talk to the professors. You get your syllabi online?"

Briar nodded, a little shell shocked, and then winced. Her neck did not like that motion. "You don't need to do that."

He waved her off. "Please. First day of classes doesn't matter, anyway. So many people transfer and drop. Most professors don't worry about who comes to class."

"But this is grad school," she argued, and she had a really tight schedule. "Forget it."

"No." Hudson pushed off the wall where he'd found a place to lean and stood at the end of the bed. "I'm not going to forget it. You're not going back to West Virginia. You heal, and you go to class." He brushed his hands across each other. "Easy."

He made it sound that way, but Briar'd had enough surgeries to know that nothing was ever that simple. She'd be on antibiotics, the graft site would ache. She'd be covered in bandages. "It might—" she argued. Would any part of her body be left unscarred?

"No arguing." Hudson held up his hand, and Briar caught Marcus hiding a smile. "I'm well aware of the risk associated with burns and surgeries. Trust me. I'll help you with this."

"We all will. We can get your books and your computer. Keep you company," Valen offered.

"Don't you have jobs?" she wondered and covered her cheeks. "I'm sorry. That was so rude. Forgive me."

"No need," Valen replied and crossed his arms, leaning back. "I don't have a job. Neither does Sylvain. Marcus and Hudson are the only ones gainfully employed."

"Oh," she replied. They must be a wealthy family. She eyeballed each of them, thinking about what little Marcus had told her, and filled in the blanks herself. Probably they were adopted by a rich, childless couple, who wanted to leave their millions to someone instead of their grasping, greedy relatives. Briar liked the sound of her story and decided to stick with it until they told her otherwise.

The other thing she liked the sound of was the way they were banding together to help her. She wasn't naturally a negative person. If she had been, she wouldn't have ventured out of West Virginia on her own. She'd have accepted her lot, and stayed in the basement, doing all of her schooling online.

These people genuinely wanted to help her and cared enough, for whatever reason, to encourage her to stay. She could continue to argue, or she could trust them. And she really, really wanted to trust them. "Okay," she answered. "I need the help, and if you want to give it, then thank you."

"That was easy." Valen narrowed his eyes at Sylvain. "Pay attention. Next time I offer something, this is how you should accept it." He pitched his voice higher, and with his long hair, and tattoos, the effect was ridiculous. "*Yes, Valen. Thank you, Valen.*"

"Is that supposed to be me?" Briar asked.

Eyes widening, Valen sputtered. "No! It's supposed—See, Sylvain—"

"I'm teasing," she said after letting him go on for a second. "I knew it wasn't me, because you didn't do an accent."

Marcus chuckled. Even Hudson, who Briar wasn't sure she'd ever seen really smile before, laughed. They were interrupted by a quick knock, and a doctor entered.

"Briar. Glad to see you're awake. I'm Dr. Sutton, the plastic surgeon. Let's take a look at you." He stepped forward, but frowned when he saw how crowded the room already was. "Um…"

"We'll step out," Sylvain said. "Hudson will stay."

"I'm a doctor, too, you know," Marcus grumbled, following them out.

"But you're a fake doctor," Sylvain retorted. "Valen explained it to me."

Briar smiled after them, waiting for the door to close.

"Brothers?" the doctor asked, glancing between Hudson and Briar and then toward the door.

"Friends." *For now,* a piece of Briar's brain added meaningfully.

CHAPTER 16
VALEN

"I want to know everything," Valen whispered as soon as the door shut. He lowered his voice, assuring no passing humans would hear them. Comments he'd let slide earlier needed to be explained. Marcus's tension and the lingering scent of their maker when they'd exited the elevator had him preparing for bad news.

"The paramedics didn't believe her when she said she would burn in the sun." Sylvain frowned, and his fists clenched. Tonight, Valen would have to stick close to make sure his brother didn't hunt those humans down. "They caused the worst burn."

"Asher arrived before you did," Marcus added.

"Why?" Valen asked, but he shouldn't have bothered. Anything Asher did was thought out and planned. If he'd appeared, it was because he wanted his sons to know he was watching. "Never mind. He knows about Briar?"

"He was the one who entered her apartment," Marcus explained. "It was a warning to us."

Sylvain stalked down the hallway, his form vibrating with anger.

"He wants us back." Sylvain dragged his hands down his face. "He's insane. I'll rip him apart for this. I—"

"How would he know, right from the start, that all of us felt something for Briar?" Valen wondered.

"He's our maker. It's not out of the realm of possibility that her scent appeals to him in some way." Marcus's voice was so quiet, even Valen, with his vampiric hearing could barely make him out.

"If it did, he'd have drained her," Sylvain countered.

"True," Marcus allowed. "We can't leave her here alone. One of us will need to be here at all times."

"What if we just left?" Sylvain said, and Valen's stomach dropped. It was an option, but everything inside him rebelled at the idea. Leaving meant not exploring this nascent connection between them and Briar.

"I'm not ready to leave."

At least he and Marcus were in agreement, and for some reason, he thought Hudson would be, too.

"I don't want to leave," Sylvain said. "No matter how much I might bullshit. I like her, and goddamn, she smells amazing."

"Don't bite her," Valen said without thinking, and Sylvain rounded on him.

"I would *never*."

"Well, I almost did yesterday." Valen remembered the scent of her fresh blood when the waitress nicked her with the knife. "I'm not saying you would, but I am saying, the temptation was so great, I nearly sunk my teeth into her in a restaurant."

"I almost bit her last night," Marcus stated, and Sylvain growled. "Not my finest hour, I know. I stopped myself, but it was one of the hardest things I ever did. Just imagining what it would be like…" He trailed off, like he was picturing the event in his mind, and it was Valen's turn to growl.

"Enough."

Marcus rubbed his neck. "Sorry."

"I'm going to find Asher," Sylvain said, quietly. "And I'm going to tear off his head."

Unlike popular myth, vampires could be killed, but it was hard. The only real surefire way to do it was with sunlight or massive body damage. Run a vamp over with a Mack truck, and he probably wasn't getting up, but the best way was beheading, an ax, a sword, or in a pinch, a twist and yank.

Sylvain was insane, though, if he thought he stood a chance against Asher. Valen had spent centuries with him. The vampire was crafty, and no doubt expected a full frontal attack. Going in without a plan, a contingency plan, and a contingency plan to the contingency plan was plain stupid. It would get Sylvain killed, and Valen had just gotten him back.

"No," Marcus argued. "He'll kill you."

"He doesn't want to kill us, he wants us back under his control," Sylvain countered. "I may be able to get close enough to—"

"You won't." Valen refused to allow it. "He knows us, Sylvain. No matter how much we may have changed, he shaped us into the killers we are. He'll know exactly what you plan to do before you do it. Attack him head-on, and you'll only lose yours."

"So what do we do?" He dragged his hands down his face and leaned against the wall next to Briar's door. "Let him get away with it? Wait for him to attack again?"

"Yes," Valen answered, and Sylvain opened his mouth, probably to swear at him, but Valen held up a hand. "For now. Marcus is right; we don't leave Briar alone. We stay nearby. Stay vigilant. And we plan."

"Maybe he'll lose interest." Marcus snorted. "Ignore me. Somehow I turned into Pollyanna for a second."

"Hey." Hudson poked his head out the door. "Doctor is leaving. You can come in."

Valen was first through, shouldering past Marcus, who gave him a well-placed elbow in the ribs. *Worth it.*

Briar was sitting up in bed, propped by pillows. The doctor was covering her neck again with bandages, but not before Valen saw the extent of the burn. For a creature who reveled in blood, it horrified him. Catching his look, Briar blanched. "I know."

"It could have been worse," the plastic surgeon reminded her, and she nodded.

"Lucky, I have long hair. I can cover it up."

"How long did it take?" Valen asked. "For this to happen?"

"Seconds," Sylvain answered for her, his voice choked. "It was seconds."

"We're going to operate this afternoon. Quick grafting and removal of the dead skin leads to better outcomes," the surgeon explained.

"We'll be here. Make sure you're okay," Valen assured her.

But Hudson interrupted him. "They worry about infection, so visitors are discouraged."

Vampires didn't get infections. They didn't get colds, or the flu, or STDs, but the doctor didn't know that. Valen couldn't very well argue Briar didn't need to worry about getting an infection from him.

"Her family is far away, so we'll be here in their stead," Hudson explained to the doctor. "We'll take all necessary precautions, but want to make sure Briar isn't alone."

"Yes, well..." Clearing his throat, the doctor glanced at each of them uncomfortably. "Speak to the charge nurse, they usually have rules about things like visitors." Turning his attention to Briar, he smiled. "Briar. I'll see you this afternoon."

"Thank you," Briar replied, sinking down the bed as if her head was too heavy for her to hold up anymore.

The doctor left the four of them alone with Briar again. "Who stays and who goes?" Sylvain asked. "I'd like to stay."

"I think I should stay," Hudson replied. "I know what the doctors are talking about and can explain it to Briar if I need to."

"I understand them, too," Briar replied, a little saucily. "I've been through this before. If you have work, you can go. All of you can. I'm going to be unconscious for a while. You don't have to stick around and watch me sleep."

The idea of standing guard between her and anything wishing to harm her appealed to Valen more than he'd admit aloud. "It's not a problem," he assured her. "We'll stay here the rest of the day. After your surgery, depending upon how many people are allowed to visit, some of us will go to your apartment to get your things, and the rest of us will stay."

"I like that," Sylvain nodded, and Valen nearly fell over. He must have looked as surprised as he felt, because Sylvain glared at him. "Shut up."

"I didn't say anything," he replied.

"You didn't have to."

"You really are brothers." Briar laughed. "I almost expect you to put him in a headlock and give him a noogie." She pointed at Sylvain before she turned on Valen. "And stop teasing him. He's being kind."

Holding up his hands, Valen shook his head. "Me?" Perhaps his face wasn't as innocent as he tried because she huffed. And then yawned.

"Take a nap," Marcus said.

The skin on her neck mottled red, the appealing color staining her throat and cheeks. It embarrassed her to have them here while she slept.

Valen understood, but she'd have to get used to it because

he wasn't leaving her alone. Possessiveness roared through him, and his fangs descended, causing him to spin around and stare out the window into the hall. Deep breaths helped him calm, but it was tenuous. Apparently with this girl, it didn't take much to have him slipping the reins.

Sure that he had control of himself once again, he faced the bed, only to catch Sylvain's glare. His brother really had all things moody perfected, except in this case, Valen got his concern.

"Hudson." They needed to put her at ease and accept their presence. All of them, without the other ones knowing, had begun to forge a relationship with Briar, but they hadn't reached the place where she could let her guard down around them. The only way to show her this was possible was with time. Valen might as well start now. "Hudson," he said again. "Are you still living out of your office?"

"No." Hudson sniffed. "I haven't done that for years. I have an apartment now."

Light dawned in Marcus's eyes, and he nodded, smiling at Valen. "When you say apartment, do you really mean *lab?*"

"I'm not squatting in my lab!" Hudson said. "At least I'm not in some hoity-toity brownstone like Marcus."

"Did you use the word hoity-toity? What year is it?" Marcus glanced between him and Valen. "Did I blink and it was the turn of the century. Gonna throw out anymore blistering insults, Hud? How about dandy?"

"You said it, not me."

Briar giggled, her eyelids drooping. "You guys are so mean to each other," she said and yawned again. It was working.

"I'm kidding," Marcus said. "Speaking of my beautiful brownstone, did I tell you about where I found the mahogany for my floors?"

Sylvain groaned. "Don't know, don't care."

"I was next door at an open house, and their foyer had

mahogany. I thought, maybe it's in my foyer, too, and beneath the disgusting tile, there it was..." He ended with a whisper, smiling at Briar who'd, in seconds, fallen fast asleep. "Home decorating. Guaranteed to put you to sleep." Marcus bowed. "You're welcome."

"I'm going to her apartment," Sylvain whispered. "I want to see who was there. See if I recognize the scents around the building. I'll grab her things while I'm there, though I have no idea what the hell I'm getting."

"I'll go, too." Marcus straightened. "I met his soldiers. I'll recognize whether it was Asher, or one of his minions."

"Or one of his sons," Hudson whispered.

Valen stood, walked to the bed, and brushed Briar's hair out of her face. "You think he's made more vampires?"

"He's spent generations with soldiers and crawlers, but we weren't the first vampires he sired," Hudson answered. "When he made me, there were three others with him. They were brothers by birth, but disappeared not long after he turned me. Those days were such a haze, I have no idea if they ran or he killed them."

"He was happy with you for a while," Marcus mused.

"I was the perfect son: bloodthirsty and amoral. It took years for the bloodlust to abate, and I've plenty of time to repent my sins. Not that there's any making up for the horror I inflicted."

"We've all made mistakes," Sylvain replied, and Valen shut his mouth with an audible click. Sylvain was the last person he expected to be making personal revelations. "It's decided then," he went on. "Marcus and I are going to her apartment, Valen and Hudson stay."

That was more than fine with Valen. Many of his old instincts were flaring to the surface. Keep her in sight. Protect her. If he was away, he couldn't do any of it. "Yes," he agreed.

"Yes." Hudson sat at the head of the bed, leaned back, and fixed his gaze on Briar. "I'd like to stay."

"All right. Let's go, then." Sylvain slapped Valen's shoulder on his way to the door. "Stay vigilant."

Valen knocked his fist into his side. As if he needed to be told what to do. "Got it."

Sylvain smirked, and Marcus followed him out, leaving Valen to smile after them. It hit him all at once. He had his brothers back.

CHAPTER 17
SYLVAIN

Sylvain couldn't help the smirk on his lips. Not even Asher's reappearance could ruin the changes he felt happening. He had his brother at his side, and the girl healing in that bed would be important, if he let her be.

Together, he and Marcus dashed through the city, back to Davis Square. As they approached Briar's neighborhood, they slowed, taking in the scents and sounds. The closer he got, the stronger the scent of decay and rot became.

"I thought it was garbage," he stated, realizing he'd dismissed the signs of soldiers and crawlers that were right in front of him.

"We've all become complacent," Marcus replied. Frowning, he came to a halt outside Briar's apartment, green eyes examining every inch of the exterior. He pointed to the side of the house where a ladder was nailed from a window to about three feet above the ground. "Look." It wouldn't have been visible to the human eye unless the light hit it just right, and then, they'd probably dismiss it as a trick of the sun. But to Sylvain and Marcus it was clear. "Slime trail."

Like a snail, crawlers left physical evidence of their path. In this case, the trail led from the backyard to the ladder, and then along a small part of the visible roof. Sylvain shook his head. "It makes no sense. Crawlers aren't effective if Asher wanted to kill Briar. They're quiet, but slow."

"But they're more in control of themselves. If Asher told a soldier to enter her apartment, he'd have a much harder time denying his instincts. He wanted a warning to us, something to catch our interest, not push us so far we become irrational." Marcus had a point.

"We haven't shown any sign that killing her would do that to us," Sylvain countered.

"We didn't have to. All we've shown is that all of us have an interest in her. Nothing more was necessary. When was the last time we did anything together?"

"Besides come to Boston every six months for a dosing?" Sylvain retorted. He left Marcus, going through the rusted chain-link gate and into the backyard. It was a mess, with overgrown grass and ancient lawn furniture. Separating this apartment house from the neighbors was a rotting, gray, wood fence, a huge hole in one corner. Flattened grass, along with the slime trail, led directly to the hole.

"Well, we know which direction they came from," Marcus remarked, but Sylvain cut him off.

"Listen!"

The next door neighbor was crying into her phone, relating the story of finding her dog dead, early in the morning. "Poisoned!" the neighbor wailed, and Sylvain grimaced. A vampire's bite was toxic, containing within it the venom which would turn a human if combined with their blood.

A crawler's bite was venomous as well, but its saliva contained a paralytic and neurotoxin. It was evolution's way of keeping down anything that was bigger and faster than a crawler, giving them a chance to feed. Rarely did anything bitten by a crawler get away.

"Poor puppy," Marcus whispered, and Sylvain silently agreed. A crawler bite was a distinctly unpleasant way to go.

"I'm going up." Without further explanation, Sylvain went to the ladder, climbing up to the window where it reached. The frame was rotted, the wood so soft he could dig his fingers into the sill and it crumbled into chunks. "Nice." Holding onto the ladder, which was groaning worryingly under him, he slid the window up, the glass rattling. Sylvain eyed the space, and peered down to the ground at Marcus. "If I get stuck—"

"Don't worry," Marcus interrupted. "I'll kick your ass through. You can count on me."

"Thanks," Sylvain replied through gritted teeth, and hefted himself through, arms first. At his shoulders, he had to suck in a breath and extend his arms, trying to narrow his upper body. No way was he doing this gracefully. He pushed off the ladder, trying to propel himself through until he landed on his head and rolled to the floor.

The window went right into Briar's room, and there was the trail, skirting the perimeter of the studio. "This place is…"

"I know." Marcus landed beside him, rolling to his feet in a move that had Sylvain narrowing his eyes. From the smug look on Marcus's face, Sylvain hadn't been able to hide his displeasure as well as he hoped. "Student apartment."

"I have no idea what you mean," Sylvain replied. To his eyes, it looked like a place that was bordering on uninhabitable, and he'd used an outhouse. It was clean, spotless, except for the pile of curtains. Obviously someone had spent a lot of time making it livable, but with the stained tiles and curling laminate, there was only so much cleaning could do.

But it wasn't even the age of the place that worried

Sylvain, it was the give in the floor he felt every time he took a step. *Rotting floorboards.* It was the stain at the base of the heating registers. *Mold.* And it was the spark and smell of burning rubber that zipped through the apartment when whoever else was on their floor flipped a light switch.

The apartment was a death trap and needed one good electrical surge to send it up in flames.

"Pack everything," Sylvain directed. "She's not coming back here."

"Thank God," Marcus agreed. He opened a door, and stopped. "Not a closet." Stepping back, he examined every edge of the room. "I don't see a closet."

"There's a bureau and a bin." Sylvain pointed to the huge plastic tub sitting against one wall. "I think that's it."

Marcus shook his head and pulled out his phone, arranging in a matter of seconds for a mover to come within the hour.

Sylvain lifted his eyebrows. "How much did that cost?"

"Why?" Marcus spat. "You offering?" Lifting both hands to his head, he sighed. "I'm sorry. I didn't... This place just pisses me off. She's probably paying something ridiculous like two thousand dollars a month, and one wrong move, and it's... I don't understand humans. How are places like this allowed?"

"Remember tenements?" Sylvain began collecting books from the bed and stacking them. He opened the bin, and finding it empty, placed the books inside.

"I do." Marcus grimaced. "Rooms half this size. No running water, no bathrooms. Families sleeping together, eating together. Some didn't have windows."

"Is this better?" One cupboard above the sink was the extent of kitchen space, and he opened it. Kitchenware—cup, plate, and bowl along with a small frying pan and pot—was all that was inside. "Won't take long to pack."

"Do you see a laptop anywhere?" Marcus asked, studying the floor and diving beneath the bed.

"No." He checked inside the bathroom and on top of the bureau, pausing to lift the framed photos knocked over. This must be her family. Briar had on her hat—the floppy, wide-brimmed one—and wrapped her arms around someone who must be a brother. Lips puckered, she tried to kiss him, but the older boy held his hand against her face while arching away from her. Sylvain chuckled and folded the stand to stack the pictures on top of each other and place them into the bin.

"I wonder if one of the cops took it," Marcus muttered. "Though I don't know why they would." He ripped the sheets off the bed, rolling them into a ball and tossing them to Sylvain. "Oh, here it is," he said as the sheets flew through the air.

Sylvain caught them and froze. The scent was overwhelming, and he couldn't help burying his face in them. The apple blossom smell was strong, but there was something else, a constellation of scents he hadn't caught before, heat, and sunlight, and ice. All of it swirled around him, and when Marcus placed a hand on his shoulder, shaking him, he growled, yanking the sheets closer.

"Okay. Keep your blankey." Marcus put his hands in the air. "What's your problem?"

Hadn't Marcus smelled it? He'd held them. Sylvain stepped toward him, a smile tugging his lips. "Smell."

Marcus's pupils expanded until they covered all the green of his irises. A rumble rose in his throat, and his upper lip swelled, pushed out by the descent of his fangs. For all his teasing, Marcus was riding the edge of control as closely as Sylvain had. He'd just been trying to hide it.

Grabbing the pillow off the bed, he shoved it in Marcus's face. "What do you smell?"

His eyelids fluttered shut, and he inhaled and held his

breath, keeping the pillow to his nose. "Heat," he whispered, voice muffled by the pillow. "Wildflowers, and apple blossoms. Sunshine and snow." His eyes popped opened, and he dropped the pillow. "Those are...Valen said he smelled snow and ice. The ocean..."

"I smelled apple blossoms," Sylvain answered.

"Wildflowers..." Marcus choked and began again. "I smelled wildflowers the first time I met her."

"I've never scented so many things at once. When Annie..." Sylvain shook his head but forged on. "Annie's scent was sweet, but it wasn't like this. It wasn't all these different things rolled into one that reminded me not only of things I love, but my brothers."

"It's as if she's made for us." Marcus grimaced and eyed him warily. Fair enough. Just a few hours ago, Sylvain would have punched him in the throat for suggesting such a thing, but now?

"To share," Sylvain added. "With all of us, or none of us."

Wide-eyed, Marcus nodded. "She's modern, and this sort of thing isn't normal."

"We're vampires, Marcus, and you're worried about normal? Which part do you think she'll run from? The undead part or the fall in love with four brothers part?"

Barking a laugh, Marcus turned away at the same time his phone chimed. "Movers are here."

Sylvain examined the room. "I think we're done for the most part." He stuffed the blankets he still held in the bin. "Let them in."

Hesitating a second, his brother nodded. As if he couldn't help himself, he lifted the pillow to his nose one more time and dragged in the scent. "Amazing," he whispered and tossed it to Sylvain. "Be right back."

It took no time to get Briar's meager belongings packed into the moving van, and then unpacked into Marcus's spare room. In fact, it took them longer to find a parking space to unload then it did to put everything away.

Sylvain had to give Marcus credit. He'd found the way to live. The vampire wanted for nothing. But for all the expensive material items, there was still an emptiness to the house, a loneliness that permeated each room. Strangely, Briar's things, even in the one room, lent it a warmth. Her scent lingered in the air now.

"You don't think she'll be angry, will she?" Marcus said, glancing distractedly at the bed as he smoothed the sheets.

"Why would she be angry?" There was no reason to be. "She lived in an apartment that wasn't fit for human habitation. We've provided her with a safe alternative. I expect she'll be grateful."

Tension drained away from him. "You're right," Marcus said. "She'll understand. *And—*" He went on. "We'll be able to help her with after care. Drop her off at classes. Hang out. Take her to lunch."

"Occupy every moment of her day?"

Marcus missed his sarcasm. "Sure. You and Valen can take the time Hudson and I are in our labs." He stopped. "You're joking."

Sylvain touched the side of his nose and headed downstairs. As he stood in the foyer, he studied the house. If Marcus's scent didn't mark it as his, Sylvain wouldn't have known it belonged to his brother. There were no personal touches.

"Where are you staying?" Marcus asked, pausing a few steps above him.

"Here and there," he hedged. "Valen usually turns up."

"Do you want to stay here?" Sylvain regarded his brother, who wouldn't meet his eyes. The tension was back in his shoulders. He fully expected Sylvain to turn him down, and do it cruelly.

"Do you have room?"

Marcus's eyes widened for a fraction of a second before he laughed. "I have three floors of rooms. There is space for all of you." He cleared his throat. "If you want."

Did he? Or a better question might be—could he? He would be truly committing to his brothers again, and reforming the family that had split apart so long ago. His heart ached, and he rubbed his chest. He'd barely survived Annie's death and their separation, even though he'd been the first to leave.

All his life, Sylvain had lost. As a human, he'd lost his wife and child, and then he'd lost his humanity. When Asher turned him and he found three brothers and eternal life, he'd thought he was set.

Then the bloodlust had faded, like it did with all newly made, and he faced what he'd done in that state, grateful he'd had brothers to keep him from the worst of his potential.

Could Sylvain take the leap, again? Throw in his lot with his brothers and Briar and accept there was the possibility of losing them all? A flicker of hope wound its way around Sylvain's heart. "Yeah. I want."

Marcus lowered his gaze, shaking his head and clearing his throat. Vampires didn't cry, but if they could, Marcus had a feeling his brother would be leaking. "You can have the couch."

"Asshole," he muttered. "We need to go back to the hospital if you're done dicking around."

Marcus leapt from the stairs, throwing an arm around his neck and nailing him in the stomach with a closed fist. The breath huffed out of Sylvain, and with a lot less strength than he could have used, he threw Marcus into the hall where he hit the wall.

"Were you hitting me or kissing me?" Marcus asked.

Sylvain opened the door. "Are you done?"

"Nope." Marcus popped the last sound of the word but closed the door and locked it behind him. Out in daylight, his demeanor changed, as if he remembered what they needed to do and what was still ahead of him. "Let's go."

CHAPTER 18
BRIAR

Briar groaned, her throat burning.
"Here's some water. Open up." Hudson's voice was as cool as the water that dripped into her mouth. Parched tissues absorbed every drop of moisture. She flopped her head toward him and moaned. The pull along her neck reminded her of the surgery. Her throat ached from the breathing tube. Something smooth touched her lips, tracing their contours, and she opened her eyes. Hudson's gaze was glued to her mouth as he traced it with balm.

"Thanks." Her voice was nothing like she was used to hearing. He capped the lip balm, and smiled.

"Here." A straw touched her lips, and she sucked greedily.

Each moment that passed, her head cleared and she became more alert. The room was dark, but she could make out the guys' forms. "If I'm Dorothy, who are you?" she joked and coughed, choking on the water.

"Go slow," Hudson replied. "Obviously, Marcus is the scarecrow."

Sylvain huffed, and she smiled. "Did it work?"

"So far so good," Hudson assured her. "You'll stay here

overnight, they'll take a look at it tomorrow, and we'll go from there."

She nodded and immediately regretted it. "Am I hideous?"

Hudson's blue eyes, usually so icy, softened. "Hardly."

"Overnight?" she asked. God, how she hated being back in the hospital. It never changed. The antiseptic smell, the weird-tasting water, the constant noise that irritated her already on-edge senses.

"Two, possibly." Tone dry, Briar got the sense Hudson wouldn't tolerate any deviating from the timetable he expected.

Glancing at each of them, Briar was struck by how comfortable they all seemed. Sylvain held the wall up, while Valen leaned, elbows on knees at the edge of his seat. Marcus stood, hands in pockets, following her exchange with Hudson. None of the tension she noted before her surgery was present now.

"What time is it?" she asked. One of the other things she didn't miss about hospitals was how there seemed to be no night or day. The only thing to really distinguish the passage of time was the nurses' shift changes.

This room had no windows to the outside, which she appreciated. She didn't have to worry about an overworked or distracted nurse opening the curtains to let in the sunshine. Absentmindedly, she rubbed a small smooth spot on her thumb, the result of a hospital stay as a child, and shade-opening 'consideration.'

Marcus glanced at his watch. "One in the morning."

Guilt swamped her. "Aren't you tired?"

"No," Sylvain answered. "I took a nap while you were in surgery." The last part was added on as an afterthought that didn't ring true.

"Hmm." She raised her eyebrows. "Did..." She paused,

choosing her next words carefully. "Have you heard anything from the police about my apartment?"

From his chair, Valen's head jerked up, and he pinned Marcus with a stare. "Yeah. Did we?"

Eyes narrowed, Marcus slowly shook his head. "No. Which is strange."

Briar dug her fingertips into the sheets. "I don't remember if they asked me anything in the ambulance. Sylvain, do you remember?"

"No," Sylvain answered. "They didn't ask you anything. The paramedics didn't anyway, and no one has been here asking anything since I've been here."

"They haven't," Hudson confirmed. "I'll call in the morning. They're probably letting you get the medical care you need before interviewing you. I'm sure they'll be by. If not here, then in the next few days."

"Someone wanted to hurt me." It was hard for her to comprehend. Her condition wasn't a secret, but she'd been in Boston only a week. The only people who knew about it, besides the admissions department at BC, were Hudson, Valen, and Marcus. A little voice inside her squeaked the question, asking if she believed they'd torn the curtains from her windows while she slept.

As soon as the voice spoke, a much louder, much surer part of her mind shut it down. Stamped it down, actually. Stamped it, and then picked it up and threw it against a wall and hit it with a shovel. *No. No way.* She didn't believe they had anything to do with what happened.

"Maybe it was a prank," Marcus spoke and winced.

"It wasn't funny, but it's possible. Do you think someone in admissions let it slip and some kids thought it'd be hilarious? Like, I've read about people hazing people with peanut allergies with peanut butter. Maybe it was something like that."

"I believe," Sylvain started, "I believe whoever did this, wanted to send a message."

Briar snorted. "Yeah. I get it. I live in a shitty apartment and it was easy to pick the locks. Wait." Thinking back to the morning, she tried to remember if her door had been open. "It was. But I had to let them in downstairs. So whoever did this..." Her stomach roiled, and not from the surgery. "Someone got in and out. Locked my door before they left. That's so creepy." It was more than creepy, but that was about as deep as she could get given the circumstances.

"Not to be unkind, Briar, but anyone with a credit card and a toothpick could get into that apartment," Marcus stated.

"I remember your opinion, Marcus," she said. Nothing could have hidden his horror at her tiny, sweet walkup. That apartment was the embodiment of her freedom, and she loved it.

"It wasn't so bad," Valen said, meeting her eyes and smiling.

"Thank you, Valen," Briar said. "You get ten points."

"For what?" he asked, confused.

"For Gryffindor."

"I'm so confused." Valen glanced at Sylvain for an explanation, but the huge man only shrugged his shoulders. "I don't know what a Gryffindor is."

"You didn't even see inside, Valen," Marcus argued.

"And I'm deducting fifty points," she said to him.

"Why award Valen ten points if you're just going to take fifty away?" Marcus crossed his arms. Smart ass.

"Because they weren't deducted from Gryffindor." She leaned forward a little, ignoring the pain and fatigue beginning to make themselves known. "I deducted them from Slytherin."

"Hey!" Marcus choked, offended.

Hudson burst out laughing, reaching for Briar's hand and squeezing it tightly. "You're Slytherin." He pointed at Marcus with his free hand and started to talk, but Briar didn't hear what he said. She was too focused on his hand wrapped around hers, and his thumb tracing circles on the back of her hand. When she thought he'd let go, he didn't. Instead, he sat on the edge of the bed, and stroked her hair out of her face. "You look tired."

"I am," she answered. "The medicine."

"And healing," he said.

"And healing."

"Go to sleep." Hudson looked over at his brothers and then back at her. "We're in for the night."

"Are you sure?" They made her feel safe. Earlier, they'd put her to sleep with their playful banter, and now, their physical presence comforted her. She swore they had a scent, something she couldn't put her finger on, that reminded her of home.

Yawning, she let her eyes close, not even waiting for Hudson's answer. If he said they'd stay, they would, and they'd stand between her and anything that tried to hurt her.

Two days passed, and the room burst at the seams with guys. Guys who were brothers, and who fought at the drop of a hat, and whose natural state appeared to be elbows out, balls-to-the-wall.

But Briar enjoyed every second of it. She'd never laughed as much as she did when Marcus gave them all online quizzes to find out which celebrity they should take to prom or which nineties-era boyband they were.

Sylvain was taking Ryan Gosling.

They also had moments of quiet when no one had

anything to say and they sat contentedly. None of them took out their phones; they were happy to sit with their thoughts, something Briar hadn't seen before, and struggled with at first. She was never without her phone, and used it as a crutch from boredom, but she had plenty to think about now.

Like, how kind Valen was. The first morning, she awoke to find he'd snuck out for breakfast so she didn't have to eat the hospital food. He did the same at lunch, and dinner, though Sylvain tagged along with him for dinner.

"He wants some of the accolades you've been heaping on Valen," Marcus had stage-whispered as they left, causing Sylvain to flip his middle finger over his shoulder and close the door with what Hudson called *extra emphasis*.

And Hudson. He would often break out of thought with random ideas and direct them at her. "What do you know about heme B?" It took her a second, because at first she thought he was talking to Marcus. But he'd stared at her and waited, and she'd realized, *he wants to know what I think*. They talked science and EPP until she was having trouble keeping her eyes open, and Marcus made a comment about never seeing science excite anyone so much.

When the doctor came to check on her, the guys gathered closer, listening intently as he examined the graft and pronounced her healing well.

Slowly, but well.

Hudson agreed with him about staying an extra night, even though Briar argued against it.

She didn't want to stay here longer than she needed to. Sure, Sylvain and Marcus brought her pajamas so she wasn't stuck in a hospital gown, but she still hadn't showered, and she was probably gross.

And that was the other thing. Every so often, she'd catch

one of the guys staring at her with something she couldn't name.

Well, she could name it, but she couldn't believe it would apply to her.

The guys were older than her, not by a lot, but Briar'd been reading Hudson's research papers for seven years, which meant he was at least thirty, and Marcus had an aura of sophistication that most twenty-somethings didn't.

Sylvain and Valen were likely in their twenties, but at times, they'd speak a certain way which had her second-guessing her estimate. Guys like them were interested in women, not graduate students who hadn't managed to make it to their first college class.

Why, then, did her stomach flutter when Valen's eyes crinkled with laughter, or when Sylvain lifted one side of his lips in a semi-smile?

The morning of the second day, Briar was ready.

Valen brought her breakfast, but her stomach was too nervous to eat. She wanted to leave, get back to her apartment, and go to class.

"I have a night class," she told Marcus when he lifted his eyebrows at her pronouncement. "I'm feeling up for it. In fact, I'm going to go crazy if I have to stay in bed another minute!"

"You may be tired by the time it rolls around," he said. "Just see how you feel. Hudson let your professors know what was going on. You have a doctor's note, so you're not penalized for being absent."

"I know." She'd thanked Hudson repeatedly, but smiled at him again in gratitude. "I'm lucky, but I want to go. I've been *waiting* to do this. Imagine if it was Christmas, but you woke up Christmas morning, and instead of presents, your parents gave you a picture of your presents. And it was everything you wanted, but you had to wait to get them. Every day you woke up, not sure if that was the day you got everything you wanted. This is my Christmas, and I can't wait anymore."

Sylvain gave her his half-smile. "I don't know that I've heard school compared to Christmas before." He glanced over at Hudson, who shook his head.

"No," Hudson agreed. "Definitely not typical."

Briar dragged the elastic out of her hair to gather the greasy strands back into a ponytail. "And I want a shower and to sleep in my own bed."

"Fair enough," Marcus said. "I understand."

The doctor arrived at that moment, and Briar clenched her hands anxiously. He asked the same questions and had her do the same motions as the day before, but it all filtered to her through a haze. Her throat burned, and she hoped if he told her she couldn't go home yet, she didn't start bawling in front of everyone.

"I think you're good," the doctor said, typing into his laptop. "I'll send the nurse in, and you can get going. Cover the wound with plastic when you shower, no pools, no heavy lifting. Do you have a pharmacy or do you need the hospital to make up your prescriptions?"

"The hospital," Briar said, groaning internally because it would mean more time before she could leave.

Nodding sharply, the doctor wrote something else down and left without another word.

"It's a good thing he is adept at his job," Valen said, glaring at the door. "Because the man is not polite."

"I'm sure he's busy," Briar replied and cleared her throat. "Could one of you drop me at home? Would you mind?"

Marcus nodded, but Sylvain sucked in a breath, causing Briar to peer at him in confusion. He and Marcus had a moment of staring—a loaded, silent conversation which ended when Sylvain looked away. "Everything okay? You don't have to, if you had plans together. I can take the T."

"No," Sylvain answered. "It's not that."

"I'm going to get my car," Marcus announced. "I'll meet you all out front."

Sylvain stared after him, open-mouthed, and Briar got the sense, as Marcus high-tailed it out of the room, he was trying to escape.

"I'm going to get my things," she said, and slid out of bed to go to the bathroom. Once there, she stared with horror at her reflection. The sunburn had faded but left her splotchy. Dark, bruised skin made circles beneath her eyes, and her hair, which she'd tried to tame into a neat ponytail, was bumpy, and greasy. "Oh, my God."

The guys' gorgeous faces flashed in her mind, and she giggled. What she'd thought was interest was definitely not that. No one could look at her right now and say she was anything but a train wreck.

"You okay?" Valen's concerned voice came through the closed door.

"Yeah," she answered and turned on the water. She brushed her teeth and combed her hair, slicking it with water away from her face and neck. It wasn't a flattering hairstyle, revealing her bandage and the scars along her throat and collarbones.

Her long hair functioned as a shield, one she could pull around her face if anyone stared at her too long. But her choices were limited. She could either showcase her scars or leave her hair in stringy mats around her face.

At least pulled back into a bun, she could have a semblance of being put together. She soaked a washcloth, gently cleaning her face and then patted it dry before leaving the bathroom. Marcus was gone, and the room was empty of everyone except Hudson and the nurse, who met her arrival with a smile.

"Here are your prescriptions," she said, handing Briar a paper bag. "I've explained everything to your brother."

Briar drew her brows together and wrinkled her nose. *Huh?* "Thank you," Hudson said, smoothly interrupting anything she might say to the contrary. "You're ready?"

"I am," she answered, and held up the small plastic bag holding her hairbrush and toothbrush.

He opened the door for her, waiting for her to slide her feet into her sneakers, set the hat on her head, grab her gloves, and follow him.

The nurses waved goodbye as they left the wing, a few of them staring a little longer than necessary at Hudson, but who could blame them? Briar was sure she'd had the same look on her face a few times, especially when he started talking about enzymes. The most she could hope for was that she hadn't drooled at any of the guys while watching them.

Hudson led her effortlessly through the hospital, keeping them to windowless hallways that were nearly empty. Briar was hopelessly turned around. She'd never have found her way through without him.

"Where's Marcus?" she asked, and he pointed to the glass fronted entrance before touching her shoulder to hold her back.

"Got your glasses?" he asked, and she slid the oversized sunglasses she held in her hands onto her face.

A black SUV with heavily tinted windows sat at the curb, hazard lights flashing. The door opened, and Valen waved from inside.

"Ready?" Hudson asked, and her stomach clenched.

It was a short distance, twenty feet at most, and she was covered. Would she ever come not to fear the sun? "This sucks," she whispered, and Hudson took her hand.

"It'll be fast," he said and nudged her forward. They

hurried through the doors and into the day. One second, two, and she was in the car and the door shut.

The passenger side door opened, and Hudson jumped in.

"Where's Sylvain?" she asked, and Marcus clenched his teeth. From her seat behind Hudson, she had a perfect view of his profile and couldn't miss the muscle jumping in his jaw.

"He's meeting us there."

"Okay," she answered, and settled back against the leather seat. A hand grasped hers, and she glanced over at Valen, who entwined their fingers.

"Are you doing okay?" he asked quietly. "You didn't catch any sun, did you?"

"No. I'm good." She couldn't feel his skin beneath the gloves, and she wished she could take them off. There was always something stopping her from fully experiencing the world, and she resented it, even if it was just learning whether or not Valen's fingers were calloused.

The traffic was heavy for this time of the morning, especially since they were headed north, except—"Marcus, you're headed the wrong way. I'm north. This is east." They should have been crossing the Charles River to head to Somerville, but instead the Charles was on their right as they drove along it.

Valen squeezed her hand, and when she met his eyes, he smiled a little nervously.

Nervously? Yes.

He couldn't hold her gaze. He stared at the floor before glancing at her again. "What's going on? Marcus?" The muscle in his jaw ticked again, and his hands clenched on the steering wheel.

Hudson smoothly turned in his seat. "It wasn't safe."

"What wasn't safe? My apartment?" she asked. "Why? What did you learn? Did the police contact you? What did they say?" Words tumbled out of her mouth, and she found herself edging forward on the seat, pulling the safety belt to give her slack. Valen squeezed her once and released her hand.

"Someone snuck in your window, Briar, and nearly killed you. Not only that, the place was a fire hazard. Marcus said he'd never seen a place in such disrepair."

"Marcus said that, did he?" Her words were a growl, and she stared daggers at the back of his head while he kept his gaze fixed on the road. *Coward.*

"So where are we going?" she asked.

"Marcus's," Hudson answered. "You can stay there."

It took everything she had not to rip into them for their high-handedness, but the truth was, until she spoke to the police, she wasn't sure she was ready to stay at the apartment right now.

She missed it; it was her home. But she wasn't stupid. Once the police assured her, as she was certain they would, it was safe to return home, she would.

"That's very nice of you," she said, the manners bred into her since birth coming to the forefront. "Are you sure?"

Shoulders slumping, Marcus let out a breath and nodded. "Of course."

"Should someone tell Sylvain? So he's not waiting at my place?"

"He's not," Valen replied with false lightness.

Gritting her teeth, Briar realized she'd been hoodwinked. She'd believed Sylvain was at her place, and they let her believe it, because they were afraid to tell her about her apartment. "Why are you afraid of me?" she asked, and giggled before quickly sobering. "Don't lie to me just because you don't want to make me angry. I'll be much angrier if you do."

"In that case," Valen began, but Marcus parking and her door opening cut him off. Sylvain stood there, smiling

163

broadly. Both sides of his lips lifted, and she wondered what caused his good mood. A full smile? Maybe someone gave him a new ax or sharpened his chainsaw.

"Hi," she said, greeting him with an answering smile. Who knew Sylvain could have an infectious good mood?

"Hi," he answered, and reached into the car, lightly grasping her elbows, and tugged her out.

"Wow." This was Marcus's house? "Holy cow."

"It's not that fancy," Marcus mumbled as he walked by and opened the door for them.

"Don't be embarrassed," Briar said. "This place is amazing! You can see the water! I can—" She stood on her tiptoes and peered over the landing before going inside. "Nope. Well, it's still really nice."

With a laugh sounding a little forced to Briar's ears, Marcus gestured for her to go inside. She did and sucked in a breath. "Everyone told me not to be a Ph.D. They said, I'd never make any money at it." She spun around and put her hands on her hips. "They *lied*. And what does your place look like?" Pointing an accusing finger at Hudson, she tapped her toe. "Huh? Golden floors?"

Hudson chuckled but didn't answer while Briar studied the interior, fascinated. Obviously, some work was being done to it. The plaster on one wall was patched, and it looked as if the floor had been gouged, but otherwise, it was beautiful. All dark wood floors and crown molding.

But as she glanced around, she noticed there were no personal touches, nothing that showed *Marcus* lived there. It was like a showcase house, perfectly decorated, but empty.

It made her ache for him. Even her tiny *fire hazard* had bits and bobs that made it unique.

"Let me show you your room," Marcus said, interrupting her thoughts. "This way."

He led her up a wooden staircase to the second floor and

pointed down the hall. The staircase went up to another floor, and Briar leaned over the railing, glancing up. "How many floors is this place?"

"Three," Marcus answered. "And servant's quarters. Those rooms are tiny, and I don't use them. I tend to seal off the floor in the winter so I don't lose heat. These old houses are drafty."

A thick carpet in deep reds and gold muffled their tread until he stopped at a door and opened it. Briar craned her neck, standing on her tiptoes to look over his shoulder when he stood in the doorway, and nearly fell over.

"I don't understand." There was her bed, made up with her sheets. Her bureau, with the framed photos of her family, sat against one wall, and her books and laptop were placed neatly on a desk.

Heavy brocade curtains hung from rods, blocking the light, but from what Briar could see, all of her belongings were in this room. "I don't understand," she said again, resting on her heels and staring at Marcus. "Why are all my things here?"

"It wasn't safe for you there," Marcus said, quietly, standing to the side when Briar walked inside, her head spinning.

"I know," she answered. "I agreed to stay here, but Marcus, not forever. I'm not moving in."

"Marcus was right." Sylvain's voice boomed behind her. "The apartment was unfit for residency. The city agreed with me, and the building's tenants have all been relocated while the landlord brings it up to code."

"What?" Briar didn't want to be shrill, but her voice squeaked. "How—that was my home! You have no right to take my things and move me here without my permission! And where am I supposed to go? Do you know how hard it is to find a place in Boston? I started looking for apartments last year, and that was the best I could find." Her head throbbed, and she rubbed her temples. "I don't know what I'm going to do."

"You'll stay here," Sylvain answered like it was the most obvious thing in the world.

She glared at him. "No. I won't."

"You just said yourself," Sylvain replied, "that it's impossible to find housing in Boston on such short notice. The other tenants have been placed at long-term stay hotels, but we declined on your behalf. Marcus won't accept rent, and there's no need for you to stay at a place any less safe than the one you just left."

"I—" For the first time in her life, words failed her. Southern manners bred into her since birth warred with her anger at the audacity and sheer presumption of these guys. Rather than spew that rage all over them, she stepped inside, turned to them, and shut the door in their faces. She didn't slam it; she didn't need to. Twisting the wrought iron key in the lock, she ignored the quiet knock from the other side.

Time was needed before she spoke to them again or else she would bring down the walls with shrieks.

Sighing, she surveyed the room. Her bureau was pathetic compared to the antiques that made up the room. Her bed had no head or footboard. It was merely a mattress and box spring on a metal frame. In her apartment, it had looked cozy, covered with her blanket from home and pillows she got at the same place she bought the bureau. There was no way her things, made of particleboard and plywood, could stand up next to the furniture Marcus had.

Briar walked over to the desk, pulled out the chair, and sat. Her laptop rested on top of a blotter, and she noted a pack of pens and sticky notes at the edge. Mashing her lips together, she tried not to care that someone had put extra thought into making her comfortable or preparing for her stay.

It wasn't in her to hold a grudge, and she recognized an effort had been made. Anxious, she stood to examine the room. She opened one door, finding her clothes hanging. The second door opened to a bathroom that had her groaning in delight.

A clawfoot tub sat in the center of the tiled floor. At the side, bath salts and body lotion were arranged neatly. She popped the top on one, sniffed, and sighed. *Holy cow.*

What was that phrase? She tried to remember. *When in Rome...* If she was going to be spending the night, she might as well enjoy all the amenities.

Soon the sound of running water filled the small room. Distracted, she sat on the edge, holding her fingers beneath the steam as it heated. The shower at her apartment had been lukewarm at best, and at times reminded her of a mist, instead of a shower. She poured in the bath salts, and the room filled with the fragrant aroma of lily of the valley. Her eyes closed, and she stripped the clothes from her body quickly, sinking slowly. At the last second, she remembered the bandage on her throat, and popped up.

Placing her elbows on each edge, she closed her eyes and let her head rest against the back of the tub. *What am I going to do with you guys?*

She was really mad. That apartment was hers and hers alone, and if it was a death trap, she should have been the one to call the city.

In her mind's eye, she saw her apartment. The grubby laminate that never really got clean no matter how hard she scrubbed. The boards on the stairs that rocked if she put her foot in the wrong spot. It was quirky, yes. But dangerous?

Sylvain wasn't a liar. Even for as short a time as she'd known him, she got that he was an opportunist, and a bit of a mercenary, but he wouldn't make something up to suit him. Therefore, if he said the apartment was a death trap, it was one.

Which left Briar with a problem. They'd gone above her head and treated her like she was unable to see reason. All they would've had to do was show her the issues in the apartment building and explain the danger. Instead, they'd taken her choice from her, like she couldn't be trusted to do the right thing.

"Grrr." She let loose a stream of air that caused the fluffy suds to pop in her face. Her mother had taught her to treat others the way she wanted to be treated, but she couldn't expect they'd been brought up the same way.

Not to mention, even though they looked only a little older than her, they acted like men who knew a lot more of the world than a typical guy their age would.

Mind set on a course of action, her muscles relaxed. It was up to her to teach these guys some manners and to show them she was up to the task of decision-making. In the meantime, she was going to enjoy this bath and stay in the water until it cooled and she pruned. It wouldn't hurt the guys to sweat a bit.

CHAPTER 19

HUDSON

"Stop smirking at me, Hudson." Sylvain paced away from Hudson, throwing himself into a nearby seat. When Briar hadn't answered Marcus's earlier knock, they'd gathered in the living room. Mired in their guilt, they'd sat, or paced, silently. Overhead, the water in the bath turned off, and Hudson heard the slosh of water against the sides of the tub.

Suddenly, he pictured Briar, hair lifted off her neck, pale, lithe body sinking beneath the water, and he couldn't smother his groan. Marcus chuckled, and Hudson wiped his face clean of emotion.

"We hurt her feelings." Valen perched on the arm of the chair next to Sylvain. His blond brother was never far from Sylvain. He no longer needed to keep up the pretense of staying away and seemed to be making up for lost time.

Valen and Sylvain were two sides of the same coin. Twins of dark and light born hundreds of years apart. Hudson was again struck by how much they'd given up.

"We'll explain again," Hudson said to Valen, falling back on facts. When all else failed, present arguments in black and white. Except, for the first time in a long time, Hudson wasn't certain of logic and reasoning. Emotion clouded everything with Briar.

"Do you think she'll be happy here?" Valen asked, and Hudson heard the unspoken question. Did Hudson think *they* could make her happy?

He didn't know.

For so long, he hadn't let himself feel anything. Even now, he was focused on how he thought Valen felt, or how Sylvain felt. He was doing everything he could not to think about himself.

"Grr." The smallest growl echoed in the bathroom above their head. Briar's soft voice with her smooth accent hid how tough she was.

"We should have asked her," Hudson said, with dawning understanding about what they'd done. "We took her choice away. She's a smart girl. We should have asked her."

"Asking is a waste of time," Sylvain argued.

"I'm going to apologize." Decision made, Hudson strode toward the stairs, not bothering to glance back to see if anyone followed him. At the heavy door, he paused, tilting his head to listen closely. Briar must have pulled the stopper in the tub, because the sound of water rushing down the drain masked all other sounds.

It was pointless to knock. Her human hearing would miss the sound until the water drained completely. And then she may choose to ignore him. Hudson clenched his fists. He hated being at odds.

Beneath the door came a waft of lily of the valley scented air and the sound of Briar shuffling her feet across the floor. He hesitated before knocking. All he had was a half-formed plan, and he didn't like it.

"Screw logic, Hud." Marcus's soft voice drifted to him from the landing, and he glanced over his shoulder. His oldest friend stood, hand on the railing, watching him closely. "Just see what happens when you speak from your heart." With that, Marcus left him, moving so quickly he was gone in the blink of an eye.

Before he could stop himself, he knocked and waited.

"Hold on." Briar's voice was muffled, as if she had her face in her blanket. Like earlier, Hudson's mind filled in the image, and he had to grip the door frame in order to keep from rushing inside, lock be damned, to see if what he pictured was a reality.

The door swung away, and he was caught in a cloud of lily and sunshine. All ability to speak left him. Nothing could have prepared him for Briar post-bath.

The heat left her natural scent even stronger. *Mouthwatering.* He curled his fingers into the wood, felt his nails sink past the shell and into the drywall.

Silently, Briar stared at him. She didn't rush to fill the silence, merely watched and waited.

"I'm sorry," he said.

The tiny pucker between her eyebrows signaling her annoyance smoothed away.

"I'm sorry," he continued, "that we didn't tell you what we were doing before we brought you here. It was disrespectful."

"I'm not stupid," she said.

Of course she wasn't. "I never thought you were stupid. You're brilliant. The way your mind works. The connections you make between ideas and theories."

She held up a hand to stop him. "You didn't include me in a decision that affects me. All you had to do was explain. I would have understood."

Wood shavings and drywall dust fluttered to the floor as he released his grip on the molding, and he prayed she didn't notice. "I know," he said, stepping forward. Immediately, she made room for him, gesturing for him to come inside. "In our defense, we went a little crazy when your safety was threatened."

The scent inside the room overwhelmed him, and for the second time, he cursed his brainlessness. He should have stayed in the hallway. The hallway was safer.

Safer for whom?

His fangs descended, answering the question his mind had thrown at him.

"Why were you crazy? You barely know me." In the corner of the room was an overstuffed chair, and she lowered herself to the cushion and curled her feet beneath her. "This, I don't understand. You're going out of your way for someone you just met."

"It doesn't feel that way," Hudson answered. All this talk of feelings—how could he explain? "Perhaps it's because I've been reading your emails for years. Your voice is familiar, even though I'm only hearing it now. I believe it is the same for my brothers."

The first time he'd met Marcus, it had been the same. They'd become brothers, and then best friends, in no time.

Something about her settled at his explanation. Her smile was softer, and she nodded and leaned forward as he spoke. "It does feel like that." She settled back into the chair, the oversized cushions dwarfing her narrow frame. "Next time, though, please ask me before you make choices that impact my life."

Her words threw him back in time, and suddenly Annie's voice screamed in his head. *"You made my choices for me and stole everything!"* He shut his eyes, but still he heard Annie's scream.

"I'm so sorry." He barely got the apology out. When he opened his eyes, he found Briar perched on the edge of her chair, reaching for his hand.

Like a dream, everything seemed to slow. Beneath her

skin, he saw her blue veins, pulsing with blood, and then her warm hand enfolded his, squeezing. "Thank you," she said.

His first instinct was to jerk his hand away, not because he didn't like it—he loved her hand in his—but because he'd become so used to denying himself anything that felt good.

Her hand was as pale as his, but smattered with golden freckles across the back. Her other hand rested against her knee, the skin still flushed from her earlier injury. "Briar."

"I know," she replied and drew her hand away to cover the redness. "I'll figure this whole daylight thing out. I already set my phone up with alerts and reminders." Something caught her attention, and she stood, glancing around the room. "I should probably call my mother."

Her mother. Briar still had a mother. She still had a family. Who was he to think he had a right to her? One misstep, and he could hurt her. *No. Let's be honest.* One misstep, and he could *kill* her. All of them walked the edge, their urges sated with a poor substitute for human blood.

And Briar smelled so good.

His growl rumbled through the room, causing Briar to spin around. "Was that you?"

His fangs ached with the need to bite, and he covered his mouth.

"What's going on?" Briar hurried to him and gripped his wrist, pulling hard.

Behind him, the door opened, admitting all of his brothers. "Hey, Hudson. Your phone is ringing. I think you have class." The excuse was weak, but he latched onto it. With his back to Briar, he finally dropped his hand. "Sorry, Briar. I need to go."

"No! Wait. I want to know what's going on. Valen did the same thing. And Marcus. What's going on?"

"You stay around people long enough, and you begin to adopt their habits," Marcus said, but his joke fell flat. Part of

Hudson wanted to turn around, drop his hand and reveal himself. But another part of him, the part that was desperate to keep Briar, made him hurry away.

"Hudson," she called after him, but he ignored her.

"We owe you an apology," Valen began, distracting her.

Once he hit the bottom step, his legs wobbled, and he sat. He'd come close, so close, to biting her. His mouth filled with saliva. She would taste as good as she smelled. He wondered if she'd taste like the wine he'd made from the ancient, sun-filled fruit.

If she was going to stay here, all of them would need to hunt more often. Or he'd need to join Marcus in his lab. Between the two of them, they might be able to find a better substitute to slake their thirst than animal blood.

One sip.

The beast inside of him began planning. *Wait until she's asleep. Drink her blood. Give her yours. Heal her.*

Turn her.

Hudson slammed his hands to his head, slapping them against his temples. The beast sent him image after image. The temptation was too much, and before he knew what he was doing, he found himself at the top of the stairs.

"Hudson! No!" Sylvain pressed his hands against his chest, fingers hooked like claws.

"One sip." The voice wasn't his, but his beast's, and just like that, Hudson disappeared, leaving his bloodthirsty monster wearing his face.

CHAPTER 20
BRIAR

A crash sounded from the hallway, and as one, Valen and Marcus spun, crouching low.

"Back up." Valen threw a glance over his shoulder before his focus went back to the doorway.

The crawlers. Briar remembered the creature's long fingers wrapping around her leg, and its weight as it pulled itself eye-level to her. Valen growled, the sound more animal than human, and the fine hairs on the back of Briar's neck lifted.

Something was wrong here. Neither Valen nor Marcus looked at her again, but she got the sense they were wholly focused on her.

As she backed up like Valen asked, their bodies shifted minutely. The cacophony of noise from the hall suddenly stopped, before erupting into something louder and more frightening. It was as if lions fought for dominance right outside her room.

Roars shook the walls. Briar jumped and rammed into the furniture. One of the framed photos from her bureau shattered on the floor, sending glass flying in all directions.

Like a flash, Valen suddenly jumped into the air to catch

the dark form flying toward her. The two figures landed with a crash so hard Briar expected to see an impact crater in the floor.

One of the forms shook free of the other, pinning Briar with a blue-eyed stare that froze her in place.

Hudson.

At least, it was a creature who wore Hudson's face and body. It twisted Hudson's features. The handsome, distant man replaced with a slavering, wild-eyed beast.

"Hudson?" Her voice shook, and the beast smiled to reveal four curved fangs along the top of his mouth. They dug into his lower lip, splitting the skin to ooze blood he then licked away.

A flash of brown leapt between her and Hudson. Marcus. Knees bent, he shifted like a soccer player guarding the goal.

Which was her.

Hudson feinted left and then right, but each time Marcus stood between them. Nearby, Valen shook off what must have been a massive body check and rushed to stand next to Marcus.

Something slammed into the door, and Sylvain appeared.

Oh God.

Sylvain's features were a mirror of Hudson's. Fangs. Sharp teeth. Wild eyes. It wasn't the sunlight that was going to be her end; it was these men. Hands clenching into fists, muscles bunching, Sylvain blurred.

Briar's brain wasn't fast enough to keep up with the action. One second Hudson appeared in front of her, straight backed and grinning, and the next, he disappeared, swept away in Sylvain's massive arms, only to reappear at her side. Each time he came close, one of the other guys stood in his way. They didn't fight, like she expected, but blocked.

They were trying to protect her, but they were also protecting Hudson.

What had she done to cause this? How could she go from conversing casually with the man to becoming his prey?

"What do I do?" she asked no one in particular. Was she supposed to stand here, frozen like a deer in headlights?

Hudson crashed into Marcus, spun away, and then crashed into Valen. Sylvain stayed at his back, arms outstretched to catch him should he try to double back or come at Briar from another angle.

"What do I do?" she asked, but no one answered her.

Hudson was tireless. He went at the guys, biting, tearing. Their clothes shredded beneath Hudson's fingers. Blood ran down their faces, and dripped onto the carpet.

They hurt. Sylvain favored one side, and Valen's arm hung at an unnatural angle.

At a loss, she called out, "Hudson, stop!"

And he did. The smile fell from his face, and he tilted his head.

"Hudson, you're hurting them and scaring me."

The smile appeared again, but a second later, disappeared. A glimmer of awareness seemed to pass over his eyes before the beast wrestled control again. He leapt, straight into the air, twisting in an attempt to go over Marcus's head. His fingers grazed Briar's shoulder, nails shredding her sweatshirt.

Reflexively, Briar swept her arm to knock his aside. "I said, stop!"

Her voice finally pierced his consciousness, and just like that, Hudson was back. He blinked, and his fangs retracted. His entire body shuddered as he came back to himself.

"Briar." Horrified, his gaze took in her trembling form. Her knees gave out, but he caught her before she hit the ground. "Briar, I'm so sorry." He helped her settle, then immediately released her, putting distance between them. "I'm so sorry." Stumbling backward, he collided with Marcus. "Marcus."

Her fear drained away as she watched Hudson come apart.

"It's okay," she said. It wasn't, but it would be. She was sure of it. "Come here." She held out her hand, but he stared at it. She wiggled her fingers. "Hudson. Come here."

He shook his head. "I can't, Briar. I—"

"Okay." She allowed her hand to drop and folded her hands together. Deliberately, she let her gaze fall on each one of the guys. "Who's going to tell me what's going on?"

No explanation was coming from Hudson, which was fine. The man—*man?*—was a mess.

"Look," she said. "Y'all..." Her accent was stronger, even to her ears. It was a dead giveaway that she teetered on the edge of losing her cool. "You know I burn to a crisp in the sun. The sun can literally kill me. And recently, I met a creepy crawly in the woods. I'm uniquely suited to understand the unexplainable. So... hit me. What's the deal?"

Marcus stared at her, his light brown skin drawn tight over the bones in his face. He opened his mouth and shut it. No help there.

"Sylvain?"

The long-haired wild man shook his head. "It's hard to explain."

"Try me."

He side-eyed Valen, looking for support, and Briar lunged forward. Cupping her hands on either side of his face, she forced him to focus all his attention on her. "Spill."

He bit his lip, and she was reminded of his sharp teeth. Without hesitating, she used her thumbs to lift his upper lip and examine his teeth. "Where'd your fangs go?"

"They retract," Valen answered for him while Sylvain stared at her.

"Is this genetic?" Briar asked, her mind whirring with possibilities. Earlier, she'd imagined a rich benefactor adopted the guys, but now she wondered if someone adopted them after they'd been abandoned. Their condition frightened off their birth parents who left them in the custody of the state. Perhaps they'd never been adopted, but had been fostered together. "What is this condition called?"

"Vampirism." The explanation came from Hudson. Briar faced him, her hands dropping from Sylvain's face. She crept toward him and perched on her heels.

"You know what I mean," she said. "They call my condition vampirism, too. What's it really called?"

Lifting his head, he held her stare steadily. "It's really called vampirism, Briar. We're vampires."

"Shut up." She clapped her hand over her mouth. "I'm sorry. I mean—"

Barking a laugh, Hudson broke away, staring at the ground and shaking his head. "I tell you we're vampires, and you apologize for saying, 'shut up.'"

"It was rude." And as her mother always said, there was no excuse for rudeness. No one said anything. Briar was struck by the lack of sound, except for her sighs. She sucked in a breath and held it, listening hard.

Nothing.

Hudson's shoulders didn't move. Sylvain's chest didn't expand.

Her breath rushed out of her. "Are you not breathing?" Lurching forward, she laid her head on Hudson's chest. "No. You have a heartbeat. So it stands to reason you'd breathe. Why aren't you breathing? There's no point to having a heartbeat if you don't. The blood brings the oxygen to your cells so they don't die. You need your lungs to—"

Against her ear, a rumble vibrated Hudson's chest. He cupped the back of her head, holding her there for a second. "We breathe. Not as often as you need to. We have heartbeats. Our body works more efficiently than yours." Gently, he set her away from him. "More efficiently than a human's."

"Vampires." There was no doubt in Briar's mind that Hudson told the truth. "But it's not genetic? It's something that happens to you?"

"Something that was done to us." Sylvain's voice was bitter, and his eyes, when she met them, were angry. "Poison."

"You were poisoned?"

"Not exactly." Settling himself next to her, Valen spoke. Each of the guys sat now. Hudson across from her. Sylvain and Valen on either side, and Marcus, perched on her bed near Hudson's shoulder. They stared at her, as though their entire beings lasered on her. Never in her life had she felt like every move she made mattered. What she said, how she responded to them, would dictate how they moved forward.

"We're venomous," Marcus said. "If we bite someone, we fill them with our venom. If we give them our blood, they will change. Hopefully into a vampire, but sometimes not. Sometimes, our venom changes them into the thing you saw the other night. A crawler. A being who will live forever in a rotted, broken form."

"What I saw the other night was a crawler and a vampire?" she asked and shivered. As long as she lived, she'd never forget the feel of the crawler's hands on her body.

"A crawler and a soldier," Sylvain ground out, his lips curled in disgust.

"A soldier is a vampire who was turned, but only given enough blood to make him immortal. They have no will, no soul. No part of the human they were is left."

"You're not soldiers," Briar said, stating the obvious.

"No. But we could have been. We were lucky. At any point in our turning, we could have been crawlers, or soldiers—"

"Or a meal," Sylvain said over Marcus.

Hesitantly, she lifted her eyes to Hudson. "You wanted to eat me?"

Immediately, Hudson's lips drew back over his teeth, and he hissed. It wasn't a threat, but anger, and it seemed to be directed at himself. "I'm so sorry. I should have controlled myself better."

"I call my vampire a predator," Valen said, his sympathetic gaze on Hudson. "Sylvain's is a monster."

"Mine is Predator," Sylvain corrected. "Yours is Beast."

"No. It's Predator."

"You're insane. I've been calling mine Predator since I turned." Sylvain crossed his arms, like it was the end of the argument.

"I'm a thousand years older than yours. If I want to call my vampire Predator, I will."

"Dibs," Briar interrupted, and both guys stared at her. She cleared her throat. "It sounds like Valen called dibs."

Marcus chuckled, and even Hudson grinned. "Our vampires are part of us," Hudson said. "But they aren't all of us. Sometimes, though, they want something, and they are strong. We fight to control them, but there are times when they remind us how much they control us."

Briar nodded. Her condition sometimes felt like another being living inside her. It controlled every aspect of her life, keeping her from the normal things a person did.

"So you didn't want to hurt me," she stated. "Your vampire did."

"My vampire wanted you. Your scent is mouth-watering. Not only to me, but to all of us. But my vampire? He wants to keep you and change you." Hudson's eyes were bleak, and she saw how tormented he was. Yes, his vampire wanted Briar, but the vampire was part of him, and so, logically, *Hudson* wanted to keep her, too.

The knowledge shouldn't have warmed Briar's heart the way it did.

"Why are you smiling?" Hudson asked, and Briar slapped her hand over her mouth. She'd smiled. *Darn*.

"I'm flattered," she finally answered. "You like me enough to want to keep me. It makes me feel good."

"You're not going to feel good if I rip your throat out," Hudson said, and Briar jerked at the image his words conjured.

"You just said you didn't want to hurt me."

"It's going to *hurt*, Briar, if I bite you. And once I taste you, I may not be able to stop myself—"

"Hudson. Enough." Marcus's voice was sharp, cutting him off.

"She should know," Sylvain said. "This is what we are. We're monsters."

"I thought you were predators," Briar joked.

"Why aren't you running?" Valen asked. "I don't understand."

Briar let herself lean against his shoulder. His body was strong and hard. The muscles in his arm had no give, but his hand, when it held hers, was gentle. In the short time she'd known the guys, she'd come to care for them.

Maybe because she'd grown up without friends, she knew how lucky she was to have found them. Before these guys, she'd never experienced the acceptance they gave her.

And so she accepted them. Being a vampire didn't change how she felt, or what she knew about who they were. If anything, it made her love them more.

Love?

CHAPTER 21
HUDSON

Once again, Hudson's logic abandoned him. Everything that should have happened, wasn't happening. Briar hadn't run, she wasn't screaming. She hadn't fainted or started to pray.

Instead, she regarded them steadily, seriously. The only sign of her uncertainty was the way she held Valen's hand. Her knuckles were white, and every so often, she'd squeeze Valen, as if she needed to reassure herself.

Reassure herself of what? That vampires surrounded her?

Hudson took in a deep breath, but she didn't smell of fear. Or even anger.

"Valen?" she asked. "Are you the oldest?"

"No," he answered and leaned his cheek on the top of her head. "Why?"

"You said you were hundreds of years older than Sylvain."

"Oh." Jealously, Hudson watched his brother press his lips onto the top of her silky head. "Hudson is the oldest. Then Marcus. Then me. And finally the baby."

Briar giggled and whatever tension was left in the room disappeared.

"Who turned you all into vampires?" she asked, and then the tension was back and ramped up by a hundred. Her gaze landed on Hudson, question evident.

"It wasn't me," he said. "We all have the same maker."

"Oh." The word came out on a long breath. "That's why you're brothers."

"Yes," he answered. "But we chose to be brothers more than anything. It was our maker who brought us together, but we decided to stay together. That's what made us brothers."

Briar grinned. "I like that. You chose each other. It makes it special." She lifted her head from Valen's arm and stared off into space.

"Briar?" Hudson asked.

She bit her lip, tiny white teeth digging into the pink flesh, and shook her head. "Sorry. Is your maker your father then? Will I meet him?"

"No!" The anger in Sylvain's voice caused Briar to wince.

"Is he dead?" she asked and frowned.

"I wish," Hudson said. "Our maker is the worst kind of vampire. He is too powerful and cares only for himself."

"He was mean to you?" Briar blushed. "I don't mean to oversimplify. I'm trying to understand. If you make someone a vampire, essentially you're choosing for them to stay with you forever, right? Are vampires immortal?"

"We are," Hudson said. "We can be killed, but we don't die of natural causes. We don't age."

"You don't burn in sunlight," she added.

"We'll get to that," Marcus interrupted. "But to answer your question. Yes. If a vampire makes another vampire, usually it is to keep them by their side for eternity. Our maker created us to be his sons and heirs. Keep in mind this was a long time ago. When Hudson and I were made, sons were an extension of power, and our maker was the king."

"We were supposed to lead his soldiers, carry out his will.

Make him the most powerful vampire ever," Valen said, his voice distant. Valen had been created specifically to lead the soldiers. As a marauder, he'd been adept at war.

Hudson, on the other hand, had come to the role with no experience. A fast learner, however, he'd soon made a name for himself as one of the most merciless and cruel generals his father had.

Marcus, when he was created, gave Hudson some competition, but neither of them could hold a candle to Valen's skill.

"Your maker sounds like a jerk."

Hudson laughed. "Evil is a more accurate term."

"Yeah," she answered. "And he's not dead?"

"Unfortunately, no." Hudson leaned his head against the mattress and dragged his hands down his face. Asher was very much alive. If he'd been stronger or smarter, he'd have killed his father when he had the chance thousands of years ago, before he'd amassed an army of vamps, or had age to add to his power.

"If I see him again, I will kill him." Next to Briar, Sylvain's fists clenched. Hudson believed him. Given the chance, any one of them would jump at the opportunity to end Asher.

"He's more powerful because he's old?" The girl was smart. She caught more than Hudson meant her to.

"Yes," Marcus answered after a moment. "But Asher is alone, for all his soldiers and strength, he has no one he trusts."

"We left him a long time ago, and as far as we know, he's created only soldiers and crawlers."

"Thank goodness," Briar said. "Except you guys didn't turn out badly."

"It took us a thousand years to get here," Marcus was quick to point out.

Briar seemed to move without thinking, reaching for Sylvain's hand. "Except for Sylvain," she teased. His brother startled, amazement dawning on his features. "You're something of a genius if you're the youngest. Took you only a few hundred years to do what they did?"

"Hey!" Marcus replied, but he smiled at her joke and winked at Sylvain, who seemed frozen. She took Sylvain's tight fist in both of hers and uncurled his fingers. "Hmm. Is he someone we need to worry about?"

Hudson didn't like the way she said "we." The last thing he wanted was Briar anywhere near Asher. The very thought sent shards of ice along his veins. She was too important, too precious to be at their maker's mercy.

Deep inside him, the general and warrior he used to be clawed his way to the surface. He'd never let Asher touch Briar, and from the looks on his brother's faces, neither would they.

"Asher is someone I always worry about." Sylvain spoke slowly, as if every word was yanked from his throat. "Just when you think he's disappeared, he suddenly shows up."

"With a diabolical scheme," Briar whispered, and when Hudson caught her eye, she winked. "I make bad jokes when I'm nervous."

He sniffed the air. Her scent had changed. She'd attempted to alleviate the tension Asher had caused with jokes. Unused to looking at the world through human eyes, he was surprised it wasn't terror he sensed. Though if any of them explained the things Asher had done, he was sure that would change.

Hudson debated doing this. The rational, scientific part of him thought if they gave all the facts to Briar, laid it out piece by piece, it would be better for all of them. Perhaps if she knew their past, and the evil which had shaped them, she'd leave.

And it would be better for them all if she left sooner rather than later.

"Asher has only made crawlers and soldiers. Is it because he hasn't been able to make vampires?" she asked, and lifted Sylvain's hand to her mouth, thoughtlessly running his knuckles across her lips. Hudson couldn't look away. "I—" Realizing what she'd done, her face flushed, and she lowered Sylvain's hand to her lap. "I'm sorry."

His brother cleared his throat. "Don't be."

"I—I was saying." Briar shut her eyes and let out a breath. "Was the crawler who I met in the woods Asher's? Or another vampire's?"

Hudson crossed his arms and leaned back, smiling. He loved how her brain worked. It was a thing of beauty. Look at her. The connections she made were split second. "I can't wait to see what you do with your brain," he burst out. "You're going to blow your professors away."

She flushed and smiled. "Maybe tomorrow."

"Tomorrow?" He shook his head. "Tomorrow's a little early to be getting back to classes."

"But that's what I'm here to do," she argued. "And..." Uncertain, she broke eye contact and stared at her and Sylvain's joined hands. "And I wasn't asking."

"Hudson is right," Valen said. "You're smart. Very smart, and you were correct in your assumption. The crawler and soldier who accosted you in the woods were Asher's. He's taken an interest in you, and we don't know why."

"Probably because you've taken an interest in me, Valen."

"Obviously," Marcus answered. "But we're all surprised he let you live."

The scent of Briar's fear blossomed like a rose, and as one, Hudson and his brothers growled. He struggled to tamp down his beast who wanted to roll in her scent. It was equal parts arousing and upsetting. He didn't want her to be afraid, and yet, fear would keep her alive. A healthy dose of it would keep her alert. "We're predators, Briar. You can't forget that."

"I know," she whispered. "But you don't frighten me."

"We should," Marcus answered, shocking Hudson. Rarely did his brother stay this serious this long. "We're monsters, as much as Asher is."

"But you won't hurt me."

"Moments ago, I attacked you, Briar. You may think we won't hurt you, but we might." Hudson hated to admit his lack of control, but she needed to understand.

Waving away his concern, she scoffed. "Can we discuss your dangerousness later? And focus on Asher and his creepy crawlers?"

Sylvain chuckled, and Hudson pinned him with a narrow eyed glare. *Not helping.*

Briar went on. "Why, as Valen noted, did he let me live if he could have killed me? I could have fed his troops. Instead, they played with me like a ball of yarn."

Her words were enough to fill the room with growls and snarls. Hudson hadn't seen her after the woods, but Marcus had. Had they injured her?

Briar yawned then hissed in pain as the movement stretched the skin on her neck.

"Enough talking," Hudson cut in. "You need rest. Take a nap, and we'll talk more tonight."

"I have too many questions to sleep," Briar said but crawled onto her bed and pulled the blanket over her body.

"You can ask them later," Hudson replied and allowed himself to sweep her hair away from her face. Her skin was so soft beneath his fingers. It reminded him of how fragile she was and how with one too-rough movement, he could break her.

She gripped his hand when he would have taken it away, squeezing tightly. The birdlike bones in her hands transmitted strength more than fragility, and he smiled. He was wrong; she was tougher than she seemed.

CHAPTER 22
BRIAR

Briar fell asleep in a matter of moments. She'd had every intention of waking up within hours, but her body had other ideas.

The room was pitch black when she awoke, and she sighed in relief. At least in a house full of vampires, they would be uniquely suited to understand, and remember, her issues with sunlight.

Or would they?

Sylvain, Marcus, Hudson, and Valen all walked in the sunlight with none of the protection she needed when she went outside. When she'd asked about it the sun earlier, Marcus had said it was a story for another time.

Briar lay in the cool, dark room and let her mind shift through everything she'd learned. She should probably be freaked out, but she wasn't. It was, quite possibly, the coolest thing in the world.

Vampires!

They were real.

Hudson's area of expertise made perfect sense now. A vampire who knew all about sun allergies? It wasn't ironic; it was serendipitous. Briar suspected both Marcus and Hudson were scientists in order to compensate for vampire shortcomings.

Pushing aside the covers, Briar stretched her toes and reached her hands over her head. Someone had plugged in her phone next to the bed, and she picked it up.

For alleged monsters, they were certainly thoughtful. Smiling, she thumbed in the password. Eight o'clock! In the morning!

Jittery with anticipation, Briar jumped out of bed and ran into the bathroom. Windowless, she didn't have to worry about blocking UV rays as she went through the motions of getting ready.

She'd bathed yesterday, so she carefully washed her face, brushed her teeth, and replaced her bandage.

Today was her first day of school. Most of her classes were in the evenings, as graduate students were eventually expected to sit in undergrad classes to support professors or run labs. But today she had two classes, one with a three-hour lab, and she couldn't be more excited.

While she'd done most of her undergraduate work online, there were some things she couldn't do from the comfort of her bedroom in West Virginia. And one of those things was labs.

She could do the basics, write hypotheses, watch videos online or take data, but her mother drew the line at sending away for fetal pigs to complete anatomy and physiology requirements.

And chemistry? When she'd order the first box of acids and bases, Mom had literally flipped out. "How do they send this through the mail, Briar? Am I going to have the Department of Homeland Security at the door because you sent away for a bomb?"

High drama in the Hale household when it came to chemistry.

So she had a couple of undergrad requirements that had to be made up, and one of those happened today.

She dug through her drawers, touched at the amount of time and trouble someone had gone through to fold each of her shirts and pants. In the top drawer, her gloves had been paired and stacked neatly in a pile.

It was a special day, and she chose her outfit with more attention than she usually did. Generally, she was limited. All she had were variations of a long-sleeved t-shirt. But some of her sun protection shirts were more expensive than others, and she had two she'd spent money on and categorized as "dress up."

And that was what she'd wear today.

Careful of her bandage, she stretched the shirt over her head and smoothed it over her hips. Gloves and hat in hand, she was set. As she was leaving, she remembered her backpack and books.

Giddy, she examined the tall pile of textbooks to find what she needed. Each book went into her backpack along with her laptop and a notebook.

School!

Practically skipping, she left her room and went downstairs, listening for the guys.

"Where are you going?" Valen's voice in her ear had her jumping and spinning.

"Holy cow, Valen!" Her heart thudded against her chest, and her pulse raced. Beneath her bandage, she could actually feel the skin stretching and retracting, and she put her hand there. "I'm going to put a bell on you if you can't give me a warning."

"Like a cat?" he asked.

"I've always wanted a cat," she answered.

Valen smiled, but it dropped away when he eyed her backpack. "Where are you going?"

"School."

"I thought we talked about this," Sylvain said, sitting up from where he must have been resting on the couch.

"That's it!" Briar announced. "Bells for everyone! Jiminy Cricket, you guys."

"You're not going to school," Sylvain said and stood. "You got out of the hospital yesterday." He walked to a curtain and, with a glance of warning, flicked it to the side. "It's full sunlight. Not a cloud in the sky."

Briar sighed. She'd been through this with her family, too, and eventually their fear of the sun enveloped her. It had taken years of studying her condition, and suffering burns, to come to the point where she was now.

"I have a nine-thirty chemistry with a lab. I'll be inside for the brightest part of the day. And I'm covered. I'm going to be careful. But—" She made sure to transmit her seriousness with her gaze. "I'm going."

"Then we'll come," Valen said.

"What are you going to do?" She threw her hands in the air, and let them fall to slap her sides. "Hold an umbrella over my head? Guys. Back off."

Valen's face shuttered, closing off any sign of emotion, and she immediately apologized. "I didn't mean it like that, Valen. I just meant please don't stop me. That was rude. I'm so sorry."

Valen nodded and stared at the floor. "Yeah. So." Without another word, he strode toward the back of the house. Briar heard the door slam, and the pictures on the wall shook. Her earlier excitement drained away, replaced with self-loathing. Hurting Valen was like kicking a puppy.

"Darn it." She slammed her fists onto her thighs. "I didn't mean to do that. Stupid, Briar. Mean and stupid."

"Give yourself a break." Sylvain walked over to her and took her tight fists in his hands. "Valen knows you weren't trying to be mean. He'll figure it out."

Angry tears leaked from her eyes, streaking down her face. She dashed them with the back of her glove. "I wasn't trying to push him away. I just want to go so badly."

She risked a glance up at Sylvain. He regarded her seriously and then sighed. "Valen is... It seems to be his lot in life to be the guy who sticks around when everyone else is pushing away."

It made Briar feel worse. She was just one in a line of people who took Valen's caring and consideration and threw it back in his face. "I have time," she said under her breath.

"Time for what?" Sylvain asked, but she'd already moved away. Backpack on her back, she followed Valen out the back door. It was eight o'clock, and she should be able to make it from Back Bay to BC in an hour. That left her with half an hour to search for Valen and apologize.

"Time to find Valen and apologize before my first class starts." She adjusted her hat on her head and slid her glasses onto her face. "I'm ready."

"You're still not going."

"Absolutely, I am." She strode by him and opened the door, but he stopped her with a hand on the doorframe.

"Briar."

"Sylvain. Do you want to come with me?"

It stopped him in his tracks. "Come with you to find Valen?"

"Yes. And then if you want, you can come to school with me. I'm in undergrad classes today, and they'll be packed. They won't notice one more person. I'm sure of it." She hesitated and studied Sylvain. With his wavy, shoulder-length brown hair, sexy scar through his eyebrow, and broad shoulders, not to mention his height and muscles, he was going to get noticed. "They'll probably notice you," she amended. "But I don't think they'll mind."

A pink flush appeared high on his cheekbones, and he rubbed the back of his neck. She'd made him uncomfortable. He shook his head. "Okay. I'll come. I wasn't doing anything else today."

Snagging his hand, she dragged him toward the door. "Great. Enough talking, let's find Valen."

They stepped into the bright sunlight, and Briar paused, instinctively expecting pain. But her clothing did its job, and all she felt was the heat of the day. From the corner of her eye, she caught Sylvain staring at her. "How was my impression?" she asked.

Drawing his eyebrows together, he studied her. "I don't get it."

"Come on!" she said, and pulled in her hands like claws before hissing. "Nosferatu?"

"Oh." He nodded. "I get it. Ha." But the corner of his mouth quirked upward, and he took her hand.

"Valen!" she yelled, and Sylvain jumped.

"Just diving right in, aren't you?" he asked.

"Chop, chop." She bounced down the steps but didn't let go of his hand. It was really nice to have him with her. Truth be told, she was as nervous as she was excited about going to class, and Sylvain was a bit of a buffer. It made it much less intimidating, and overwhelming, to have someone with her to work out the kinks of her new routine. "Valen!" she yelled again. "Do you know where he'd go?"

"Not far," Sylvain answered. His gaze raked her from head to toe, and she felt her cheeks heat. With the back of his hand, he pressed it against her face. "You're not getting burned?"

It was hard to find her voice when his skin touched hers.

"No." *Nice Minnie Mouse impression.* "No," she said again. "I feel good. Are there any graveyards nearby?"

He narrowed his eyes and tilted his head. "Huh? What are you—graveyards?"

"Crypts? Coffins?"

"You're joking." He glanced away from her and examined the street ahead of them.

Only a little, actually. Marcus had a home, but she had no idea where Valen and Sylvain spent their time. There were still so many things for her to learn about vampires. "I don't know where you guys stay."

"We're staying with Marcus right now. My bedroom is across the hall from yours, and Valen's is near the stairs," Sylvain replied as they strode down the street. At each alley he peered inside and took a deep breath before giving her a light tug to encourage her onward.

For her part, Briar stood on her tiptoes and did an impression of an old fashioned cat clock, eyes darting from side to side. "So no coffins?'

"Are you honestly asking me this question?"

"No," she answered. "Sorry." She took a deep breath and yelled, "Valen!"

The wind ruffled her hair, blowing the locks into her face and into her eyes. When wearing gloves, it was difficult to grasp the silky strands and tuck them behind her ear. The hat didn't help, as it had a string to catch below her chin and her hair tangled in it.

"Are you all right? Why are you yelling?" Valen stood in front of her and reached toward her face, extracting her hair and pushing it back behind her ear.

"There you are," she said, and held his hand when he would have pulled it away. "I'm so sorry. I was rude and mean. You didn't deserve that." She stared up at him and wished she could take off her glasses and hat to see him better, and so he could see her and know she was genuinely sorry. He didn't answer, and her belly ached. "Valen, I'm so sorry."

The thought of having offended him more than he could forgive terrified her, and she threw herself at him, wrapping her arms around his waist.

His hands hung at his side as he stood there like a statue. Briar squeezed harder, and then began to release him. If he didn't forgive her, that was how it went. She'd just have to work harder to earn it.

"Wait," he grumbled, and pulled her forward, arms going around her shoulders, careful of her bandage. "I forgive you."

"I was a jerk," she mumbled into his shirt but held onto him even tighter. Valen's heart beat beneath her ear. One thump, a long pause, then another.

Earlier, Sylvain said Valen tried to hold things to him, especially when they wanted to go. She didn't want to be one of those things Valen was unsure of.

Her friendship and love weren't contingent on anything.

"Sylvain's coming with me to school," she said, and he made a sound of agreement. It vibrated against her ear, tickling her. "Do you want to come, too? Come to my chemistry lab?"

Valen stepped back and stared down at her. "You want both of us to come to school with you?"

"Why not?"

Over her head, Valen watched someone and finally nodded. "Okay. You won't be embarrassed?"

"Why in the world would I be embarrassed? I'll have the two of you with me. I won't be alone. I'll have someone to get lost with, someone to eat lunch with, or next to because we have so many vampire details unclear." Briar took a breath. "We can stop in and see Hudson. Oh no!"

Sylvain and Valen had identical expressions on their faces.

They watched her wide-eyed, and opened-mouthed and every so often, glanced toward each other. "What?" Sylvain asked.

"I didn't say goodbye to Hudson or Marcus. Or say thank you for—" Embarrassed, Briar turned around to speed walk home, but Sylvain caught her shoulder. "Hudson is at work, as is Marcus. They would have come to you when you awoke if they'd been home. I believe Marcus left a note."

Briar let out a breath and allowed Sylvain to spin her back around. "Okay."

The excitement of the morning finally caught up to her, and a wave of nausea made her swallow hard. She had run out of the house without eating, and it'd been a full twenty-four hours since she'd last had a pudding cup. "We have time for coffee and a muffin," Briar said. "Do you mind stopping?"

"Of course not," Sylvain answered, but Valen interrupted him. "Actually..."

Glancing around, Valen spied what he'd been looking for and snagged a paper bag on the ground. "Here."

Inside was a still-warm muffin.

"Oh," she said. So after she'd yelled at him, he'd gone to a bakery to get her breakfast. Tears pricked at Briar's eyes, but she sniffed and blinked them back. "Thank you, Valen." Hopefully, he wouldn't be able to tell she was close to tears. She risked meeting his eyes. "This was very sweet. Especially after how mean I was."

"You weren't mean." He held her shoulders and began to walk with her. "You were frustrated. I get it. Believe me. I hang out with this guy, and he's the king of push and pull."

Sylvain shrugged and ambled next to them, hands stuffed in his pockets. Briar nibbled the muffin. It was delicious and exactly what she needed. Her stomach settled, and she could concentrate on what the day would bring.

When they got to Boston College, Sylvain and Valen navigated like they'd been there a million times. They knew the names of different buildings and where to find them.

It took all the guesswork out of Briar's day, which was nice. Though she'd been careful to explore the campus before classes started, with everything that had happened this week, she was completely discombobulated.

If the guys hadn't been with her, no doubt she'd have gotten lost, and probably would have missed some of her class.

Like she'd expected, Valen and Sylvain got a lot of open-mouthed stares, most of them from girls. Briar didn't blame them. Together, Valen and Sylvain were a sight.

And when they sat on either side of her, dwarfing her, while she listened to a lecture on matter and measurement, she couldn't have been happier. Every so often, she'd sneak a peek at them. To their credit, they listened intently. When once Sylvain caught her staring, he lifted his eyebrows and glanced toward the front of the room as if to say, *pay attention*.

Briar nodded, focusing again on the lecturer.

Her day flew by. Both her first class and her lab were in a room without windows. So she could have her hat and gloves off and function like a regular student.

It was wonderful, and she practically skipped out of the class when it finished. "I'd like to find Hudson, if you don't mind."

With a nod, they led her through the building, winding their way past offices and classrooms. None of it looked familiar to her, probably because she'd been unconscious the last time she was here, but eventually they came to a lab with a nameplate on the door. Professor Hudson Nors.

Lifting her hand to knock, she caught Sylvain side-eying her. "What?"

"You don't need to knock," he explained, and the door opened.

"She doesn't. But Briar has manners, and you do not." Hudson smiled at her, a flash of white teeth. "Hello, Briar."

Suddenly shy, Briar's face heated. "Hello, Hudson."

His hand was cool through her glove. He tugged her toward the inside of his space. She stared at it, taking in all the details she'd missed the last time she was here.

"Ohh," she breathed. "A Storm 860 Molecular Imager." Nodding, she examined each piece of equipment. "Nice."

"Have you seen these before?" Hudson asked, and she shook her head.

"No. Well, yes, in photos. I know what they are and what they do, but I haven't used them before."

He smiled, the skin near his eyes crinkling. "Do you want to?"

"Yes," she answered. "What are you working on?"

"I was using gel electrophoresis to separate DNA of individuals with EPP. Would you like to be one of my subjects?"

It had pretty much been her dream to hear Hudson utter those words, and the surreality of hearing him say it wasn't lost on her. "Yes, please."

Hudson nodded and walked over to a bench, pulling out cotton batting and handing it to Sylvain and Valen before shoving some up his nose. "What are you doing?"

"I'll need to draw your blood, and after last night, I think it's better for all of us if we don't smell it," Hudson said.

"Oh." He was afraid he'd smell her blood and kill her. "The cotton will work?"

"Yes," he answered. "I treated it for this. You're not the only human I have to draw blood from. Even if you're the best smelling one." He winked at her, and Briar laughed. She liked seeing this side of Hudson, the mix of silly and commanding. She got the sense he didn't let this aspect of his personality emerge much.

Which made it all the more special.

"Here." Hudson gestured to a chair and Briar sat, shoving her sleeve over her elbow. Sylvain and Valen exchanged a glance and then sat as well, their eyes glued to the inner curve of Briar's arm.

"Will you be okay?" she asked them. "I don't have to do this." She turned to Hudson. "You don't have to do this if you have other things to do."

Silent, he wrapped rubber tubing around her arm and pulled on gloves. "I'm not. I want to. You can use the equipment, and I'll have another sample of DNA from a person with EPP. Win-win."

"Okay," she answered quietly, still watching Sylvain and Valen, who hadn't answered her question. "Guys?"

"Fine," Sylvain answered, and she giggled. The cotton had changed the resonance of his voice, leaving him to sound as if he had a bad cold. A second later, though, she stopped when Hudson slid the needle into her vein. The room went silent as he drew back the plunger, filling the tube with her blood.

"There," he said, and swept a pad over the insertion point before using cotton and tape to cover the wound. He glanced up at her, and she stared at him.

The calmness in his voice belied his tension. The muscles along his jaw twitched as he ground his teeth together, and his skin was taut. His eyes, usually a bright blue, were dilated, the black pupils huge. "Give me a moment, and I'll be fine." Standing, he released a breath, and then brought the vial over to a small incubator. "I think I may have overestimated my control."

"Again," Sylvain muttered.

"Yes," Hudson agreed. "Again. It seems to be a habit with you, Briar. You make me illogical."

"So we can start?" Briar rolled down her sleeve and approached the incubator. Visions of gel castors and ethidium bromide danced in front of her eyes.

"I—" Hudson stared at the incubator. "I'm sorry, Briar. I need a little while. Perhaps if I expose myself to your blood without you here, I'll have better control."

"Oh," she answered, disappointed. "What about other people's blood?"

Hudson was silent.

"Perhaps it's better if we keep blood and Hudson separate for a while," Valen suggested.

"I think so." Hudson's shoulders slumped, and Briar frowned in sympathy.

"Hey." She took a step forward before stopping. "Is it safe if I approach you?" she asked.

He nodded but didn't turn toward her.

"I'm going to touch you," she warned him, and when he nodded, she grasped his shoulders. "It's fine. We'll get there. I'm sure there are other things in the lab you could show me. Like..." She examined the room. "I see a computer. Do you have protein sequence analysis software?"

He scoffed. "Do I have protein sequence analysis software?" Finally, he faced her and saw her grin. "You're teasing me."

"I am," she said, failing to keep her grin from widening. "I'm trying to distract you."

"Horrible," he said, but smiled, a slow, soft smile that made her heart clench. "Do you want to see my most recent analysis of Chromosome 18?

She nodded excitedly. Chromosome 18 was the site of the mutations that resulted in her condition. "Definitely."

"When's your last class, Briar?" Valen asked.

"In an hour," Briar answered. "It's my art history class."

Hudson swiveled in the chair, pushed it across the lab, and typed his password onto the computer. Immediately, a magnified image of a chromosome appeared on the screen, and like a ghost, Briar floated toward it. "Don't let me forget what time it is, Valen. The science is sucking me in."

Behind her, Valen chuckled. "You got it, little one."

The hour passed by in a blink as Hudson pointed out recessive and dominant patterns of inheritance in various samples. Briar was in heaven. It was everything she wanted to learn, and now she was hearing it from the leading expert in the field.

She bounced on her toes and leaned forward, her hand on Hudson's shoulder as she pointed out a spot of incomplete penetrance on the arm of the chromosome.

Valen stepped to her side, and grinned down at her. "Briar, it's time."

She blinked at him, piecing together what it was time to do. "Right!" she said. "Thank you."

"Will you come back after your class?" Hudson asked.

"Yeah," she answered and mashed her lips together to keep from grinning like a dope. "Yes."

"Great. I'll see you here."

"Okay." She scooped up her backpack from next to the stainless steel counter and put it on her back. Sylvain and Valen waited for her near the door like bouncers.

Briar adjusted her backpack and held out her hands. "Ready?" she asked.

They didn't hesitate to take them. Sylvain opened the door, and they strode out. "Thank you," she called over her shoulder, and then squeezed the guys' hands. "You all are the best."

CHAPTER 23
HUDSON

Hudson waited to approach the incubator until the door closed behind his brothers and Briar. There, the vial of Briar's blood seemed to gleam, beckoning him.

It tempted him, but he fought his instincts to upend the liquid into his mouth, and instead, gloves in place, he began the process of extracting her DNA from the sample.

Each time his mind would focus on the fact that it was Briar's blood in front of him, he pushed the thought away, burying it under the steps he needed to complete. The logical process distracted him, and soon, he was completely absorbed in the familiar task.

He wanted to have Chromosome 18 displayed when she came back so he could show her the site of the mutation that resulted in her condition. But as he worked, digging deeper and deeper, unease gathered in the pit of his stomach.

Something was wrong.

There was the mutation on the long arm of Chromosome 18, but it was different. Not like any other mutation he'd seen with people who had EPP. It was close enough; he understood why a geneticist looking at this had thought EPP.

But it wasn't.

Hudson pushed back his chair and rubbed his hands down his face. How was this possible?

He thought back to everything he knew about Briar.

Valen had seen her eat. Hudson had seen her wounded. She hadn't healed in moments; her body was still recovering from her burns.

Though, she did have much more energy than a person who was healing from a physical trauma generally experienced.

Still. It was within the range of normal for human recovery.

He dropped his hands and shoved his chair forward again, narrowing his eyes at the screen as if what he saw would have changed in the seconds since he'd pushed away.

But it hadn't.

Impossible.

A short, soft knock sounded on his door before it opened, and Marcus walked in. "What are you looking at?" He stood next to Hudson, hands shoved into his pockets as he leaned over. "Is that Valen's?"

"No."

"It looks like Valen's chromosome," Marcus replied. Hudson glanced up at him, and Marcus pulled his eyebrows together. "What? Is it Sylvain?"

"No, Marcus." Hudson rolled away from the computer so Marcus could look more carefully. "It's Briar's."

"It can't be." If Hudson hadn't been watching so closely, he'd have missed the tiny misstep Marcus made as he leaned closer. He gripped the edge of the table tightly and leaned forward. His gaze bounced along the screen, taking in each aspect of the magnified image. "How is this possible? I don't understand."

"It's the same marker we have, just a slightly smaller mutation. It's why she has the diagnosis she does. But she doesn't have erythropoietic protoporphyria, Marcus. She has vampirism." If he hadn't been the one making such a pronouncement, he'd never have believed it. But there it was, clear as day.

If Hudson displayed images of his chromosomes, or any of his brothers', they would be identical. Only someone like Hudson, who knew what he was looking for, would be able to see the subtle difference that meant one of them would burn in sunlight and the others would catch fire.

"But—" Marcus rubbed his hand across his short dark hair and strode away from the computer before coming back. He zoomed in on the chromosome, and finally, shook his head. "How the hell is this possible?"

"The implication is that a vampire isn't only something that can be created, it is also something that can be born." Hudson fell back on the science, as if to remove himself from the emotions churning inside him. He'd lived thousands of years, and he'd never once seen anything to make him believe this was a possibility.

"We don't know if this is an inherited trait or a mutation," Marcus whispered. "We can't know unless we have samples of her family's blood."

"We do." Hudson remembered one of the first emails Briar had sent him, years ago. It compared her DNA to her family's and had as a question on the subject line. "Why me?" He thought the email would contain a whining narrative, but instead, she'd gone into detail about recessive genes and mutations. "I drew her blood today to give her a chance to go through the process, use the equipment. But I wanted to surprise her with this image. She'd never had the chance before, though she did have this." He searched his saved documents and brought up her email, then expanded the image she'd sent. Opening four separate windows, he gestured for Marcus to sit closer, then enhanced the images.

Together, they examined her brother's chromosomes. "There's nothing there," Marcus stated, finger tracing the image. "What about her father's?"

Hudson brought up the image, magnifying it closer and closer. "There."

"And her mother's?"

He did the same to hers. "There."

"Two recessives passed on to the daughter, not the son." Marcus shook his head.

"I know how gene inheritance works, Marcus," Hudson snapped and then closed his mouth, teeth clicking together. He sighed. "I'm sorry."

"Is this why she appeals to us all?" Hudson wondered aloud.

"You mean we're sensing genetic compatibility?" Marcus asked.

"Yes," Hudson answered. "Her scent. It's nature's way of drawing us in, attaching us to her, and then—"

"We're not animals, Hudson," Marcus said. "Maybe it is what drew us to her, yes. But it's not the only thing."

Some of Hudson's worry drained away. His beast was a creature of instinct, one he was constantly fighting. He didn't want it to decide on Briar because she was genetically compatible with him.

Hudson wanted a choice, and *he* chose Briar. Not the vampire.

"Somewhere out there, Hud, or somewhere in time, the first vampires were born. And they had children and those children had children, all down through the ages." Marcus spoke quickly, excited. "It's incredible. Think about it; think about the evolution of our species. There's nothing else like it!"

"That we know of," Hudson answered. "I haven't even heard a whisper of vampire children born. Not for all of my existence. Have you?"

"No. Do you think it's possible for us to have children?" Rolling back in the chair, Marcus widened his eyes. "Jesus, Hudson, what if Briar—?"

"That's getting ahead of ourselves, don't you think?" Hudson stared down his nose at Marcus. "She has no idea we feel anything for her."

"She knows," Marcus said. "You've always been oblivious to things like this. But we didn't move her into our house and walk with her to class, and *analyze her DNA*, because we want to be her buddies."

"Do we tell her?" Hudson asked, glancing at the clock on the computer screen. "She'll be back soon."

"Yes." There was no delay in his response. "Absolutely. She knows about us." Marcus rubbed the muscle along the side of his neck.

Something about the movement jarred Hudson, and he stared at Marcus, trying to figure out what it was that hovered at the edge of his mind. "The medicine."

"What?" Marcus stared at him in confusion. "What are you talking about?"

"Marcus. If she doesn't have EPP, but what she has is a genetic marker for vampirism, the medicine that works on us might work on her."

A slow smile spread from one side of Marcus's face to the other, reminding Hudson of the Cheshire cat. "By God, old man, I think you may be right."

The door to the lab opened, and Sylvain held it, gesturing for Briar to pass through. She smiled when she saw them, but her eyes focused over Hudson's shoulder. "Is that me?" she asked and hurried to the computer. "That's me, isn't it?" she repeated but then paused. Moving closer, she leaned over and squinted at the image. "No. That can't be. That's the mutation, but not—" She straightened. "What's going on?"

CHAPTER 24
MARCUS

"It's complicated," Marcus answered and earned a glare from Briar. "But it is you. It's the reason you react to ultraviolet light, and—" He stopped himself before he could say *and the reason why we're drawn to you*. Because that wasn't true. They may have initially been drawn to her because of how this ephemeral vampire element appealed to them, but it was *her* who made them want to stay.

Look at them. Sylvain and Valen were poised on a knife's edge, ready to fight if it would take the worry out of Briar's voice. It wasn't the scent of wildflowers that made them act like that. For goodness sake, if it did, they'd be hovering around the outside of a soap shop in a mall.

"It's not EPP," Briar said, distracting him. "I've never seen the mutation that close before. I never would have noticed it otherwise." Along her cheekbones, her skin flushed, and she stared at the ground, as if embarrassed. Marcus reached for her hand and removed her glove. When she glanced at him, he winked and shoved it into his pocket. "Don't be embarrassed. You didn't have the equipment to do this sort of investigation."

"I want to show you something," Hudson said, interrupting. Similar to his lectures, he barreled over everything and anyone to make his point.

They crowded around the computer, even Sylvain and Valen, who wouldn't necessarily understand what they were looking at, but who were definitely picking up Hudson's unease.

He switched between images, showing her each of his brother's chromosomes, and the exact spot that mirrored the mutation in her own chromosome.

"This is Sylvain." Hudson pointed to each image. "Marcus. Valen. And me."

"It's similar," Briar said, eyes wide.

"I took Briar out to breakfast, and she ate yogurt. This morning, I got her a muffin. She ate it. She's not a vampire if that's what you're suggesting," Valen interjected. He crossed his arms, a mountain of a man ready for battle.

But what was he supposed to fight? Biology?

With a flash of insight, Marcus realized that Valen had made a study of Briar. If she was upset, or somehow disgusted with what Hudson and he were explaining, Valen was ready to step in.

"If we have a similar genetic mutation, does that mean I'm part vampire?" Briar laughed then shook her head. "No. I'm kidding. What is this?" She'd hit the nail on the head, and when no one said a word in disagreement, she choked. "What? I'm right? Is this true for everyone with EPP?"

"Not everyone with EPP has this mutation, Briar. We're the only ones with something similar." Hudson smiled at her, and Marcus grinned in response. It was good to see his brother smiling again.

"But you don't burn," Briar argued. "I've seen you in the sun, and you don't burn."

"We would," Sylvain said and knelt next to Briar when she

sat back in the chair Marcus had vacated earlier. He spun her toward him and then dragged the rolling chair forward. "Hudson has made something, a medicine, and it keeps us from turning to ash in the sun."

Eyes wide, she reached for Hudson's arm and shook it. "Afamelanotide?" she asked.

He shook his head. "No." Then he began to describe a series of amino acids and chemicals that had Briar nodding her head in excitement.

Even Marcus, with his Ph.D., didn't feel the level of fascination with Hudson's study.

"I always thought it was magic," Valen said quietly, and Briar turned her attention to him. "I thought it was a combination of curses from my gods and magic. I've lived a thousand years. I'm not convinced it isn't."

"If turtles can live four hundred years," Briar said. "Why not a man? Or species? Just because we don't understand why a thing is the way it is, doesn't mean it isn't supposed to be that way. I think it's a little magic." She reached past Sylvain for Valen and squeezed his hand.

Again, Marcus's humor failed him. He could only watch in awe as Briar found a way to astonish, and ease, all of them. Even Sylvain, in the past week, had gentled. Marcus no longer feared his brother running away should any of them make a misstep.

Her draw bewildered him. How was it possible after all this time they would all find a person to appeal to them so completely?

Unable to stop himself, he edged past Sylvain and Valen, and kneeling, pressed his lips lightly to Briar's.

Shock reverberated through her body, but she touched him gently on the back of the neck and returned his kiss. Marcus had a second to fear her scent would overwhelm him, but she made a small sound of pleasure. Her tongue shyly touched his, and all worry left him.

His vampire was as enamored of her as he was. In fact, the vampire inside him *purred* in satisfaction. Marcus touched her arms, curling his fingers around her slight-boned body, and it warned him, *careful.*

Reluctantly, he drew away and opened his eyes. Briar stared up at him, her blue eyes glazed. Her rosy lips were swollen, and he didn't even try to stop himself from tasting them again.

"Your scent is just the hook. It's getting to know you that really makes you dangerous," he whispered. "*You're* the ultimate predator."

"Marcus," she whispered, and then her face flamed. As a human, she couldn't sense his brothers had moved away to give them the facade of privacy. Darting a glance at them, she met Marcus's eyes, confused. "I—"

"It's okay," he reassured her and peered over at his brothers. Valen met him with a rueful grin, one that said he wished he'd been quick enough to kiss her, while Hudson narrowed his eyes at him.

But Hudson wasn't angry. Marcus knew him well enough to know he was upset with his timing. He probably wanted to talk science with Briar for another inordinate amount of time.

Time that was much better spent kissing.

Sylvain on the other hand. Sylvain stared at them, but it was like he wasn't seeing them. Suddenly, his face cleared, and he growled, low and long. The sound filled the lab, bouncing off the concrete walls.

Near him, Briar's heart pounded. Marcus could feel the heat coming off her body from the blood pumping fast through her veins.

Now the scent of wildflowers and fear, a mouth-watering

mix filled the air. His fangs descended, lengthening, and his mouth filled with saliva, but he fought down the vampire.

And the vampire let him. He didn't want to frighten Briar.

"Sylvain." Marcus stood, and his vampire flashed his fangs at his brother in warning. "You're scaring her."

Sylvain shook his head. "That's why Asher's reappeared, Marcus. She draws us to her. Like you said, the scent is her hook. It draws him to her as well."

His vampire hissed and snarled at the threat. He'd tear Asher from limb to limb before he came close to Briar.

"He's our maker," Hudson said, voice tight. "Of course she'd appeal to him."

"It's basic biology," Briar said quietly. "The female of one species is designed to appeal to the male. And vice versa." Her eyes widened, and then she wrinkled her nose. "Pheromones."

Marcus chuckled, and even Hudson smiled. Valen took a step back to her, and dipped his head into the curve of her neck, breathing in. "What are pheromones? You smell like winter."

"That's good, right?" Briar asked squeaky-voiced and flushed.

"Very," Valen answered, and kissed her skin, lingering against her before he drew back. "Very good."

"So maybe if I mask my smell, I won't be interesting to him," Briar said after a second. Along her forehead, Marcus could make out a sheen of sweat. All of their attention was overwhelming her.

Until now, she'd been sheltered and protected. Marcus suspected she had no experience with men, and certainly not with men—vampires—like them.

"I don't think that will work," Sylvain replied. "You drew him in, and before that, we were drawn to you. The combination will be too much for him to resist. The only way he'll leave us alone is for us to kill him." The words were matter-of-fact, but the situation wasn't clear cut.

Asher was the most powerful vampire in existence, and even with all their knowledge and experience, he could easily destroy them all.

But they had Briar now, and if Marcus was a betting man, he'd bet on them.

CHAPTER 25
BRIAR

Briar couldn't think of anything except having her first kiss.

Her first kisses.

Marcus, and then Valen. She'd kissed one man, *vampire,* and then seconds later, Valen had leaned into her, and his cool lips had pressed against her skin.

Briar touched her lips and then her neck. The ghost of sensation remained, and she shivered. Glancing up, she caught Marcus watching her with a knowing smile, and she slapped her hands to her cheeks to hide her flush. The temperature seemed to rise, and her clothes stuck to her back. She pulled her sleeve over her hand and touched her forehead to catch the perspiration beading there.

Hopefully, they wouldn't notice.

What was she thinking? They smelled everything. *Smell like winter?* She hoped so, because she really didn't want them smelling her sweat.

"—kill him."

The words cut through her haze. Sylvain narrowed his eyes at Marcus, and one-by-one focused on each of his brothers. Nausea threatened, and Briar swallowed hard. "I thought you said the older the vampire, the more powerful they were," she said.

Sylvain paused and frowned, but Valen interrupted anything he would have said. "Asher has a plan, and we need to know what it is. I suspect he is more interested in us than you. He thinks of us as his sons, and he wants us back."

"You think I distracted him for a moment," Briar said. It made sense. From what they'd told her, Asher had spent millennia creating the perfect family, only to have it splinter. It had finally re-formed, but without him. "He's jealous. You came together again, and he wants in."

"Jealousy will make him act without a plan," Valen said. "He relied on Hudson for strategy. We all tempered his responses."

"He was stronger with you," Briar said, understanding from the little they'd told her about their maker that he'd truly recognized the brothers' strength. And used them. "If it wasn't for you, he probably wouldn't have lived as long. What did you do for him? Protection? What was his purpose?"

Sylvain looked taken aback. "His purpose?"

"Yes," Briar said. "What does he want?"

"Power," Sylvain answered.

"I thought he had power? Age makes him powerful. So if he's old, it stands to reason he's powerful. Why want you so badly? I'm not trying to be difficult," she said. "I'm trying to understand. This is a modern world. What does he want that he can't get?"

Hudson smiled at her, and she blushed. He stared at her like she was something special. "You hit the nail on the head, didn't you? What can we give him that he doesn't already have?"

"His pride," Sylvain answered. He shook his head from side to side, realization dawning on his features. "It's always been about pride for him. He had no reason to create me, except I didn't want to be a vampire. He hated that. The way he thinks, if he was to bestow eternal life, I should be eternally grateful. And none of us have been grateful."

"He wants you because he can't have you?" Briar asked. "That's it?"

"There are other vampire families in the world," Hudson explained. "Not as powerful, and nearly as old. It is rare for a vampire family to break apart. Like you, it's something I've never heard of before."

"And another reason he'd want Briar. A human with vampire tendencies," Marcus said.

"You mean all the foibles and none of the cool stuff," Briar said. "Which you still haven't described."

"Quick healing, strength and speed, immortality." Marcus listed them off on his fingers, point-by-point. "Moving on."

Briar giggled, but held out her hands. For some reason, he didn't want to have this conversation about vampires, but it needed to happen. "Nope. Back up the truck," she said and wiggled her fingers. "One—do you sleep? Two—where do you sleep? Three—Do you read minds? Four —Do you—"

"Do not say glitter," Sylvain stabbed a finger toward her. "Do. Not. Say. It."

"Sylvain, did you just make a joke?" she asked.

He narrowed his eyes then lifted the corner of his mouth. "Perhaps."

"I think you did. I think you made a joke," she said. "And I wasn't going to say glitter, but I was going to say, do you turn into bats?"

"The bat shifting comes from speed," Hudson said. "We are so fast we often blur. It gives the impression of a cloud, or fog, of bats or bugs. But no. We do not turn into bats. As for the rest—yes, we sleep, in a bed, though not as often as a human. We do not read minds, and we don't glitter. Though some may say I have a glittering personality."

Briar threw her head back, barking a laugh. "Two for two! First the unlikely Sylvain, and now Hudson for the win! Come on, who's next to dazzle me?"

She edged toward the table to rest her back against it, but on her way by, Sylvain snagged her hand. With a firm tug, he pulled her into his lap and wrapped his arms around her, nuzzling her shoulder.

She didn't know what exactly had changed. The tension from earlier was gone, and now, all of them were comfortable hugging, or kissing, her.

It filled a hole in her she didn't know she'd had. Closing her eyes, she let her head drop back onto Sylvain's chest. His heart beat slowly, and subconsciously, she began to count the beats. It was much slower than hers, or a super athlete for that matter. It was hypnotic.

"Can you hypnotize people with your gaze?" she asked, eyes still closed.

"No." Sylvain's voice vibrated against her ear, and she shivered.

"Mind control?"

"I think that goes along with reading minds or hypnotizing," he said. "So, no."

"Okay. Why do you think I'm so drawn to all of you?" she asked. *Oh, pooh.* The thought had slipped out of her mouth before her brain even had time to process it. She opened her eyes, gazing at each guy before staring at the floor. "I mean—"

"When you say 'drawn to all of you,' " Hudson said, "what does that mean?" One perfect, dark eyebrow lifted, and though he didn't smile, his lips twitched.

Breath huffed out of her, and she relaxed until he spoke again. "Why do you think you're drawn to us?" he asked, turning the question around, just as he had done earlier when he'd shown her his lab.

"You're all very kind, and you go out of your way for me," she answered honestly. Why lie? While it may save her pride, she had the sense that if she took the risk, it would be worth it. "I think—" Briar tapped her finger on her lips as if contemplating the question, but once she'd given herself permission to be honest, the reasons came easily. "Hudson drew me in with his brain, and his passion. And Sylvain with his gruff nature. The first time you said, 'get out of my way.' " Briar lowered her voice to do a Sylvain impression, but tempered with a grin she threw over her shoulder. "Marcus was sweet, and funny, and he didn't get mad when I slapped his face with my glove. I believe you still owe me a duel, sir."

"I think I might," he replied, bowing low. The move was so graceful and natural. It struck her, suddenly; these guys were old. Ancient. Her brain understood that fact, but until Marcus bowed, like he'd been bowing to royalty for centuries, she hadn't really gotten it.

Swallowing hard, she glanced at Valen before she cleared her throat. "Valen, your heart. First, you cared that Sylvain upset me. Then you took me to breakfast and gave me my first taste of friendship." Her lip wobbled, though she didn't mean it to. She hadn't expected to get emotional. "So, that's it." The smile she gave was a little less genuine because she was trying not to cry, but she wasn't sad. "Everything about you drew me in. All of you."

Sylvain tightened his hold on her but remained silent. "We've kept you out of the house longer than we meant to," he whispered, changing the subject. Was the topic too hard for him to discuss?

"Sylvain's right," Marcus said. "This is your first day of school, and I'm sure you have homework."

She thought about the syllabi in her bag. Before her next

classes, she had hundreds of pages to read and questions to answer. In her art history class, she even had a paper to write. "I do," she answered. "But you don't have to come home with me. I can make it on my own."

"What about our conversation, and what we've revealed, makes you think that is a safe choice?" Sylvain asked.

When she tried to turn to see his face, he squeezed her, as if he didn't want her to move. *Fine.* "I'm not used to thinking about vampires," she said, "if you're referring to Asher. Which reminds me, do you have the medicine you mentioned earlier? I'd really like to see it with some of your equipment."

Hudson stood. He walked over to a small stainless steel refrigerator and reached inside to withdraw a vial.

Briar tapped Sylvain's arm, a sign for him to let her up, and he did. As she moved closer, she could sense the others watching her. "So this is it."

"Yes. It's what allows us to walk in the sun."

The implications of what Hudson said weren't lost on her. Her mind immediately connected the dots. Her DNA was similar to theirs—Chromosome 18, the marker which identified her as having vampire characteristics. It would stand to reason then that the medicine that kept them from burning could work for her.

"Can we try it?" she asked, reaching out for the vial. Hudson let her take it, and she held it up to the light.

"No," Hudson answered.

Hurt, she met his steady gaze. "Why not?"

"Because you are not immortal. I was able to test it on myself, and Marcus, for years in order to perfect it. I'm not willing to give it to you, then let you walk in sunlight only to receive third degree burns." He pointed to the bandage on her neck. "I'm not willing to risk that."

"I'm not going to take it and stand in the sun at noon. We can do skin tests. There are plenty of ways to try this." If

Hudson expected her to accept his reason, he had another thing coming. "I accept not trying it right this very minute. But you've studied the trials pharmaceutical companies did with afamelanotide. We can do something like that. I volunteer."

"No," Sylvain interrupted. "You're not testing it on her."

"I have to agree," Marcus added. "Afamelanotide hasn't worked with you, right? That's why you're not getting it now."

"Right, and now we know why." The vial in her hand caught the light from overhead, refracting through the glass and casting a beam of white light on the table. "But this is different."

"*You're* different," Hudson said bluntly. "Not to be unkind, Briar, but you're not wholly vampire and not wholly human. I'm not saying never to this, just not right now."

Fair enough. She understood what he was saying, but she didn't like it. It seemed like her cure was right in front of her. She'd never been so close.

And she couldn't have it.

Hudson was right, it probably wouldn't work on her since her mutation differed from theirs. Things were never easy.

"Okay," she whispered.

"You can work on it with me." Hudson took the vial carefully from her fingers. "I'll talk to your advisor. It can be your graduate research if you want."

"I feel like I have an unfair advantage," she said and slapped her hand over her mouth. *Talk about making assumptions.*

Hudson considered her and shook his head. "I'll admit, knowing you makes me want to have you close by. But I wouldn't offer if I didn't think you deserved it. Your emails, the papers you sent me, all of it speaks to an intelligence and drive I respect. But if you don't want to work here, I understand."

"I want to," she answered. "I do. But you promise you'd have asked me anyway?"

"I wouldn't have asked you anyway, but I'd have considered you. I probably would have asked you next year. But knowing you now, I want you." Hudson held her gaze, and his words repeated over and over in her mind. *I want you.*

"Yes, please," she said. "I want to work with you, too."

"And you can work with me sometimes," Marcus said. "I have a lab. My area of expertise might not be as sexy as Hudson's, but I like your brain, too." He blew on his nails and rubbed them on his chest. "It's at Harvard."

"Oh ho!" Hudson crowed. "Here it comes!"

Briar giggled. "Here what comes?"

"What?" Marcus asked. "My lab is at Harvard. It's a place. She'd get lost if I didn't tell her where it was."

Sylvain and Valen chuckled. "Don't these guys exhaust you?" Valen asked. "All this ego in one place? I know I'm exhausted."

The good-natured ribbing went on, and Briar leaned against Valen's arm. He extended it, tucking her beneath it, and continued to tease his brothers. Her yawn caught her by surprise, but all at once, the guys stopped. "Come on," Valen said. "Time to go home."

"Okay." Too tired to argue, she let them bundle her up. She accepted her hat from Valen and tucked her hair beneath it before pulling on her gloves. "I'm ready."

"I need to do a little more work," Hudson apologized. "I'll be home later." He took the chair vacated by Sylvain, and rolled to his computer.

As she passed by, Briar leaned over and kissed the top of his head before she could overthink it. "Don't be too late."

He snagged her hand and pressed it to his lips. "I won't."

She imagined she could feel his cool lips and wished she hadn't already put on her gloves. With one more wave, she followed the guys out of the lab. The closer they got to the exit, the quieter they became. Sylvain was tense, and Valen seemed to be scanning the crowds of people. Even Marcus was off, glaring at people who crossed in front of them or accidentally knocked into Briar.

At the exit, Sylvain hesitated and faced her. He studied her from head to foot, and she took the sunglasses from her backpack and put them on. "Ready."

Silently, he pushed open the door, walked through, and then held it for her. She went next, then Valen and Marcus. The three of them surrounded her, and she scoffed. "Guys."

They didn't answer but kept walking. With Sylvain in front of her and Marcus and Valen on either side, she couldn't see where she was going. Sylvain could lead her off a cliff, and she wouldn't know she was there until the ground disappeared. "Sylvain. I can't see over you."

"You don't need to see over me. We're walking to Marcus's car, and then we're driving home."

"But I want to see," she argued. This was her school. She wanted to look around, see the sights. People watch.

"Unnecessary," he answered.

She opened her eyes wide and glanced at Marcus, hoping he would see how silly Sylvain was, but he shook his head. Annoyed, she mashed her lips together and stopped completely. The guys took two steps without her, but she got what she wanted. Now she could see.

It was a bright, warm evening, and students were milling about everywhere. Some of them were perched on the steps of buildings, while others had found shady nooks under trees. It looked exactly the way she imagined college would look. In fact, it was a pretty accurate reproduction of the booklet cover she received when she'd sent away for information from BC when she was a senior.

"What are you doing?" Marcus asked, striding back toward her.

"I want to see," she said. "I told you. I can't see over your massive shoulders and Sylvain's big head."

The big head in question glared at her but didn't attempt to bundle her up or throw her over his shoulder.

"You're right," Valen said. "We're sorry. *I'm* sorry. We're not used to this, and our instincts can make us overprotective."

"Doesn't mean our instincts are wrong," Sylvain countered. "Why are we standing in the sun? Are we trying to tempt fate? Marcus's car is two minutes away." He clenched his fists, like it was all he could do not to grab her, and she decided to have pity on him.

"Let's go, Sylvain." She linked her arm with his. "I'll stay close, but I want to look around. This is my first day of school."

His muscle relaxed under her hand, and he sighed. "I'm sorry. You're right."

The rest of the walk was much less tense, though she was out of breath by the time they reached the car. They were walking fast for sure, because she wasn't so out of shape she couldn't walk two minutes without panting.

Briar climbed into the backseat when Marcus unlocked the car, and they drove home. Her appetite had returned full force, a sure sign she was healing, and she went straight to the kitchen.

Even there, blackout curtains were in place. She stared at them, feeling guilty. Had Marcus done all this for her? Had she relegated the guys to the shadows now that she'd moved in their home? The thought made her stomach clench, chasing away her appetite.

"Fridge is stocked," Marcus said, passing by her to open

the door to the giant side-by-side, stainless steel refrigerator. He glanced at her and paused. "What's the problem?"

Slowly, she took off her hat and gloves and placed them on the marble island. "I feel bad you did all this for me."

"Did all what?" he asked, looking around. "The food? Don't. I have groceries delivered every week. They just won't go to waste now."

"The curtains," she said. "You have medicine so you can walk in the sun, and now you have the curtains drawn all over your house."

Marcus shrugged one shoulder. "I don't care about that. They're blackout curtains, yes, but I still would have the curtains drawn. This is Boston, sweetheart. You don't want people peeking in your windows. Because they will if you're not careful."

"Really?" Some of the tightness in her belly relaxed.

"Really," he answered. "It's not a big deal."

It was a big deal. Not even her mother had gracefully done the things these guys had done for her.

And her mother was supposed to love Briar unconditionally. It bothered her mom to no end to live in a cloudy city in a dark house.

"What do you want to eat?" Marcus asked.

Refocusing, Briar peered over his arm into the fridge and pointed to the apples and then the cheese. "Please."

Marcus took out the fruit, adding some items to the pile before shutting the door. He stacked it on the counter, and then nodded at the chair. "Sit. I've got this."

"I can do it."

But he shook his head. "I can cut up cheese and fruit."

His hands blurred and in a matter of seconds, he'd made her a plate of snacks. "Here."

"Were you showing off?" she asked, and he shrugged.

"Maybe."

"Definitely," Valen answered as she took her plate.

"Do you mind if I eat and work?" she asked, and Marcus shook his head.

"Go on." He gestured with his chin toward the door. "I'll bother you in a little while."

Standing, she shook her head. "You won't bother me." With her plate in hand, she left the kitchen and went into her room. Someone had brought her bag up, and she sighed, equal parts grateful and overwhelmed.

Briar placed her plate on the desk and grabbed an apple slice. She needed to find some way to give back to the guys. Sylvain and Valen had dedicated their entire day to her. Hudson had set her up in his lab, and Marcus had pretty much redecorated and bought food he didn't need.

There needed to be more give and take because right now, all she did was take.

Briar settled at her desk, syllabi on one side of the surface, books on the other, and got to work. Soon, she was deep into a chapter and blissfully unaware of anything except Roman *bas-relief*. She studied the photos in her art history book closely, amazed that someone with a chisel could add as many details into stone as the artists a thousand years ago could.

She yawned, jaw cracking and laid her head on her hand as she turned the page. Her belly was full, and the room was warm. It got harder to keep her eyes open, and rather than fight it, she took her book to the bed and lay down.

Chapter two. She'd made it pretty far into the assigned reading and could take a little nap. Curling on the side opposite her bandage, she snuggled into the pillow and shut her eyes. In a matter of moments, she'd fallen asleep.

"You're the girl who has my sons tied into knots."

Briar blinked. She stood in a bright green field, the sun shining down on her. *A dream.*

"Briar." Someone snapped their fingers. "Focus."

A haze appeared in front of her, like the waves of a mirage. Slowly, it formed into a man shape. She could see through it at first, and then it became opaque.

"I thought they said you couldn't read minds."

The man laughed. *Asher.*

"You're their maker," she whispered. "This is a dream."

"Not a dream, Briar," he said. His features changed, morphing from human to vampire. He didn't hide it the way the guys did. But even as he'd first appeared, she'd never have mistaken him for human.

He was too golden, too ethereal.

Too beautiful.

Tall and long limbed, with dark hair that swept the middle of his back, he was otherworldly.

Like an elf king.

He could have stepped out of any fairy tale.

But his eyes were cold, and his teeth, sharp. He walked toward her smoothly, and his feet didn't touch the ground. "Not a dream." He breathed in deeply. His eyes closed as he leaned closer to her. When he opened them, she froze. She was caught in the gaze of a snake, and all she could think was *guys, you were wrong.*

Asher laughed. "I did not share all my tricks with my sons. And I won't share them all with you. But I will give you a choice."

Wake up.

"Listen, girl." He sighed. "This is a place of in between. It is not dreaming. It is not awake. It just *is*. *And I decide what is real.* Shall I show you?" The scenery changed. The grass crackled and wilted. Green to brown, and then to ash, it disintegrated. Everything around them swept away until it was only the two of them on a barren, rocky plain.

He held out his hands, palms up. "You're going to be a message to my sons."

She shook her head, but he reached for her. She'd expected pain. Instead, his hands were gentle as they settled on either side of her face and moved her head up and down.

"Yes. I want them," he said slowly, as if he was speaking to someone of questionable intelligence. "I want them to return to me. They are mine." He stepped back and brushed one hand over the other.

"Why tell me? They've only just met me. What do you expect me to do?"

Asher leaned closer. "They think they have a choice. Let this be a lesson. I take what I want." He whirled away from her, and if he'd had a cape, she could have seen it billowing around him. "I am patient, and I am forgiving, but I am their maker. I am their *master*."

Briar shook her head without thinking. Their master? In no plane of existence could she imagine Sylvain and Valen, Marcus or Hudson being mastered.

"You underestimate me as well," he said.

If only they'd been right about him not being able to read minds.

"Fine. Let this not be a message to tell, but to *show*. I'll send you back to them in pieces." He moved then, faster than any of the guys had ever moved. One second he stood in front of her, the next, he wrapped his cold hands around her shoulders and dragged her into his arms.

Like Valen and Sylvain had earlier, he dipped his face into the curve of her shoulder. She froze for a moment, and then fought him. She wasn't stupid, she knew what vampires did. But still, the first slide of his teeth against her skin, *through* her skin, stunned her.

Fire spread from the bite through her veins.

Was she always going to burn?

It hurt as badly as anything had ever hurt before. The hands on her shoulders tightened, and then pierced her like claws. Against her throat, Asher moaned. She felt his tongue slick from her shoulder to her ear, and then he bit again.

Unable to move, to cry out, to do anything to help herself, Briar stood paralyzed in his hold.

"It's the venom," he whispered, withdrawing his fangs. He kept his lips against her, the words he formed moving them against her skin like a perverted kiss. "It holds you still, keeps you from running or screaming. I wish you could scream. Next time..."

No next time.

"Yes," he answered. "Over and over. I promise to visit you here. You'll close your eyes and see me. And feed me. God." Asher groaned and embraced her, drawing her closer to his body. He held her so tight, and all she wanted to do was escape. Each brush of his lips was sandpaper, scraping the skin from her bones. "God. You taste so good. You make me rethink everything." He drew back, his eyes wild and bright. "What do you think, vampire girl? Shall we see what it is Hudson's discovery means? Could you and I be the creators of a new breed of vampire?"

He may have been able to control her movement, but nothing could control the nausea that made her retch and heave. Immediately, he dropped her, and she fell to the ground, knees slamming into the rocky earth. Over and over, she gagged, body and mind in complete agreement, rejecting what Asher proposed.

With his absence came control of her body. She dug her fingers into the ground, holding herself from hitting the ground face first.

"I should be offended, but I'm not," he said. "I'll let you think about it. Perhaps I spoke too soon." He knelt next to her and touched her. She felt his fingers graze her neck, and then he held her chin in his hand, forcing her head up. As she watched, he placed his fingers, covered in her blood, in his mouth and closed his eyes. When he opened them, they were black. "So much to consider now." He stood, lurching to his feet. "Forget my message. Forget my sons. Everything has changed now." His long fingers dug into her hair, sliding back through the strands. "A kingdom of vampires. A queen and king. Your blood is life, and I need more."

Briar fell back, dug her heels into the ground, and shoved away, but he was too fast and too strong. He was on her, lifting her to her feet and embracing her. Again his teeth slid into her neck, and he drew hard against her veins.

Unable to fight, hands limp at her sides, all Briar could do was scream in her mind. *Sylvain! Valen! Hudson! Marcus!*

Their names were her prayer and plea, but no one came. Her eyes closed, and in her ears, her heartbeat thudded. Once. Twice. Pause.

They're going to know. I'm going to remember.

"Oh, little vampire girl, no, they won't. Go to sleep, and forget all this." His voice seemed far away. "Goodnight, sweet Briar."

CHAPTER 26
SYLVAIN

Sylvain couldn't explain his anxiety, but it nipped at his heels. He took the stairs, two at a time, pausing for a second outside Briar's door. Through it, he could make out the smooth inhalation and exhalation of her breath.

Carefully, he opened the door, then found her curled on her side, book tucked under one arm. She didn't rouse at his entrance, so he risked getting closer.

Her breathing hitched, and beneath her eyelids, her eyes tracked from side to side, signifying she was deeply asleep. She was fine, taking a much-needed nap.

But something was off; Sylvain could sense it.

Unwillingly, he thought of Annie and the last days of her life. He'd known something was wrong with their wife, he'd felt the same sort of foreboding, but he'd overlooked the signs. He'd ignored the pit in his stomach, and the way she seemed to look through all of them.

It was a mistake he wouldn't make again. If something felt off, he would investigate it, figure out the source of his unease, and fix it.

In the back of his mind, Sylvain counted Briar's breaths. Her rhythmic heartbeat was the soundtrack to his thoughts.

What was she dreaming about? Her breath came faster, tiny pants, while her eyelids twitched. Hopefully, she was having a good dream.

Cheeks rosy, she continued to dream, and he continued to watch her. He wished he could be in her head, see what she was seeing.

Perhaps it was wrong to watch her while she slept, but he couldn't make himself move. Sylvain studied her face and found the small scars that hinted at burns. Beneath one eye, the skin was smoother, and beneath that scar, one side of her mouth dropped a little lower than the other. Funny he'd never noticed it before.

It was cute. She had a perpetual smile on her face. Gently, so as not to wake her, he touched her face with the pad of his thumb. A small spot, the side with the scar, lacked freckles, but on her other cheek, they scattered across her skin likes stars.

Wrapped up as he was in her freckles, at first he didn't notice her skin cooling. But all at once, the golden dots stood out starkly against her skin. Scowling, he touched her cheek with the whole of his palm. Her skin went from cool, to icy, all at once, and her pulse which had been thumping steadily, stuttered.

"Marcus!" Sylvain wasn't a doctor, but he knew this wasn't normal. People didn't go to sleep and stop breathing. They also woke up when someone yelled in their face. "Briar. Wake up." Her eyes continued to move, but she didn't wake up. "Briar!"

Nothing.

"Move." Pushing him aside, Marcus took his place next to Briar. He touched his fingers to her pulse, and a wrinkle appeared between his eyebrows. Valen arrived as well and stood on the other side of her bed, staring down at her. He reached for one of her hands and squeezed it. "Come on, little one. Wake up."

"Briar." Marcus spoke firmly, but not loud, and shook her shoulder. "Briar, wake up."

She didn't move and even her eyes stopped twitching. "She's so cold," Marcus muttered. "I don't understand. Briar! Wake up!"

Sylvain held his breath. *Wake up.* He willed her to do it. "Briar. Wake. Up."

"Do you smell that?" Marcus asked, glancing back at him.

Sylvain sucked in a lungful of air. It was off, as if her natural scent was so light, it had nearly disappeared, and beneath that was another scent. Fear. Pain.

Why pain?

"Under the sink, I have a first aid kit. One of you get it." Marcus was abrupt and kept his fingers on her wrist. "Hurry!"

Sylvain dashed past his brothers and shoved the door open so hard it slammed into the wall behind it. In the bathroom, he dove beneath the sink, sweeping everything out of his way until he found the small white box. A heartbeat later, he was back, pushing it into Marcus's hands. "There."

Marcus opened it, and pulled out a small plastic cylinder. He tore it open, and waved it beneath Briar's nose.

Beside him, Valen was still, his eyes glued to her face. When she took a breath and her eyes popped open, the three of them let out a collective breath.

Her face was white, down to her lips. The only bit of color on her were her golden freckles, but she stared at them confused. With a wince, she sat up, and ran her fingers through her hair, but she wobbled, and grabbed her pillow to steady herself. "Whoa."

"Look at me," Marcus directed, and held her face in his hands. He turned her head from side to side, staring into her eyes before dropping his fingers to her neck and taking her pulse. "What happened?"

"I fell asleep," she answered, looking between them. "What's going on?"

"You wouldn't wake up," Sylvain answered. "You were cold as ice."

She lifted her hands to her face, but Marcus stopped her. "Wait." He finished taking her pulse and gently pinched the skin on the back of her hand, then sat back. "Well, that was exciting."

"She's okay?" Valen asked.

Marcus nodded. "Pulse is a little slow, skin is still cool, and she's dehydrated. But body temperatures drop during sleep. With all the excitement and healing, I think you just fell into a deep sleep faster than normal."

"That wasn't normal," Sylvain said. Nothing about what happened was typical. From his sense something was wrong, to her scent of pain and fear, to her waking up now. Something was off.

"It's not typical," Marcus said. "But it is normal. Her body is healing, of course she's exhausted."

"Why is she so pale?" Sylvain asked and breathed in. "And her scent is different." Breathing in Briar was like walking through an orchard in full bloom. Now it was just a ghost of a scent, mixed by residual fear and pain. "Do you hurt? I smell pain."

Briar moved her neck from side to side and stretched her arms over her head. "I'm a little sore. My neck is stiff like I slept wrong. I should probably check the graft and change the bandage."

"Come on." Marcus held out his hands. "Since I'm in doctor mode, I'll check you out."

Briar stood and wobbled again. She fumbled for something to hold onto, but Marcus caught her, and Sylvain held her arm. Nearby, Valen had jumped at her first step off the bed. They had her surrounded.

"Sorry." Grasping his arm tighter, she stood motionless. "Okay," she said after a moment. "I think I'm good."

But Sylvain didn't let go. He held onto her arm all the way into the bathroom, and kept holding on when she sat on the toilet seat and let Marcus remove her bandage.

"How's it look?" she asked, and Sylvain winced. It looked strange. The injury wasn't a perfect shape, but ragged, which the stitches around the outside emphasized. Netting covered the skin across the top of the injury. He wasn't a doctor, though, and couldn't say if it was healing well or not. Marcus examined it closely. It was bright pink.

"Good," he answered. "Healing well."

"How many of these have you had?" Sylvain asked. It might have been healing well, but it still looked painful.

"This is nothing," Briar said as Marcus covered it again. "You should have seen this one." She pointed to her cheek and the bone directly beneath her eye. "I'm lucky I have movement in this side of my face." She yawned. "Sorry."

"You're exhausted," Valen said from his place at the door. He crossed his arms and stared at her. "You should go back to bed."

The air in the bathroom filled with the scent of Briar's panic. "I—" Her breath came rapidly, and she shook her head. "I—"

Sylvain pushed Marcus aside and scooped her into his arms, he strode down the stairs into the wider living room space. "Breathe," he said.

She nodded, and when he sucked in a breath, she copied him. Eventually, her heart rate slowed.

"What was that?" Marcus asked. Sylvain hadn't even realized he'd followed them; he'd been entirely focused on Briar.

"I don't know." Tears leaked from her eyes, and gently, Sylvain swept them away. "I don't know."

Sylvain didn't know either, but he suspected it was related to his earlier sense of something being off. Something had triggered Briar's response, and even if she couldn't name what it was, she'd felt it.

"I don't want to go to sleep though," she said. "I'm not tired anymore."

"Are you sure?" Valen asked. "You—"

"I'm positive," she answered and stood. She walked to Valen and embraced him, leaning her head on his chest. "I'm sure. I have a ton of homework, and I'm going to do it. Thank you for waking me up. Even if it was just a deep sleep, I needed to wake up." Valen smiled down at her, but Sylvain knew his brother well enough to see he was worried.

She took a step toward the stairs and hesitated, as if she didn't want to go up. "Do you mind if I study down here?" she asked, glancing at Marcus and then him.

"Please," Marcus said, and Sylvain nodded. He'd been reading Hudson's research papers, trying to understand what it was Briar thought she had. He had so many questions, and he hated not having the answers.

Or he hated asking Hudson and Marcus for the answers.

Sunlight wasn't something he could fight, nor could he design a formula that would allow her to walk in the sun like him. He needed something to punch. He was great at punching.

Valen walked upstairs with Briar and came down minutes later, books and laptop in his hands. Briar trailed behind him, each step downstairs seemed to take more energy than it should. He stood, walked to her and took her hand. "Sit with me?"

She nodded, her skin tight over the bones in her face.

How was it she seemed even more frail and insubstantial than ever?

Valen placed her books on the coffee table and the laptop on the couch. Sylvain patted the sofa, and she sat, shoulder against his. "What are you studying?" he asked.

"I fell asleep reading art history. But I should focus on chemistry now." She glanced over at him and the computer he'd stolen from Marcus. "What were you doing?"

"Shopping," Marcus said, from his seat near the window. He idly turned a page, as if disinterested, but Sylvain caught his smirk.

"I was reading Hudson's research," he said, shooting a glare at his brother.

"Oh," she breathed and scooted closer to look at the computer. "Can I see?"

He tapped the keys to wake the computer. "This is his first one. It's a summary."

Briar nodded. "He took all the other research out there and compiled it. It's a good place to start. But it's pretty dense. Hold on. When I first started researching, I tried to dive right into Hudson's work, too, but there's a better place to start. Can I see your computer?"

Without waiting for him to answer, she slid the machine into her lap and began to tap away. "Here." After a moment she handed it back. "This is a summary, in lay terms, about genetic mutation. Those freaky little chromosomes have one bitty change, and suddenly you're toast." She shook her head. "Crazy."

"What do you think about what Hudson and Marcus discovered yesterday?" he asked as Valen sat on her other side. From across the room, Marcus lifted his head and then pretended to read again.

Briar shrugged. "I think it's interesting, but practically speaking, it doesn't change anything. I'm still allergic to the sun. I still have to cover myself head-to-toe. As far as it affects me, it doesn't. But—" Her face lit up, and her breath came rapidly. "What I really think is fascinating is that there is a biological basis for vampires, and science has the answers. What else might exist in the world? Werewolves? The Loch Ness Monster? Vampires were supposed to be myths, but they're not." Her respiration quickened, and she sat against the back of the sofa, hand over her chest. "Phew." She focused on breathing and then started again. "So tell me, do you have a werewolf friend I haven't met yet?"

"Sadly, no," Valen answered for him. "Sylvain is the closest thing I've ever seen to a werewolf. You should have seen him four hundred years ago. You wouldn't have been able to tell the difference."

Briar groaned. "You can't say things like, 'four hundred years ago,' when I have two chapters of chemistry to read!"

Marcus chuckled from the corner, but Sylvain merely glared at Valen. "You should talk. Tattoos from head to foot. Helmets made of horns. Scared off the villagers the minute you set foot in the territories."

Briar shut the book with a snap. "That's it. Spill. 'The territories?' And what helmet with horns. And these tattoos?" She reached for Valen and traced the curled edge of one tattoo that snuck out from the collar of his shirt. "What is it? Hudson said you were a marauder. Does that—" Her eyes widened. "Holy cow. You're a Viking."

"When I met Valen, he was called a Varangian," Marcus said, closing his book. "He was a sword man and a bodyguard."

"He was already a vampire when I met him," Sylvain said.

"I don't know as much history as I do biology," Briar apologized and yawned. "Sorry. I wish I'd paid more attention so I could know the timeline we're talking about. You became a vampire a thousand years ago, Valen?"

"Fourteen hundred, give or take. Hudson is the oldest one of us, but he and Marcus stopped counting at two thousand years," Valen said.

"Sylvain?" she asked. "You said hundreds."

"I was a colonist," he said. "Came to the colonies from Canada. My father was a trapper, and my mother, an Abenaki."

Briar waited, encouraging, but Sylvain didn't want to get into his history beyond that. It was too hard, and he was already on edge. As much as Briar, and his brothers, seemed happy forgetting what had happened earlier, he was not.

The whole event left him unsettled, and he had to work not to snap at his brothers to take it more seriously.

The front door opened and shut, and Hudson dropped his bag. "Hi," he said. He walked to Briar, and kissed her cheek, breathing in. "You smell off. Are you okay?"

"She's not," Sylvain answered over Marcus. "She fell asleep and wouldn't wake up. Twice, she's nearly fallen when she stood, and she's cold and pale." He crossed his arms.

"Your skin is cold," Hudson said. Sliding away the books, he sat on the coffee table, reached for her wrist, and touched it with two fingers.

"I've already taken her pulse, and she's—"

"Shh." Hudson glared at Marcus and refocused. "It's slow. And you've been dizzy?"

"She has," Sylvain said, and Briar side-eyed him.

"I know you're worried, Sylvain, but she's fine," Marcus said.

"She's not fine. I knew something was wrong, went in her room, and watched her turn pink to white and warm to cold. That's not normal." Sylvain dared Marcus to cross him. "I don't need a medical degree to know that."

"The house is secure," Valen said. "I was down the hallway and heard nothing until Sylvain went into her room."

Hudson stared at the wall and shook his head. "I don't know. You're feeling better though?"

"I am." Briar held up her hand when Sylvain would answer. "I really am."

"Then we watch." Hudson's face was grim. "We assume the worst until we know better."

Sylvain liked the sound of that. Assume the worst. He might just make it his personal motto.

CHAPTER 27
BRIAR

The rest of the evening was spent studying. On his way home, Hudson had picked up dinner for her, and Briar ate it, though no one else did.

"Food loses its flavor after a while," Valen explained. "When it doesn't fill you up or satisfy you, there's no point."

Hudson had brought her soup from a Vietnamese restaurant, and she ate slowly. For a while, she wasn't sure if her stomach would accept the food, but she forced it down.

She hated to admit it, but what happened earlier really freaked her out. There were times when she brought the spoon to her mouth, she was afraid she would drop the utensil. It seemed to be taking more energy than she had. Her muscles were a weird combination of loose and overexerted.

Once, she'd lifted weights with her brother, and she had the same sort of feeling. Like she could barely close her fist, she'd overtaxed her muscles so much.

By the time she finished supper, she was completely done, but each time she thought about returning upstairs and falling asleep, she panicked.

"It must have been a nightmare," she said to no one in particular.

Sylvain nodded. "Maybe." Of everyone, he was the most concerned. "Do you remember what it was about?"

Briar paused, thinking back. Her last memory was curling up on her comfortable bed before jolting awake. There was no in between. "No."

"I'll come up with you." Sylvain held out his hand. "Someone made me walk around Boston today. I'm tired."

Briar paused, worried. "You don't have to come with me if you don't want to."

"Nice," Marcus said.

Briar shushed him with a look, but Sylvain just ignored him. "Are you finished?"

She was. For some reason, her stomach was in knots. She didn't think she could swallow another spoonful. "Yes, please." Sylvain hadn't followed her train of thought so she clarified. "Yes. Come up with me. If you don't mind."

Sylvain jumped to his feet. The chair almost crashed to the ground but he caught it, and righted it. "Okay."

"Goodnight." She waved to Marcus and Valen, wondering if she should give them a hug, or kiss, but they decided for her. Valen kissed her cheek gently, and Marcus blew her a kiss.

Hudson stood, swept her hair back from her face and smiled at her. If someone had ever told her looking into another person's face could be done in a non-weird way, she wouldn't have believed them. But Hudson managed it. He kissed the tip of her nose and stood back. "Get some rest."

Sylvain took her hand, and together, they left the kitchen.

"I need to wash my face," she told Sylvain when they got to her room, and he nodded. He jumped onto the bed, landing with a gentle thump and crossed his ankles, one hand behind his head. "Smooth," she said before she shut the door. "I'm jealous."

"I can't tell if you're serious," he called, and she giggled.

"I am," she answered. "I absolutely am."

She glanced up into the mirror as she shut the door, and watched the smile drop from her face. Death had more color than she did. If it wasn't for the off-white tape, she'd be the same shade of white as the bandage on her neck.

Leaning forward, she touched beneath her eyes and pressed on her lips. Slowly, the pink filled in. All of the injuries she'd suffered recently, as well as the stress, had probably left her anemic, and she made a mental note to get an iron supplement.

A knock sounded on the bathroom door just as she stuck the toothbrush in her mouth. She opened the door a crack and peered out.

"Here." Sylvain shoved some clothes at her. "I thought you'd want these."

It was her pajamas, striped sleep pants and a t-shirt she'd stolen from Jamie that had a picture of Bill Murray on it. "Thanks." She spoke around the toothbrush and reached for the clothes, hoping she didn't drool.

Sylvain nodded once and shut the door.

It took her no time to wash her face and slap on some deodorant, but she lingered for a moment before opening the door. The idea of getting back in bed and closing her eyes caused her heart to pound, and she felt sweat trickle down her back.

The door suddenly opened, forcing her back.

"What's wrong?" Sylvain asked. He looked past her, examining every inch of the bathroom for what it was that must have frightened her.

"I don't know," she answered. "I think about sleep and

I…" She placed her hand over her heart, thumping to demonstrate. "Weird. I know."

"Come on." He held out his hand, waiting for her to take it. It was warm, and his fingers rough. He led them to the bed, where he'd already turned down the covers, and waited for her to climb in.

Feeling awkward, she did. Instead of climbing in after her, he tucked her in and went around to the other side to lie on top of the covers. Immediately, he faced her, curling on his side. "I'm here, and I'll stay here all night. You can go to sleep, and you'll be safe, got it?"

In response, she curled to face him and shoved a pillow under her head. "You don't have to."

"I want to," he said. "I'm not smart like Marcus and Hudson, so I can't make a medicine to cure you, or take your pulse to figure out if you're healthy, but I can fight. Give me something to fight, Briar, and I'll do it."

"Thank you." She grasped the crook of his arm. "You're sure?"

"Yes."

It worked. Telling her she was safe with him made her feel safe, and her body relaxed enough to finally fall asleep.

JUST LIKE HE'D PROMISED, SYLVAIN WAS THERE WHEN SHE woke up. He must have moved during the night, but not far, because he held her favorite book in his hand. As if he could sense her eyes on him, he placed it, pages down, on his chest. "Sleep well?"

She nodded. "Yes. Thank you." Toes pointed beneath the blankets, she stretched and lifted her arms over her head. "You stayed here all night?"

"Yes." Such a simple answer, but he couldn't know what it meant to her to have done it.

Next to her bed, her phone chimed, and she reached for it. "It's my mom."

Sylvain stood up, walked to the bookshelf, and slid the book in place. "I'll let you talk," he said.

"Thanks," she said then took a deep breath before answering. "Hi, Mom."

"Briar Rebecca Hale, it has been days since you have called me." *Uh oh.* Briar's full name only came out when she'd done something wrong.

"I texted you yesterday. I had class all day."

"Mmhm, and you couldn't call your momma at lunchtime?"

Briar caught herself just as she was about to sigh. "I'm sorry."

"Briar…" Mom was silent and then continued. "So you had a nice time in your classes?"

"Yes, ma'am. I had a chem lab and then art history."

"Why are you taking art history?" her mother asked, and Briar smiled. This was the first normal conversation she'd had with her mother since she'd been gone, and she hadn't once asked her about her health. *Baby steps.*

"Something different. I have the time, and I'm interested," she said, pushing back her covers and padding to her bureau to get her clothes out for the day.

"I took art history at college, too," her mother said dreamily. "I don't suppose much has changed since I took it. Art is art."

"I don't know," Briar joked. "Maybe we can compare notes?"

Her mother giggled and sighed. "Don't let too much time pass before you call again. I miss you."

"I'm sorry," Briar said. "I'll be better. I miss you, too."

"Well, have a good day and do your homework."

"Yes, ma'am," Briar answered. "I love you."

"Love you, too, Briar. Be good. Bye, now."

"Bye, Mom," she said and waited until her mother hung up before she disconnected. Her mother wasn't asking a lot, merely for her to call more often. A call every other day was do-able, and she could text throughout the day. It must be hard for her mother not to know every detail of Briar's life. For so many years, Briar had been her focus, and now she was gone, doing exactly what she wanted, when she wanted.

Briar hurried through her morning routine and rushed downstairs. "Morning," she said, greeting the guys who'd gathered in the living room. It was only Sylvain and Hudson.

"Marcus and Valen gone?" she asked.

"They went to Marcus's lab," Hudson told her, packing his laptop into a messenger bag. "Want a ride to school?"

Briar nodded. "That'd be great." Eyeing Sylvain, she cleared her throat. "Are you coming today?"

The set of his mouth tightened, and he eyeballed Hudson. "I thought you could go to one on your own, and then I'll meet you later."

"I'll be nearby, and Sylvain can go hunting," Hudson explained.

"Oh," Briar breathed. "Good. That's good. Do you have a place you like to go?"

Sylvain smiled, and maybe it was just her imagination, but his teeth looked sharp. "North of the city."

"Do you drive there?" she asked. "Will you be gone all day?"

He shook his head. "No. I'll run, and I won't be gone long. Back before lunch."

Her head was spinning. *Run?* She had a million questions. How fast did he go? Did he follow the highway or was there a more direct route? Had he ever tried to flip a coin into a tollbooth on the Mass Turnpike?

"Where'd you go?" Hudson asked, waving a hand in front of her face.

"I had a vision of Sylvain flipping a quarter into the toll as he ran by," she answered, and Hudson chuckled.

"I haven't done that since they invented EZ Passes," Sylvain said and winked at her. "I'll find you later." His boots hit the floor with a thud, and he stood. Mouth dry as she watched him walk toward her, she swallowed hard.

"I'll see you," she said as he came to a stop.

"See you, Briar." But he entwined his fingertips with hers to keep her from leaving. He bent at the waist, eyes on hers. "You snore."

She jerked back. "I don't!"

Quick as a flash, he wrapped his arm behind her back and touched his lips to hers. Despite his size, Sylvain was gentle, and his kiss lasted only a few seconds. He held his lips against hers, waiting until she was the one to move. She pursed her lips, capturing his, but he drew her lower lip into his mouth, nipping it before releasing. "Stay out of trouble."

"I'll try," she replied, and he set her away from him.

He faced Hudson and straightened, rolling his shoulders back. "Keep her safe."

"I will," he said. "The only time she'll be out of my sight is for class."

"You can't go with her?" Sylvain asked.

"He can't." Briar shook her head. "Hudson is a rock star in the science world. If he comes to my undergraduate class, he'll be attacked by a horde of nerdy fans like me. They'll throw graphing calculators and beg for him to sign their laptops. Pandemonium."

Hudson rubbed the back of his neck, embarrassed, but

Sylvain smiled. "Fine." He took her hand once more, and then released it before leaving.

"Come on," Hudson said, straightening her hat and handing her the sunglasses she must have left downstairs the day before. "I was thinking you could spend some time in the lab with me today."

"Yes!" When her voice echoed down the street, she drew her shoulders to her ears. "Whoops. I mean—yay!"

Hudson smiled and opened the car door for her. She'd only seen his car at night, and she was struck by how flashy it was.

Flashier than Marcus's SUV, at least.

The windows were tinted, like Marcus's, but she expected the glove box to open and a robotic hand to offer her a martini—or a gun.

"How long have you been in Her Majesty's employ?"

Hudson pulled into traffic, accelerating smoothly. "I don't understand."

"But you understood my wizarding references," she complained.

"The Queen employs wizards? I'm lost."

Briar huffed but grinned. "Never mind."

Jerking his chin in the direction of the glove box, he asked her. "Will you hand me my sunglasses?"

Briar reached forward.

"But don't hit the red button. Q installed a missile launcher."

Whipping her head toward him, she smirked. "You knew. You knew who I meant."

"Of course I did. I might be two thousand years old, but I know who James Bond is. I don't live under a rock." He gave her a small smile, eyes crinkled at the sides. "But seriously. My sunglasses?"

"Oh!" Moving fast, she handed him the sunglasses she was sure cost more than her rent.

"How do you manage not to teach any classes?" Briar asked, rubbernecking as they drove by Fenway Park.

"Money," he answered simply.

She wrinkled her nose at his one-word answer. "Grants and endowments."

"Yes, but my own as well. I've accumulated wealth," he explained. "So I'm in the position to pay for my own equipment or supplies. It helped more in the beginning, when I started out. But then again, when I started out, the university system was quite different."

They were getting closer to Boston College, and their conversation only led her to have more questions. "How long have you been researching?" She wondered if he published research under another name. "You weren't also known as Gregor Mendel, were you?" she asked, referring to the early nineteenth-century geneticist.

Hudson barked a laugh. "No." He continued to chuckle as they parked and he opened the door for her. Taking her hand, he pulled her to stand, but held onto it as they walked.

Suddenly, there was a spotlight shining on their hands, and Briar imagined every person they passed stared at it pointedly. If Hudson was uncomfortable, he hid it well.

Every so often he would chuckle, or shoot a grin her way, but he seemed completely at ease. "Have fun." He paused in front of her classroom and smiled down at her. "You ready?"

"For Human Parasitology?" she asked. "So ready."

"I want to kiss you," he said without preamble, the smile disappearing. "But—"

"It's bad enough we're holding hands," she answered for him and dropped his hand, stepping back. "I understand. It doesn't look good."

He studied her, eyes roaming her face. "I should have thought this out."

His words hurt, but she understood. Things had moved really quickly. One day, she went to his lecture, and the next, she was kissing his brothers and taking up space in his house. Now, he'd offered her a position in his lab and held her hand across campus.

The last thing she wanted to do was mess up his life or damage his professional reputation.

"Briar," he whispered and shook his head. In a flash, he took her hand and pulled her away from the door. Down the hall he dragged her into a bathroom. After a quick check of the stalls, he rushed to her and picked her up.

"I don't care about anything except you. I know you're smart, and if I hadn't met you at my lecture, I'm sure I would have sought you out later. You're one of the smartest students here, and eventually, I'd have put you in my lab."

She stared at him in disbelief, shaking her head.

"Yes," he answered, punctuating his point with a kiss. He turned his head from one side, to the other, placing kisses at the edge of her lips and along her cheekbones. "Yes, I would have." He drew back. "But I don't want anyone second guessing you or calling into question anything you do. Do you understand?"

It was hard to understand anything when his body was against hers, his hips and hands holding her against the cold tile wall. All she wanted was more of his kisses, but she closed her eyes and ran his words through her head one more time.

The third pass through, she got it. He wasn't worried about his reputation, but hers.

"Hudson," she said. "I…" She hesitated, but anything she would have said was cut off when the door started to open.

Hudson reacted, blocking it with his arm. "Custodial staff. Use the bathroom down the hall."

He let her legs fall to the ground but didn't release her until she was steady on her feet. Telegraphing his movement, he leaned closer, giving her time to stop him.

She didn't want to stop him, but she also didn't want to be the girl who ditched class to make out with her boyfriend.

Boyfriend?

Hudson touched his lips to hers, tracing her lips with the tip of his tongue, but then stepped away. "Later."

Biting her lower lip, she nodded. He opened the door, peered out and then went through, dragging her behind him. Side by side, they walked back to her class. "I'll see you in the lab," he said. "You remember how to get there?"

When her kiss-addled brain cleared, she was sure she could find it, so she nodded.

He waved and left her. Halfway down the hall he spun and walked backward. He lifted his hand again, and then turned around, hurrying away.

Boyfriend? The word hit her like a sledgehammer. No. She needed to get her mind wrapped around biology, not Hudson's lips.

❧

NO ONE NOTICED BRIAR AT FIRST when she came into the classroom and slid into a chair near the door. The professor was already there, setting up her PowerPoint, while the other students chatted with each other.

Briar took out her laptop and book, and waited for the lecture to begin. She drummed her fingers on her leg and happened to glance over, catching a student staring at her. Guilty of people watching herself, Briar smiled so the girl didn't feel embarrassed. But it happened again a few seconds later, this time with a different student.

And then another.

She lifted her hand to her mouth, checking to see if anything was on her face, but the white fabric of her glove was clean when she peered down at it.

Oh. It was her clothes. Inside this classroom, made up of one wall of windows, Briar couldn't take off her hat or gloves. She was fully protected against the sun.

That was why everyone kept glancing at her. In the days she'd been with the guys, and yesterday when most of her classes took place in cave-like auditoriums, she'd taken off her hat and gloves.

But she couldn't do that here, and so she stood out. Grasping the corner of her hat facing most of the class, she tugged it lower. This way, her peripheral vision was blocked, shielding her from her classmates' curious stares.

The professor lifted her gaze to the class and lingered for a moment on Briar. Would she demand Briar remove her hat?

Before she could create any more worst case scenarios, the professor moved on, diving right into the meat of the topic.

For the rest of the class, as long as Briar stared straight ahead, she was good. Anytime she looked to the left, though, she'd inevitably catch someone staring at her in confusion.

Well, let them stare. Hopefully, she'd actually meet some of the other graduate students soon, and once they knew why she dressed the way she did, the side-eyes would stop.

When the professor dismissed the class, Briar hesitated. She wondered if she should take the opportunity to introduce herself and risked making eye contact with a girl heading to the door.

"Hi," she said.

The girl smiled, her gaze flitting to Briar's hat. "Hi," she answered and beelined it to the door. The results were the same with the next two students she tried to engage, and finally, she gave up.

At least she'd made an effort, and she could try again next week.

Hudson's lab was in the below ground level, and it wasn't easy to find. Briar'd been distracted the second time she was there, and unconscious the first, so she got turned around. Eventually though, she found herself in front of Hudson's door and knocked.

No one came, and she knocked again before jiggling the handle experimentally. It turned, and she walked in. "Hudson?" No one answered as she let the door shut behind her. "Hudson?"

The stainless steel countertop was covered with things—syringes and test tubes, a simple microscope. His computer was on, a magnified image Briar recognized as her sample expanded on the screen. She sat in the rolling chair and scooted toward the computer, careful not to touch anything.

Hudson was sure she didn't have EPP, and she could see the difference in her mutation compared to the images she'd seen of other chromosomes from people with EPP.

She wondered what other signs she may have missed. When he got back, she wanted to see if he'd show her the images he'd shared of his and his brothers' genes. She'd never asked if there were other places on the genome that were different for vampires.

Now that they were thinking vampirism could be an inherited trait, there should be some commonalities between genes. They'd need to find other vampires and take their blood.

Briar chuckled at the irony. "I want your blood... sample." She tried it out loud with a bad Eastern European accent. It needed work, but she was going to try it on Marcus later, nevertheless.

The door opened behind her, and she spun, ready to greet whoever it was. But when Valen walked through the door, followed closely by Marcus, she paused. Their eyes landed on her but then skidded away.

"Are you okay?" she asked, standing.

"Yes," Valen answered, but his voice was strange, hollow sounding. It was as if someone had made a Valen puppet and moved his mouth. There was none of the rolling cadence and personality that colored even his one-word answers.

"What happened?" she asked Marcus and stopped. His shoulders heaved with each breath he took, his nostrils flaring. "Marcus." Tempted to snap her fingers, she started toward him.

"Stop." The words ground out of him, his muscles barely moving like he was the Tin Man before oil. "Don't move."

Frozen, she stared at him. His eyebrow twitched, and the muscle below his ear jumped. Next to his sides, his hands fisted and un-fisted, and every so often, he would lean forward, and then pull back.

Still, Briar didn't move. She had the impression he was fighting something, each bob forward was countered.

"What can I do?" she asked, but he didn't reply. His lips seemed to swell, and she saw the white tips of his fangs dig into his lower lip.

Oh no. Where was Hudson?

As if thinking of him made him appear, the door opened and he came inside, followed closely by a heaving, messy Sylvain. Leaves and twigs stuck in Sylvain's hair, and his t-shirt was ripped along his chest and sleeves. She could imagine him running through the forest, uncaring of trees or bushes or rocks. One of his boots was even missing, and he stood off-balance, one leg lower than the other.

Sylvain's eyes were wild, similar to Marcus's, and she decided then and there she preferred the wildness to Hudson and Valen's dead eyes.

Sylvain held onto the doorknob, and beneath his hand, the metal groaned and suddenly snapped.

"Sylvain, look at me." His eyes tracked to hers, and he sucked in a breath, growling deep in his throat. The rumble seemed to encourage the others, who in a flash of motion, surrounded her.

In a heartbeat, Briar went from freaked out to terrified.

These were not the guys she knew. Sylvain had called his vampire Predator, and she could easily see it in his eyes. He followed her, his body shifting if she so much as leaned in one direction.

Valen called his vampire a monster, but he was empty. The only sign of a monster was his fangs, which were visible with each snarl.

Marcus had stopped twitching, and instead moved smoothly around the room. All of them did. They were a well-oiled machine with one purpose—corner her.

She didn't realize that was what they were doing until her back hit the wall.

"You're scaring me," she whispered. "Stop."

At her command, Hudson blinked, and for a second, she thought she saw awareness, but in a flash it was gone. Almost as one, their pupils dilated, and they stepped forward.

"Stop it," she said again, but their only response was an angrier growl. Valen stepped in front of Marcus, fingers curled into claws. Knees bent, Briar got the impression he was about to launch himself onto her.

She had some self-preservation, and she lurched to one side.

"Don't run," Marcus said again, and for just a second, his eyes bled to green.

Whatever controlled them, they were fighting. At first, she thought Sylvain broke the door because he didn't want her to escape, but now she wondered if he was holding himself in place.

"Stay still," Hudson ground out, his eyes becoming icy blue before being swallowed whole by the black.

It went against every instinct she had to stay in one place. The guys had been replaced with beings who had only one purpose, to feed.

"Back off," she said when Sylvain had snuck forward. His head cocked to the side, like it wasn't attached to the rest of his body. The way he regarded her was singularly wrong. "Sylvain." She wondered if saying his name would wake him up. "Sylvain!"

She wanted to run. She wanted to run so badly. But how would she get away from them? They'd take her down in a second, and when they came to, they'd be wrecked.

Briar knew, she absolutely, one hundred percent knew, the creatures in front of her were not the guys. Even in those moments when Hudson had attacked her, she'd seen a glimmer of himself. As if the vampire he caged inside him was merely a stripped down version of himself.

These creatures were not like that. They were closer to the creature in the woods, the one who had climbed her body, than anything she'd seen from the guys before.

Which meant one thing: Asher.

Yeah. They'd said that Asher couldn't control them, but there was no other explanation for what was happening.

The guys were fighting for control. In those few seconds when Marcus and Hudson had spoken to her, it was clear that whatever was happening wasn't something they wanted.

So what did she do? How did she get them back?

"Hudson." She made her voice as firm as possible and swallowed down her fear and terror. "Hudson. Help me."

He blinked, ice blue, then black again. But it was there.

"Sylvain." She turned her attention to the man who

seemed more predator than human and raised her voice. "Sylvain. I'm scared. Help me."

He growled, but stepped back. Next to him, Valen's fingers uncurled, and he shook his head, wincing.

"Valen." He opened his eyes, but she couldn't see him there. "Valen. You don't want to hurt me. You protect me. Help." He growled and snarled, but whirled away, and to her horror, threw himself at the wall, head first, over and over. "Valen," she choked.

Marcus's entire body twitched, almost like he'd stuck his finger in an electrical socket. Of all of them, his struggle was the clearest. He fought for control of his body. "Don't hurt me," she whispered. "Marcus. Please, don't hurt me."

Marcus yelled out, gripping his head, and fell to his knees. "Stay there!" he yelled, clawing at his temples.

"Don't move." Hudson's voice was hoarse, like he had to push it out of his throat. "Briar. Please. Don't move."

She didn't, though her knees shook, and she wasn't sure how much longer she could stand.

Then, like puppets who had their strings cut, the guys collapsed. First Valen, then Sylvain, and Marcus, and Hudson. They hit the ground, eyes closed, crumpled in a heap.

That was it for Briar. Her legs gave out, and she fell to her butt, hard enough to bruise her tailbone. Hot tears spilled down her face, and she let them fall. It was all she could do at that moment to keep breathing.

"It's okay," she whispered to herself and crossed her arms over her chest. A shiver began at the base of her spine, and zinged her all the way to her shoulders. "It's okay," she said again and pressed her hands against her cheeks. "I'm okay."

CHAPTER 28
VALEN

Valen awoke slowly. His eyes didn't want to open, but he fought them. For a moment, he wondered if Hudson's medicine had stopped working, and the sun dictated his sleep.

From a distance, he heard a hiccuping sob, and suddenly, horribly, everything crashed into place.

"Briar!" Desperately, he scanned the room and found her sitting, her back against the wall, staring back. He crawled to her, and when he got close enough, reached for her face.

His heart broke when she flinched.

"Are you okay?" he asked, pulling back his hand.

"I'm okay," she whispered. She pressed her lips together when a small sob escaped.

"Briar!" Sylvain woke up next and leapt to his feet. The scent of fear pervaded the room, but Valen's monster was not tempted by it. If anything, he was hunkered down, arms over his head, hiding in shame.

"Briar?" Sylvain whispered and knelt next to her. She peered at him nervously, gaze jumping from Sylvain to Valen, and then to Marcus and Hudson who still lay unconscious in a heap.

Marcus and Hudson had kept Briar alive. Valen, completely disconnected from his body, had had no control. Even his vampire was stripped down, until all they'd smelled was Briar and all they'd wanted was her blood. If Marcus and Hudson hadn't begged her to stay still, he'd have devoured her.

And if the terror emanating from Briar was any indication, she knew it.

All he wanted was to comfort her, but the last thing he wanted was to frighten her. Like a signal coming in and out of range, her words had filtered through to him. *"You don't want to hurt me. Help."*

He'd been powerless.

"Briar," he choked and took a deep breath. "I'm sorry. I never..."

"I know." She rested her cheek on her knees, turning her head to face him. "It wasn't you."

Behind them, Hudson roared awake, and Briar screamed. The sound of it pierced his already bleeding heart.

Together, he and Sylvain whirled to face Hudson, but whatever it was Hudson was ready to fight, it wasn't them, and it certainly wasn't Briar.

If he lived another thousand years, he never wanted to hear her scream again.

Hudson stayed utterly still. "Are you okay? Did we hurt you?"

"You didn't hurt me," she answered. "I'm okay." The words seemed to reassure her as much as them.

Hudson held out his arms and then dropped them. "I need to touch you."

A fresh scent of fear spiked, but then drained away as she

nodded. "Okay." She stumbled when she pushed herself to her feet, but Hudson was there to catch her.

Why hadn't he thought to ask? Jealously, Valen watched Hudson enfold her in his arms, face buried against her neck. "I'm so sorry, Briar. I'm sorry."

"It wasn't your fault," she said. "I know it. I know whatever that was, it was out of your control."

"It was." Marcus had awoken, but Valen's total focus was on Briar, and he hadn't heard him rouse. *Stupid.*

You protect me. Valen had done a horrible job protecting her. Would she ever trust him again?

She lifted her head from Hudson's chest, almost as if she'd heard his thoughts, and held out her hand. "Come here."

Valen went without pause, taking her from Hudson and wrapping her up. He held her like she was made of porcelain and one too-brisk movement would crush her.

"My turn," Sylvain growled, and reluctantly, Valen passed her to him. A moment later, Marcus intruded, and Sylvain was forced to do the same. Eventually, though, he had to relinquish his hold and they all had to face what had happened.

"Asher," Hudson said.

One word—it explained everything and made it all so much more complicated.

Their master had effectively fired a shot across their bow. It was up to them, now, to respond, and the only thing to do was go to war.

And Valen was very good at war.

CHAPTER 29
HUDSON

Two thousand years ago, a vampire had turned him from a man into a general. His only purpose was to fight and destroy.

Over millennia, Hudson had honed his skills until he was the most ruthless leader of vampires the world had ever seen. It was a role he thought he'd left behind him.

He should have known better.

The four hundred years they'd existed without Asher had all been a ruse, and they'd fallen for it.

Hudson and his brothers had become complacent. He was a scientist for God's sake.

Not anymore. If Asher wanted a war, he would have it, because he'd threatened the one person who, in two thousand years, had not only brought him to life, but brought him and his brothers together. Briar had healed their broken family, and there was no way, no way, he'd allow Asher to destroy it.

He'd destroy him first.

CHAPTER 30
SYLVAIN

If Sylvain's brothers were the brains of battle, he was the battle-axe. He would hew and rend without discrimination.

Deep inside him, the predator roared for vengeance. If Briar had moved, if she'd blinked, he would have ended her and would have awoken with blood on his hands.

He was the one who decided who lived and died. For years, he'd been the good son, the loyal son. All it had gotten him was pain. Until Briar, that was what he'd come to expect from his existence.

His human life had been torture, and his early vampire life one of bloodlust and selfishness. But perhaps, it had all been leading to Briar.

So he was going to hold onto her, tightly, and no one would take her away from him. Especially not Asher, who for some reason thought he could wield and control him.

If Asher wanted blood, Sylvain would drown him in it. And then he would rip Asher's head from his shoulders and stick it on a pike as a warning to any creature who tried to come between him and Briar.

CHAPTER 31
MARCUS

Marcus had never fought so hard in all his existence. The battle he'd just fought against his own thirst and Asher's control had nearly annihilated everything he wanted. From the looks on his brothers' faces, they knew it as well.

Long ago, Marcus had made a choice. He'd chosen to live as a vampire and wreak havoc. He'd taken human lives and hadn't given them a second thought.

Since Annie had died, he'd tried to make up for what he'd done. His research now was his attempt at finding a way for vampires not to need humans to feed at all. Ever.

Animal blood eliminated the hunger, but it didn't sate the vampire. Only human blood did that.

He was a scientist and logical, but unlike Hudson who was ruled by reason, Marcus believed in karma. He'd put bad out into the world, and he had bad coming to him.

His scale was unbalanced. He'd taken and taken and taken. Losing Briar seemed like the universe's way of evening things out.

It was the most horrifying thing he'd ever considered. A

huge sword hung over his head, and he didn't know when it would fall.

Marcus needed Briar in his arms again, to assure himself she was there and he hadn't destroyed the bright spot in his life. The one person whose presence had given him everything he wanted.

Briar came willingly and wrapped her arms around his waist. He breathed in her scent, the wildflowers masked by the pungent aroma of fear.

"Don't be afraid," he whispered against her hair. "Please."

"You've got me," she said, and then, because he was completely undeserving, "I'm safe with you."

CHAPTER 32
BRIAR

The guys brought Briar home, and they sat together in the living room. The curtains were drawn, but she held her hat, turning it in her hands.

She leaned against Valen, seeking strength in his nearness, and he seemed to need it as well. Every so often he kissed her head or touched her knee. All of them sat close by, at times watching her or staring off at nothing.

Something had changed. The guys exchanged glances, and she got the sense as soon as she went to bed tonight, they'd open a door to a secret room and a giant map would descend from the ceiling.

Then they'd begin to lay the plans for their counteroffensive.

"So, Asher can use mind control. If it was Asher who did this," Briar said, proud of the way her voice didn't shake.

"Yes. It would appear so," Marcus replied.

Sylvain and Valen shut their mouths, and Sylvain gnashed his teeth. "Though it is a newly developed skill."

Briar nodded, and then narrowed her eyes. Was it? These guys were honorable men—vampires—and from what they described, when they'd been with Asher, they'd murdered and fought. What if Asher had controlled them and they didn't realize it?

What if everything they'd done, and had described to her shamefully, hadn't really been them?

"Are there levels of mind control do you think?" she asked. "Marcus, I could see you fighting him, whereas Valen, you were absent. I couldn't find you when I looked at you."

"Little one," Valen whispered and shook his head. "I'm so sorry."

"I'm not trying to guilt you," she said. "I promise. I just want to understand. Maybe Marcus could fight because he could barely control all of you. Or maybe there's another reason. I don't know. But I wonder..." She took a deep breath. "Do you think he was controlling you all along?"

Hudson sat straighter. "For the entirety of our vampire existence, you mean?"

Briar nodded. "Yes. It wasn't until there were four of you that you left him. Maybe he couldn't continue to control all of you at once. If he could control you without you knowing, or, I don't know, be the devil on your shoulder—the kind who whispers excuses making bad things not seem so bad—think of his power. He could manipulate you to do whatever he wanted, and if you balked, then he just gave you a mental shove in the direction he wanted. Maybe his control was like that."

From their wide-eyed stares, the thought had never occurred to them. "He wanted to show you how powerful he was today, but what he actually did was show you how strong *you* are."

She fixed each of them with her gaze, wanting to impress upon them what she thought of them. "You fought him, and I'm alive."

Slowly, Sylvain grinned. First one corner of his mouth

lifted, and then the other until he threw his head back and laughed loud. "You're right. And he's revealed himself to us. We won't underestimate him again."

"Exactly!" Briar snapped her fingers. "See? We've got a leg up."

Hudson and Marcus exchanged a glance, one that was loaded with the promise of strategic battle planning. They would use this to their advantage.

"Whatever happens," Valen added, catching her attention, "we will fight to keep you safe."

"Yes," Sylvain answered and took her hand, bringing it to his lips and kissing it gently. "You're with us now. We're a—"

"A team?" she joked, and then shook her head. This was serious. "We've got each other's backs. We take care of each other."

Hudson nodded and stood before kneeling in front of her. "I promise you, Briar. I will do everything in my power to protect you."

"And each other." Briar looked around the room. "Promise me. You'll protect each other. You're family."

"Well, you're part of this family now," Marcus said, and leaning down, kissed her lips. "Consider yourself one of us. Vampire-lite."

Briar giggled and held out her hand. One-by-one each of them touched her, and she smiled at them. Her heart thumped, and even if she couldn't say it aloud yet, she wanted them to know how much she cared for them. "Family. Forever."

Sylvain swallowed, Adam's apple bobbing in his throat, and he glanced at his brothers before answering. "Forever."

ABOUT THE AUTHOR

Ripley Proserpina spends her days huddled near a fire in the frozen northern wilds of Vermont. She lives with her family, three magnificent cats, and one dog who aspires to cat-hood.

Printed in Great Britain
by Amazon